OPPOSITION REFLEX

Ron Vergona

Published by:

*S*hepherd *H*ill

Coeur d'Alene, Idaho

To my wife Addie, and children Jessica and Michael, for their love and support.

PART ONE

CHAPTER 1

San Francisco, California

STEVE CASELLA JOLTED AWAKE. HIS blue eyes darted in the pre-dawn light seeping into the stark cinder-block room. Cold sweat clung to tense muscles trembling from his father's image on the video. The biting words echoed in his head. It was the same damn dream. And his father was still dead.

Steve exhaled and glanced at the watch he'd tossed onto the tiny bedside table. No more sleep tonight. A night fragmented by typical minor incident responses. None close to the once-in-a-career, testosterone-driven call every firefighter craved.

Steve's brain ricocheted between the intensity of the nightmare and the lunacy of his squad's last call. A drunk driver attempting to pull over to a non-existent shoulder to vomit. Instead, he bounced down an embankment, covered with what he was trying to deposit outside his brand-new Prius. No one, including the hapless drunk, was seriously injured. Not this time. And he'd gotten the best damn gas mileage ever on the final hundred feet of his journey. Plus, an expensive trip to the E.R., followed by a night in lock-up.

The edgy features on Steve's face relaxed, anticipating his shift ending in a couple of hours. More so on the realization he'd have the next three days to recover and get some needed work done around the house. Resigned, he checked his email as another unbidden thought flashed across his brain.

Two years ago, events catapulted Steve into the final chapter in what he called his dad's farewell party. He recalled the brief email but couldn't remember who'd sent it.

It read: *Steve, click on the WildFlix link below.*

He shook his head, trying to push those images back into the dark recesses. The harsh clanging of the bell and the all-too-familiar voice blaring over the intercom snapped him back to reality.

"Let's get to it, ladies. Time to rock and roll. The residents of San Francisco have summoned Dogpatch to another barbecue."

CHAPTER 2

Morristown, New Jersey

"YEAH, NANA. RIGHT. SURE."

EDIE Pauling cradled the phone while struggling to pull open a stubborn drawer in her thrift shop dresser. She had lost the battle against filling her suitcase with useless stuff she didn't need to lug all the way to the West Coast.

"Yep. I'm getting ready to leave tonight. No. I told you; I'm covering the AHA conference for several newspapers. What? No. It stands for the American Heart Association. It's a medical convention. No. I'm not going there to find a husband. And no, for the third time, this trip has nothing to do with any investigation into Dad's death. Why would you think that?"

Caught in the lie, Edie's eyes targeted the papers sticking out of her open laptop case.

"Yes, I'm being paid to write these stories." Edie extended her chin and leaned against the dresser. "That's why I went to college. Remember? To be a journalist."

All true. If she could put together something those cranky editors considered worthwhile printing, she would get paid for one of her stories. But nothing would come close to covering her expenses if she saw this impulsive scheme through to the end.

"I'll be careful. I'm not a baby anymore. Well, maybe to you twenty-five seems young. Don't worry. No one's gonna be pushing me around."

She stretched herself a little taller and tucked back some errant strands of straight black hair from her face.

"You might've forgotten, but they don't make us sit in the back of the bus anymore. You're missing the point. And I've seen plenty of pictures from back then."

She smiled, recalling some stories of her own she'd written on that subject.

Edie's face clouded over as she listened. She stopped what she was doing and stretched herself across the only vacant part of the bed she could find.

In a subdued voice, Edie said, "I know Dad would be proud."

She thought back to the last time she saw her father alive. Back in the hotel room almost two years ago, the former Navy SEAL's words still echoed in Edie's ears.

"I just need to check up on a few last-minute things at the embassy. You should stay here and finish packing. We certainly don't want to miss our flight. I'd say it's about time we get the hell outta here and catch up with the rest of the family to celebrate the Fourth. Even though we'll probably be a little late."

CHAPTER 3

San Francisco, California

FULLY AWAKE AND PUMPED, STEVE climbed into the rig. He covered his dark brown hair with his helmet and readied himself for action. The old wooden door creaked and rumbled open at the historic Dogpatch fire station in the Potrero Hill section of San Francisco. The gleaming engine rolled out of the station and turned left onto Tennessee Street. Another left onto Twentieth, shattering the dawn's stillness as it cut its way through the slumbering neighborhood and under the 280 Freeway. Before the crew had a chance to savor the building adrenaline rush, they completed a jarring turn onto Mississippi Street, their destination yards away.

Twenty-nine, and just shy of six feet, Steve did not have an ounce of excess fat to slow him down. While in top physical condition, his mental psyche was more fragile. He had been working on C Shift for almost four years and was living his dream. His real dream. Not the nightmarish memories he encountered a few short minutes ago.

Those nightmares started when he was twenty-two and completing his first year as a volunteer firefighter with the Glen Ellen Fire Department, about an hour north of San Francisco.

******

Steve had scarcely finished polishing the last brass hose fitting on the vintage engine when he got the call.

"Hey Dad, what's up?" His voice sliced to silence by the news his mom had been rushed to the emergency room.

"I… I'm on my way," Steve said.

Steve jumped into his Jeep Wrangler and headed for the Highland Hospital campus of the Alameda Medical Center in Oakland. Barely concentrating, he negotiated the convoluted MacArthur Maze. Exiting the 580 Freeway at MacArthur Boulevard, Steve jumped from his parked Wrangler and burst through the doors of the Koret Critical Care and Clinical Center at Highland Hospital.

He stopped short at the sight of his father. In a fraction of a second Steve grasped the news was horrific. The stunned look on the face of Tom Casella was all Steve needed to confirm his fears. His mother had died on the operating table. He hadn't realized it then, but in the thousands of times he replayed that instant, Steve's memory also summoned up something else on his father's face. A deeper, darker image of a hidden ire lurking behind the grief. To this day that foreboding vision still haunted Steve.

******

Steve bounded out of the truck with the rest of the crew and shook himself back to the present. He primed himself for Capt. Jordan's orders.

They were faced with a single story detached residential structure, wood-framed and sided. Garage underneath with a set of open wooden stairs to the main living level. Steve saw minimal smoke escaping around the edges of the two hinged carriage-styled garage doors. He noted no visible flames.

Heavy boots thumping, gear and helmet clanking, Higgins sprinted from the alleyway alongside the structure. "No signs of any involvement to the rest of the structure, captain."

Higgins looked over his shoulder and acknowledged the old woman shuffling toward the group of men. "This lady lives next door. Her bedroom window looks across the alleyway and out to the street. A barking dog woke her up. She heard shouts from inside the house. She got a whiff of scorched wood and saw light shimmering off the wet concrete in the driveway. So, she called it in."

The captain stepped forward, springing into action.

"Casella and Parkinson. Get up those stairs. Start at the main level and check to see if anybody's still inside. Work yourselves down to the garage. Higgins and Bartley. Check the perimeter again and be ready to back them up. Now move out. I'll check on the E.T.A. of the wagon."

Though heavily geared, Casella and Parkinson easily scaled the stairs which groaned from the intrusive assault. At the top they found the door unlocked. Casella shrugged, deep-set, intense eyes flashing with a tinge of regret. Not needed, the axe remained clasped to his belt. A resounding crash followed the solid push on the door causing it to bounce off the side wall of the empty living room. They proceeded to a hallway opening up at the far end of the room. To the left, a bathroom, and to the right, two bedrooms. All empty with no signs of any smoke or fire. Similar findings in the kitchen located at the back of the house.

At a closed doorway on the left side of the kitchen, Steve paused and motioned to Parkinson. "Come here, Parky. Listen up. You hear that?"

"Yeah, it's coming from down there. Like scratching sounds and something else. A whining."

Senses heightened, Steve checked the handle and surface for signs of heat and nudged the door open. It hit them in the face like an old recurring foe.

"Ah shit," Parkinson said. "Is that what I think it is?"

"Let's move it." Steve's face reflected the same dreaded certainty he'd seen on Parkinson.

They descended the rickety stairs, finding a body spread across the exposed doorway leading to the interior opening of the garage. Through his tinted face shield Steve scrutinized the slender, middle-aged man with shredded and charred clothing. The lower part of the body and extremities covered in burns.

As Steve crouched down beside the man, he noticed a slight movement in the man's ribcage and a brief fluttering of the eyelids. Facial injuries appeared limited to first degree burns, but judging by his labored breathing, Steve suspected swelling and possible airway burns.

"Give me the canister," Steve said. "He's still breathing. Go check the rest of the garage. The fire could've started in there."

As he said this, a rasping sound came from the man's lips.

Steve leaned closer, straining at the quivering, fading voice. "Amber. Where is she? Is she okay? I tried. But couldn't get her out the back door." A sudden coughing fit interrupted, subsiding almost as quickly as it began. "Couldn't budge it. Must've jammed. You find her? She okay?" The last words fading away. But no more coughing.

Face shield pulled up, Steve said, "Who's Amber? Your wife? Daughter? Who else is in the house?"

The man exhaled, face contorting, his words a whisper. "My dog. Just me and her. Nobody else in the house."

Parkinson reappeared from the garage speaking simultaneously into his mike and to Steve, "Conditions are stable. The guy had an extinguisher and must've knocked down the fire."

Steve turned away from the injured man and said into his own mike, "Captain, we need the paramedics in here pronto. We've got one victim located with severe third-degree burns. Probable airway and lung damage. No other known occupants. Except there may be a dog loose in the house. So, give the guys a heads-up."

"Roger," Capt. Jordan responded. "Paramedics are three blocks out. Higgins and Bartley are right behind you to double check for other possible victims."

To Parkinson, Steve said, "Nothing you can do here. I've got it covered. You might as well go help the guys with the final walk-through."

As Parkinson left, the man's shaky hand yanked the oxygen mask off his face. "Please… make sure she's okay. Don't let them take her to any shelter. My wife and baby—they've been gone for a while."

The man paused, fighting to take a breath. "There's no one else to take care of Amber. You gotta promise. I know they'll put her to sleep. Please. Tell me you'll help her."

Steve repositioned the man's mask and struggled to maintain a professional detachment. "Easy now. Try to breathe. No more talking. The paramedics will be here in a minute, and then we'll make sure Amber's safe. I promise. I'll find her and take good care of her."

Even before these last words left Steve's lips, the man took his final breath. A tear formed and slipped down his swollen cheek, disappearing in the charred remnants of his shirt.

Steve's concentration broke as Parkinson's voice rebounded across the hallway from the back room. "Hey, Steve. We've got us a big, white, and very much alive puppy dog."

Steve's eyes shut for a moment, then reopened with an unfocused gaze. "Holy crap. God help me and Amber."

CHAPTER 4

Newark Liberty Airport

AS THE UNITED AIRLINES JUMBO jet rolled back from the gate, Edie eased herself into the economy class seat. Was it possible an airline seat could make her five-foot, 100-pound body feel fat and cramped? She looked around at the majority of her fellow passengers on the non-stop flight from Newark to San Francisco and had to consider herself more fortunate. At least there was no danger of gaining weight between here and San Francisco. These days flying was akin to being tossed into a holding cell with all the inmates on a hunger strike. There'd been no time for a decent meal before rushing into the waiting cab for the ride from her Morristown residence. She anticipated some great meals at San Francisco's finer restaurants, or maybe one of the vendor stands at the Moscone Convention Center. Whichever her meager budget tolerated.

Edie glanced out as the mammoth airliner climbed toward its cruising altitude, looking down at the Statue of Liberty, and imagined the iconic figure saluting her departure. She closed her eyes and prayed this symbol of liberty was not too old and tarnished to help right the injustices weighing down her spirits. They were much heavier than the damn carry-on bag she'd stuffed into the overhead compartment. With that task she had the help of a fellow passenger.

Would she get the help needed after reaching her final destination? Could she convince Steve Casella to abandon his own stubborn beliefs to join her in the battle to expose the cover-up of events surrounding her father's death? Not to mention rewriting his own father's legacy.

CHAPTER 5

San Francisco, California

"JESUS CHRIST. THE FREAKING DOG tore off my glove." Parkinson slammed the door to the back room shut and turned to Steve. "Goddamned lucky I still got all my fingers. Let's get animal control over here so we can finish this up without having to deal with this monster."

"Give it a rest, Parky," Steve said. "I thought you said it was a nice big puppy dog?"

"Yeah? Well, see for yourself. I think it changed into the big bad wolf. Either way, we don't have to handle it, so the quicker we call animal control, the quicker we get back to the station and wrap up this shift."

"Here's the thing." Steve's head buzzed, trying to wrap this foolish idea around his own head. "The owner asked me personally to take care of Amber."

"Who the hell is Amber?"

"Must be the one in there who has your glove. I'm gonna go in and see if I can get acquainted with her. Hang tight." Steve stripped off his helmet along with some of his bulky gear. Not a good idea to look too threatening for his first encounter with Amber.

Steve eased open the door while grasping onto an object he pulled from his pocket and disappeared inside. The early morning light cast deep shadows and exaggerated the uneasiness he was experiencing. He found the room packed with boxes, garden tools, old furniture, and an array of discarded belongings representing a life that had once seen brighter days.

A low rumbling growl came from behind some boxes piled on the floor near the far-right corner of the room. Steve kneeled down with his right hand holding the object out in front of him, hoping to calm the frightened animal.

"Here, Amber. Come on, girl." Steve shook the chain collar and leash he found on the floor next to the dog's owner. "Come on, be a good girl."

At his first glance of the trembling dog, Steve neglected his instinct to turn and run. He knew he shouldn't stare, but something in the dog's eyes cut into his heart. He jingled the collar again and it broke the dog's returning glower. Steve had little experience in handling dogs, but he knew enough to turn sideways, not approach her, or make any sudden movements.

He whispered the dog's name and quietly spoke anything that came into his head. There were tentative padding and clicking sounds against the cold concrete floor. He didn't turn his head until he felt a wet sniffing nose in his ear.

Steve emerged from the room with Amber on the leash, walking by his side.

"Here ya go, Parky," Steve said.

He tossed over the missing glove.

Amber suddenly wrenched Steve around the corner, straight to the lifeless body. He watched as the dog tried to conjure up a response from her deceased owner. The dog spiraled between frantic nuzzling and whining; and then sprung back to a kneeling Steve. She knocked him off balance, licking his face. Gently grasping Steve's hand in her mouth, Amber tugged. Whimpering, she led him to the body and placed her head on the man's face, her eyes fixed on Steve.

******

"You gotta be fuckin' kidding me," Parkinson said after listening to the extended version of why Steve thought taking Amber home was the smart thing to do. Well, maybe not the smart thing, but something he needed to do.

"You better listen to him on this one, Casella," Capt. Jordan said, easing around the corner. "I heard enough of your story. I'm telling you this is a bad idea; not happening on my watch."

Steve glanced down at Amber, noting the dog's narrowing eyes, folded back ears, and quivering lips. Amber was showing an overabundance of sharp canines. Wisely, he resolved to preserve his own facial features in a more neutral condition.

CHAPTER 6

EDIE SHUT HER EYES, ATTEMPTING to block out the cacophony of human sounds blanketed by the underlying white noise of the rushing air and engine din surrounding her. The toe of her stocking foot bumped the side of her black and tan leather laptop case stowed under the seat in front of her. The shock reminded her of why she was on her way to the West Coast. But it didn't give her any confidence in what would happen or any guidance in how to proceed. With her usual approach to things, Edie got on the plane and tried not to look back. Neither did she look too far ahead. She told herself that was why she never attempted to contact Steve Casella before making this decision. Kind of a blind date. Right? Except she had the advantage of already knowing who Steve was and what he looked like, along with this desperate idea of what she wanted from him.

A growing sense of paranoia kept Edie from pulling out the troubling email. Her eyes darted about the cabin. Maybe she was being too dramatic. But she didn't need to re-read the email. The emblazoned words were etched on her brain like the memory of when her first so-called true love initiated his version of passion. The back of a 2001 Chevy Astro minivan. Not a 'Space Odyssey' for either one of them.

At this point Edie wasn't sure how the Wildflix video or the Casella family fit into the embassy bombing. But this email had revived her hopes of finding new answers. And this trip was as good a place as any to resume her efforts that had frustrated her since returning from Pakistan.

CHAPTER 7

San Francisco, California

TWENTY MINUTES AFTER RETURNING FROM the fire, Steve walked into Capt. Jordan's office. The captain signaled to Steve he'd be off the line in a minute and pointed him at the dreaded wooden chair in front of his desk.

"Right, chief," Jordan said. "I understand the regulations. Don't worry. I'll see what I can do."

Steve detected the frustration in Jordan's voice.

Dropping the handset into the cradle, Jordan took two deep cleansing breaths, bleeding off the tension sequestered in his rutted bulldog neck muscles. He stood with an effort reminding Steve of an overstuffed Pillsbury doughboy extricating himself from an ungreased muffin tin. Albeit a muscularized version of the pale pasty character.

"Casella," the captain said, "you can make this all go away. We can pretend calling animal control was the first thing you did when you saw the damn dog."

"Captain, I—"

"No, let's not make this about you. This is about the department. Its policies. The supposed cooperation we have between management, meaning me, and the union, meaning you. Let me state the obvious."

Capt. Jordan set his gaze above Steve's slouching pose and recited in a well-practiced tone. "I do not have any discretion at this time for this particular matter."

He shifted his eyes directly at Steve. "Or in a way you might understand—there's no pissin' room here to deal with this kinda shit. As you're aware, the official departmental regulations say, and I quote: 'No one is to accept any gifts and/or appear to be involved with compensatory offerings by anyone outside of the department for performing his or her duties within this jurisdiction.' And can I add for the record? In this case, since the owner of this certain property is deceased and can't confirm or deny what you've said, well…"

"Captain, I—"

Capt. Jordan backed off, raising his hands. "Casella. Hold on. Look, we both know this is all bullshit, but as a member of local 7980, you're no longer an individual, but part of our one big family."

Steve watched as the captain's face and tone transitioned from the look of a frustrated bureaucrat, to an agitated boss, and finally to a concerned friend and colleague.

"I'm sure once the investigation into this is completed," Capt. Jordan said, "you'll be cleared. But until then I have no choice but to place you on a thirty-day paid suspension. You have the right to file a grievance with the union."

Holding up a hand, he paused. "Before you answer and tell me you're keeping the damn dog… Do you remember a story from a couple of years back? The one about a firefighter back east? A suburb south of Chicago. She took it upon herself to rescue some big motherfuckin' dog. If you recall, a week later they found her mauled to death. I'm just sayin', Casella, just sayin'…"

"Soooo. Is it my turn to speak, captain?"

"Cut the shit. And wipe that smirk from your smart-assed Sicilian face."

"Captain," Steve said, his posture relaxing. "I appreciate the position I've put you in. But I'm sorry, I gotta do this. I was there, listening to this guy. Critically burned. In stifling pain and near death. He pleaded with me to take his dog. It was the only thing that mattered to him. What else could I do? It's about family, captain. Something I don't have such a good track record with. As we both know."

He mumbled his last few words as his face lowered.

Recovering, Steve said, "And no. I won't be filing any grievances. In fact, this is exactly what I need to get acquainted with my new canine friend. And by the way, if you thought those not-so-subtle union cracks would've swayed me, you're wrong. I'm not only an upstanding dues-paying member, but I've also spent a lot of my free time over the last two years doing those memorable public service promotions for the union. Not to mention the political appearances in support of my union's favorite candidates. Remember seeing my pretty face now?"

******

"Hey Parky," Steve called out as he cruised into the recreation room. "I see you got all your fingers and other body parts still intact. How's my girl doing?"

Steve crawled across the glossy black and white tiled floor to greet Amber. She had stretched herself as far away from Parkinson as the leash allowed.

"Who's ready to go for a ride?" Steve said, roughing up Amber's coat.

CHAPTER 8

AFTER LANDING AT SAN FRANCISCO International Airport Edie grabbed her first gourmet meal on the run at the Boudin's Bakery and Café. She juggled her turkey sandwich on sourdough bread, along with the rest of her traveling necessities, as she dashed through Terminal Three to the taxi loading zone area. She barely had enough time to gobble down her food in the short cab ride up the Bayshore Freeway to the Marriott Marquis across from the Moscone Center.

Edie looked out of the cab as it exited the freeway and negotiated its way toward downtown San Francisco. They'd passed a few blocks west of yesterday's early morning house fire where Steve Casella failed to save the only human occupant, but succeeded in walking away with a large, white dog named Amber.

At home, Steve rested in bed, Amber curled up at his side. The first girl he'd got into his bed in quite a while. Steve's prospects had been bleak. He couldn't find anyone who kept his interest beyond the first dinner and a movie. Steve had pleaded with Parkinson to quit trying to set him up on any more disastrous blind dates.

CHAPTER 9

EDIE SPENT THE FIRST FEW days at the Moscone Center carrying out her role as a working journalist. Or as she should have recognized, postponing her real mission. She covered lectures, seminars, symposiums, and scientific sessions. Following up on several newsworthy stories, she succeeded in getting a few in-depth interviews with key scientists involved in the research. Edie made several frustrating attempts to add human interest angles to her stories by struggling to squeeze some personal perspectives out of her subjects. She concluded that these lab-type guys and gals weren't from this same planet.

She had a talent for this work and completed a couple of solid stories. After emailing the material out to potential clients, Edie checked out of the hotel room and headed north in a rental car for the next phase of her journey.

She traveled over the Golden Gate Bridge, leaving San Francisco behind, on a quiet Sunday morning. She headed up the Redwood Highway through Marin County and gradually emerged from the dark and encompassing fog. Like a newborn baby out of the womb. The computer-generated voice from the GPS app on her smartphone provided Edie with companionship and guided her across the southern borders of the wine country and to her destination in the Sonoma Valley. She entered the town of Sonoma via a broad expanse of roadway, fittingly designated as Broadway.

"Left turn ahead," the computer voice announced.

Edie obeyed after gazing at the stately Sonoma City Hall. It stood at the end of a tree-lined entranceway in front of her at the southern end of the Sonoma Plaza.

"Your destination is ahead on the left," the computer voice informed her. "You have arrived at your destination. The guidance will now stop."

Edie turned into the parking lot of the Sonoma Valley Inn and muttered a reply to the computer voice. "I'm not quite at my real destination. And I sure as hell am going to need a lot more guidance in the days ahead."

CHAPTER 10

Sonoma, California

STEVE ENDED THE CALL AND sat back in his old dark brown leather recliner, saying out loud, "Well, I'll be damned. Amber is a pure-bred German Shepherd. I've never even heard of a white German Shepherd."

Steve didn't know if this was a good thing or not. At least she wasn't part wolf or coyote. He looked down at his scribbled notes. He was pleased to see that at eighteen months old Amber was up to date with all necessary vaccinations and in good health. Steve had tracked down the key information from the tags on Amber's collar. It had included the phone number for the veterinary clinic taking care of her since she was a puppy. His eyes lingered on the last bit of information he had just jotted down. Amber's owner had expressed concerns about her disposition. According to the vet, she'd shown definite signs of aggressive tendencies. He glanced at the notes citing several behavioral incidents that worried him. Amber's records also contained some temperament testing results that didn't make a whole lot of sense to Steve. The vet had also mentioned that Amber's owner was trying to get her trained and certified as a protection dog. They had even begun taking classes. Nobody thought this was best for the dog. Or its owner. The vet wasn't sure how far the training had progressed, or if it had done anything to stabilize Amber's behavior.

"That's great. It's gotta be why the owner didn't want the dog sent to any animal shelter. He knew the dog would be euthanized. One way to fix the problem."

Steve shook his head, realizing he was doing a lot of talking to himself.

A loud burst of serious barking interrupted his reflections. He also heard something else. Steve wasn't sure, but it sounded like a scream.

"Oh shit. I left the damn dog outside. Amber. Amber!"

He charged through the front door and skidded to a halt at the spectacle confronting him on the edge of his driveway. He focused on the scene playing out on a patch of ground that could never be confused with an actual front lawn.

"Why the hell are you just standing there, Casella? Get this freakin' wolf off me."

The sounds came from a girl pinned down beneath Amber. From where he stood, he couldn't get a decent look at the girl.

"Well, miss, I'd say you've got me at a disadvantage. You seem to know who I am, but I haven't a clue who you are."

Steve leaned sideways, peering around Amber to get a better look at his visitor.

"Still, I'm not the one on the ground with my ears being slobbered. I might even be a little bit jealous." The last part he said under his breath.

"Amber. You come here, girl. Let's go." Steve grabbed for her collar, and one by one lifted her paws away. His eyes stared at what they left behind.

"Your dog could've killed me. Can't you control it? Or at least keep it inside?"

"Maybe all her licking could've drowned you, but otherwise you didn't seem to be in any real danger." Disturbing glimpses of potential temperament and behavioral issues flashed across his mind.

"Sorry about your T-shirt," Steve said. "Amber's been rooting around in the mud all day. And with our infamous mud, your shirt will never be the same." He tried not to stare at the muddy paw prints splotched across her chest.

Steve let a small smile spread over his face.

Amber relaxed and Steve offered his hand to help the young lady back up on her feet. She brushed off his help and pushed herself up from the ground while keeping a guarded eye on the dog.

Again, Steve extended his hand.

"Steve Casella. But you already know that."

This time the girl responded with a brief clasp of his hand. "I'm Edie Pauling, and I've come a long way to talk to you."

She caught her breath, gazing at the view. A panoramic display of the western hills and valleys outlined against the clearest blue sky she had ever seen spread out beyond the cozy A-frame cabin. Far below, the town of Sonoma lay nestled at the southern edge of the vibrant, slender valley. Beyond the small town spread the fertile rolling hills and lowlands of one of the world's best wine producing regions. They merged with the northern boundaries of the San Pablo Bay. Further still, she got a glimpse of the taller buildings of San Francisco peering out from the fog, resembling misplaced fence posts above a blanket of newly fallen snow.

Steve smiled, savoring this rare opportunity for someone to enjoy his little place nestled on the hillside. "Come on, let's walk around the deck. From the back of the house, you can get a better look across the valley. And then you can tell me why you're here."

"I need to get my laptop case and notebook from the car—"

Almost letting go of Amber's collar, Steve interrupted. "Whoa. Hold on there. Don't tell me—you're—a—reporter?"

"Well, I'm a freelance journalist, but that's not why I'm—"

"Goddamn it. Can't you fuckin' people leave me the hell alone?"

Having started this explosive response, Steve couldn't stop until it all poured out, even as Edie cringed and withered in front of him.

"That part of my life is over. It's been almost two years and you still can't give it up. He's dead. Back then I did all the interviews and talk shows you guys could throw at me. I'm done talking. It's over. Can't you people understand that?"

Edie waited for Steve to take a breath, but he never stopped.

"And I sure as hell never defended what he did or said. He never got over his bitter hatred. It screwed up his whole life."

Still talking, Steve took a step forward, but Edie planted both feet on the ground, meeting his challenge.

"Let me make this clear," he said. "I am not my father. I deplored what he became and the violence he caused. But he might've accomplished one thing. He exposed those reactionary fools who took over his life. They filled him with their damn poisonous ideas. And all that venom convinced enough people to make sure those assholes didn't win the last election. But it didn't erase the violence and the deaths he caused in Pakistan. Did it?"

As Steve finally took a breath, he saw several tears rolling down a face shrouded in darkness. In the few short minutes after Edie had appeared at his doorstep, he witnessed a kaleidoscope of expressions transform her captivating image. Ranging from fear, to anger, to joy, to determination, to surprise, and ending in sadness. It didn't take him long to realize he preferred a smiling Edie.

He stared at the features on Edie's face, as if appreciating her for the first time.

Steve looked into her eyes, and said in a soft voice, "Amber…"

Edie looked down at the dog.

"No," he said. "Your eyes. They're amber."

Edie stood straighter and regained her resolve. She wiped her eyes and squared herself off in front of Steve.

"Good speech, Mr. Casella. But I'm here to convince you that you're dead wrong about thinking any of this is over. Let me make this clear. I'm not here as a reporter. So save your insults for someone else. Again, my name is Edie Pauling. My dad was Chief Petty Officer Chuck Pauling. He was a Navy SEAL. Retired. After getting out of the service he worked as a civilian security consultant for the State Department. Up until his death two years ago. When, by the way, he was killed on July 4th while on assignment at the U.S. embassy in Islamabad, Pakistan."

Both enlightenment and confusion tore at Steve's emotions as he processed the words being hurled at him.

"So, you've come all this way to kick me in the ass?"

"Well, I'm thinking about it," she said, "but I'm doubting it's for the same reasons you've got in mind."

******

Steve and Edie faced each other across the glass-topped wrought-iron table on the back side of the wrap-around redwood deck. It overlooked the Sonoma Valley far below. They both toyed with their glasses of iced tea Steve had placed on the table, staring at the mugs as if the condensing water dripping down the side was the most beguiling spectacle in the world.

Edie had retrieved her laptop case from the rental car without any further outbursts from Steve. Having arrived at this juncture, she was at a temporary loss of how to begin. With a nervous expression she glanced down at the dog now resting near the side of the table closest to the railing. She no longer feared the dog but needed to find the strength to continue.

This journey started at least two long and frustrating years ago. There were so many missing pieces to what happened back then she couldn't be sure where or when everything went so very wrong.

CHAPTER 11

Islamabad, Pakistan
(early June, two years ago)

ASSAD MAHMOOD REGARDED HIS TWO compatriots as he entered the dark and smoke-filled room.

"Praise be to Allah," he said. "I have returned with the awaited answer to our prayers."

Assad Mahmood took a seat at the remaining rusted and shaky metal chair at the far end of the battered table. The men seated around this table would be at home discussing their business on filthy beds of scattered blankets and rugs in caves along the rocky mountainside near the borders of Afghanistan and Pakistan. As others had done for over a millennium.

Today the three men were cloistered in the dank and cramped office space in the loft of a leased warehouse. The building itself was inconspicuous, located amongst many similar structures along a neglected and crumbling alleyway off the east side of Marvi Road, in an area between Bhittai and Nazin-ud-din.

Housed in the main section of this rundown warehouse were two identical late model minivans. Or at least they had been at one time. At present, one vehicle delivered kegs of draft beer and other ancillary supplies to the various nightclubs and restaurant establishments within the Diplomatic Enclave of Islamabad. The other vehicle was now being prepared for the one-time delivery of a specific package.

This industrial area was located approximately five miles from the main entry point to the Diplomatic Enclave, which contained among other structures, the main compound and complex of the American embassy. This warehouse location warranted no particular scrutiny from any of the local authorities. Given the current political climate in the region, they could have placed an Al Qaeda logo on their front door with little fear of any real reprisal.

Assad Mahmood, thirty-nine, was older than the other two men at the table. Born in Cairo, Egypt, he was the only non-Pakistani in the small local Al Qaeda cell. This cell had twelve active members. The core participants for this operational plan were all in attendance tonight.

Assad Mahmood was olive-skinned and slender, but he was the only one with a full and bushy beard that shrouded his facial features. Abu Wajid Khan, thirty-two, maintained a more modern profile with a neatly trimmed beard and short, carefully combed black hair. At twenty-eight, Abdul Ali Qadir Ahmed was the youngest. He portrayed the most western of appearances with a clean-shaven face and a cropped head of hair.

Assad Mahmood lit a cigarette and glanced around the already smoke-filled fetid atmosphere dominating the room. He exhaled with an unnatural force as if to expel this habitual fatwa in direct opposition to the teachings of the Qur'an. Pushing an overfilled and reeking can that served as an ashtray to his left, he placed the documents on the table.

With a palpable air of authority, Assad addressed his two compatriots. "In front of me are the communication documents sanctioning our proposed holy mission.

Mustafa al-Zawahiri and his generals in Abbottabad have expressed one important stipulation regarding this mission. We are not under any circumstances to execute this assault on the anniversary of the 9/11 attack on the World Trade Center as we have discussed."

Assad's eyes scanned the faces of the other two men, trying to see any hint of displeasure at the news, but saw nothing.

"Mustafa," Assad said, "believes those arrogant bastards are not foolish enough to ignore the possibilities of our using that date to strike another blow for Allah. He is certain they will issue orders to increase the security threat levels at all their foreign embassies to the maximum on the days surrounding that anniversary. Even though their leaders have declared that their military and covert operations have all but decimated our core organizational structure and our holy commitment to Allah, they also realize most of their rhetoric is just for the sake of political expediency. The generals in Abbottabad have issued their decree for us to strike on what they believe to be a more powerful event to defile the infidels. They have chosen the day on which the American pigs indulge themselves in an egotistical demonstration and celebration of their perceived superiority to a world they hold in disdain. A day on which they would be so involved in their own self-importance with their vulgar display of national pride they would not consider themselves vulnerable.

"So my friends, the time is short. We must accelerate our efforts. Our leaders have ordered us to strike on July 4th. The day the pathetic Americans celebrate their independence and the birth of their vile nation."

The recognition and approval transforming the stoic features of Abu Wajid Khan and Abdul Ali Qadir Ahmed pleased Assad.

He lit another cigarette and spoke in a more animated tone. "We will show the stupid bastards they will have no independence from the aggressive onslaught of our brave jihadists. We will strike them right here in Islamabad. On the nearest sanctioned American soil to their cowardly raid and murder of Osama Bin Laden led by their spineless so-called warriors. Those who have repeatedly defiled our land and homes. Their drones will be powerless to stop us."

All three men recited a brief prayer to Allah.

Assad closed his eyes, and his voice took on a reverent cry for revenge. "Let us all picture in our minds and hearts how the impotent, spineless political leaders back in their repulsive city of Washington will look as they are sitting around the same table where they laughed and cheered at the death of Osama Bin Laden. You must remember the scenes of self-congratulatory blustering they broadcast to the world on that dreadful day. This will remind them that the murder of Bin Laden was the impetus cementing our brave warriors to fight until the arrogant infidels are eradicated once and for all time. The fools look to their failure on 9/11 as a wake-up call to unite an apathetic American people. But to Al Qaeda and the rest of the Muslim jihadists, it was the beginning salvo which will ultimately lead to the end of their unfettered meddling in the just causes of Islam. The world of Islam can only be at peace after we have exterminated the immoral behavior of the non-believers."

"We will not fail Allah," Abu Wajid Khan said when Assad had finished. Abdul Ali Qadir Ahmed echoed the sentiments.

"We must now discuss the final aspects of this vital mission," Assad said in a more relaxed manner. "Abdul, I am eager to hear the status of your progress. And I must tell you, Mustafa al-Zawahiri wished me to convey his acknowledgment of the martyrdom you have vowed to accept."

"Yes, thank you," Abdul responded. "I am grateful to all our great leaders for the opportunity to serve Allah. And I am pleased to inform you that I have tested our planned routes and schedules. I have staged the expected activities. There have been no indications anyone suspects my movements and the ultimate purpose of our supposed services."

"That pleases me," Assad said, nodding his approval.

"Yes, Assad," Abdul said. "And I have been fortunate to have configured credible schedules to coincide with several major public events hosted by the diplomats at the American embassy. This has allowed me to observe first-hand how the security guards at the main public access gate handle the arrival of civilian vehicles. This will facilitate my ability to penetrate those same barriers before they have any chance to react to the unexpected intrusion. Our vehicle has become a normal part of the daily traffic patterns in the immediate vicinity of the American embassy. It will not be perceived as a threat. I have also made certain my face is familiar to the American fools who guard the embassy gate. I wave at them every day while delivering the vile brew to their neighbors across the street. With my adopted western clothes and mannerisms, I am positive I would have no trouble passing for one of them."

Before continuing, Abdul bowed his head. "I am sorry if you are offended by my western appearance. It is necessary for this mission to succeed. It will assure their guard will be down."

"Yes, I understand," replied Assad. "You have done an excellent job in establishing the pathway for our mission. I can assure you; your martyrdom will soon be rewarded."

Assad turned to his other compatriot. "Now, Abu. I pray you too have made the expected progress."

"Yes, Assad," Abu said. "I have procured all the needed components for our mission. We have sufficient quantities of the explosive ingredients. The specialized containers have been installed and welded in place in the back of the second minivan. For all outward appearances this vehicle is identical to the one Abdul has been using for the real deliveries. I am in the process of filling the containers with the explosive mixture. In two to three days, I will be ready to begin the intricate task of wiring the detonation circuit. There should be no problem having the vehicle ready by the new targeted date."

Abu placed a hand on Abdul's shoulder and gave his friend a brief smile. "I have already explained to Abdul the correct procedure to arm the explosives at the proper time for the detonation. When Abdul delivers his payload to the selected position within the American compound, I am confident the force of the explosion will exceed our requirements to do maximum damage and produce significant bloodshed to the celebrating infidels."

"Excellent, my friends," Assad said. "I am most pleased with the progress you have made and will immediately report your efforts back to our leaders in Abbottabad. I am confident the success of this important mission will spearhead the battle taking us right to the hearts of our soulless enemies."

Assad pounded a fist on the battered table. "Remember, this is not merely a revenge, but a resurgence of a jihad to trample the fields of their despicable beliefs."

Assad slowly turned and looked at Abdul Ali Qadir Ahmed.

"Our enemies," Assad said with great force, "will hear our thunder and fear the lightning bolts of our martyrs."

CHAPTER 12

Islamabad, Pakistan
(July 4th, two years ago)

THIS MORNING AFTER EDIE HAD left the hotel room, his uneasiness returned with a vengeance. Chuck Pauling leaned back in his chair and kneaded the muscles beneath his graying temples with his extended fingertips. After resting them on his neatly trimmed salt and pepper mustache, he proceeded to tent them aside the bridge of his nose. His elbows came to rest on the desktop, with head and hands assuming a prayer-like pose. Forcefully exhaling, Pauling attempted to purge the tension and frustration plaguing him all morning. Rising up and drifting toward the window, he gazed out from the fourth floor of the Serena Hotel to the large expansive pool area below. There he saw Edie grabbing a few last moments of relaxation before returning to the room to finish preparing for their long journey home.

At forty-nine, Chuck Pauling, a former Navy SEAL, was still fit and trim, although the rigorous activities he had forced his body to endure while on active duty had taken a toll on his aging six-foot-two frame. Edie had told him the emerging gray and thinning of the hair about his temples served to make him look more distinguished. For a moment he considered taking his distinguished body down to the hotel gym and sweat out the achiness and tensions in his stiffened muscles. Early tomorrow morning they'd be boarding the long flight back to New York. He knew there'd be little chance for anything physical during those twenty plus hours of confinement.

Pauling had been working as an independent civilian security consultant for the State Department since his retirement from the Navy. His current two-week assignment to perform a routine security audit at the American embassy in Islamabad was complete except for finishing up his written report. He planned to do it on the long flight home. His next task was to enjoy some needed down time with Edie, her two brothers, and Nana back in New Jersey. He was looking forward to this diversion, as it had been quite a while since they managed such a family gathering.

The original plan was to be back in time for the Fourth of July holiday, but once again Pauling's work got in the way. So far at least, Edie had been silent on this topic. He could sense if he didn't get his act in gear, a reminder would be imminent.

He had been reluctant to bring her along on this trip, but as always, she had a pervasive manner in getting what she wanted. He admitted it had turned out to be a unique and positive bonding experience. There were a lot worse things she could have asked for as a college graduation present.

It was still hard to believe how life had unraveled with the death of his wife, Maggie, killed by a drunk driver. Pauling had been on duty overseas. Another time he wasn't around for his family. At the time of Maggie's death, Edie's brothers were grown and out on their own. Edie was fifteen and, for the most part, mother and daughter were by themselves while Pauling was out fighting terrorists around the world. Pauling's own mother stepped up to the plate as usual. She guided a devastated Edie through the last formative stages of childhood and played a major role in helping to mold the young lady who had now accompanied him to Islamabad. By the time Pauling had retired from the Navy, Edie was entrenched in college work and her own blossoming interests.

Every moment they spent together on this trip had been an eye-opening experience for Pauling. He was getting to know his daughter. Not as the impulsive and often stubborn little girl he always remembered, but as an intelligent and determined young lady. As an added bonus, she had taken an inquisitive interest in his consulting work and had a habit of asking questions in a way that both challenged and inspired him to re-evaluate his sometimes status quo mentality.

With renewed energy, Pauling directed his attention back to what had been gnawing at him since he woke up yesterday morning, causing him to reschedule their flight home in the hope he might come up with some solid answers. In an effort to help connect the dots, he thought back to yesterday's conversation with Edie.

******

As had become the norm for the trip, Edie rooted herself right into the problem. They'd just returned to the room after a quick breakfast down in the hotel lobby. Edie curled herself up on the sofa next to the desk.

"So if you think the security systems and protocols at the embassy are adequate and managed properly, what's got your panties in a bunch?" she asked.

"First of all, young lady, Navy SEALs don't get their panties in a bunch. They get bugs up their ass. And I can at least point out some minor improvements to be made, but none of it means shit if something breaches the embassy gates. Any asshole can see they don't have the firepower to stop anything larger than a small crowd of crazy protesters. But the guys on the ground over here sure as hell don't need me to tell them any of this."

Edie edged forward in her seat and tilted her head. "Remember what we saw on the BBC last night? The anti-Muslim video put out by that new conservative group? I'm talking about the Restraint in Government Alliance. The RGA? It's gone viral. Ya think the embassy people need to be concerned about any backlash from the local Muslims?"

"What makes you think there's anything to that crap besides its potential as a political time bomb to wake up the president's voter base? Nobody in President Connor's camp is going to miss the opportunity and leverage this gives them to tie this new RGA movement to the more extreme fringe elements in the right-wing conservative groups. With a little help from the right kind of media exposure, they can use this as a soapbox to derail the republican convention before that tired old elephant can figure out what the hell kinda hat he's gonna wear and join the rest of the animals in the circus tent."

He stopped for a moment, chuckling to himself. "But let's get back to reality. The embassy folks have pounded the drums since the Bin Laden raid precipitated all this unrest. But the bureaucrats in Washington don't have the guts to acknowledge there could be a problem. The security people on the ground here have even demanded every person in the compound, suits included, be trained in the use of firearms. Can you imagine what the hell would happen with the desk jockeys parading around with guns? What chance would they have against a full detail of screaming armed terrorists storming the compound?"

He shuffled through some papers and tapped his finger on the memos he pulled out. "You remember these State Department intelligence briefings I got from my buddy in the Bureau of Intelligence and Research back in Washington?"

"Sure. You started brooding over them on the flight over here two weeks ago. The BIR is the State Department's intelligence gathering operation, isn't it? Don't they process and assess data from different sources regarding threats from terrorist groups?"

He nodded his head at her description and then pointed again for emphasis. "This here shows a definite step-up in communications activities from Al Qaeda cells in the Pakistani regions close to Islamabad and Abbottabad. There's been chatter about potential plans of retaliation for the killing of Osama Bin Laden. The first messages were intercepted around the anniversary of the Bin Laden raid. Happened almost two months ago, but the BIR officials chose to ignore this as any meaningful threat to the embassy. If you ask me, they don't want to admit to anything that doesn't fit with the pretty picture the White House is trying to paint about damaging Al Qaeda's ability to launch any more significant attacks. You've heard of the OTPA? It's a new department in the executive offices."

Edie shrugged and took a quick peek at his notes. "No, but we sure can use another administrative department in Washington."

"Right. And I need to put on another twenty pounds to stay in shape. But anyway, it stands for the Office of Threat Perception Assessment. I hear they were put in place to make sure the White House is shielded from any bad publicity of this nature. Their job is to spin these reports and make sure they are consistent with how the administration views the results of its foreign policy agenda."

Shaking his head in disgust, he said, "My assignment was scheduled at least six months before any of this took place, so I would have been here anyway. This has all been made clear to me and the embassy staff. The higher-ups in both the BIR and the OTPA don't want to give the impression there is any concern about increased threats of violence, especially if there is anything that suggests Islamic extremists might be involved. I heard some stupid bastards in Washington tried to postpone this audit so there would be no hint of any potential problems in the region."

Pauling grumbled a few incoherent words that Edie missed before he got himself back on track. "Well, I can't do anything about this election rhetoric. Regardless of all this political crap, my job is to assess the ability to detect and respond to specific threats. But I don't know how in the hell they can respond, if they're not given the opportunity and resources to be prepared."

Edie walked to the window, trying to absorb the discordant information her dad was struggling with, but was at a loss for how to help. With an apologetic look she asked the next question.

"What does RESURCON have to say about this?"

Edie was referring to a prototype software program being developed by Survidiware, a start-up software company. Before Pauling left for this assignment, the company's founder had talked him into working with the development team to evaluate and do extensive beta testing of the program.

RESURCON was being designed to evaluate digitized video data for the purpose of analyzing surveillance video images. It explored potential recognition patterns with the ability to separate and scrutinize random events by comparing them to recurring patterns to predict if security compromises or threats could be discoverable in a pre-emptive manner. At least those were the exact words from the company's promotional statement given to Pauling.

"Good question. But I think I need to review the results this program has been spitting out with the developers when we get home. I'm not sure I can handle all the data from here. Sometimes I think I'm getting to be too damn old for all this fancy new technical crap. I'd be better off trying to interpret Hieroglyphics. As far as my limited ability can decipher, the program has flagged out a number of anomalies to certain events, such as delivery frequencies, particular vehicle types and routes, driving patterns, scheduling discrepancies, and so on."

"Couldn't that be important?" Edie asked.

"I suppose," Pauling said, "except the primary focus of these things doesn't appear to have anything to do with the embassy itself. It's targeting traffic activity around an adjacent facility, not part of the American embassy compound. And this property belongs to the French, so who in the hell can make any sense out of what they're up to?"

Edie knew better than to counter any references her father made about the French, so she nodded and let him continue.

"Besides," Pauling said, "I've also reviewed the same surveillance videos by the old-fashioned method, and so far there's no specific threat activities I can point to with any certainty."

Edie could tell he was bothered by the statement.

"It's unfortunate, but I'm limited by a couple of things," he said. "So far, they've only given me access to the last thirty days of embassy surveillance videos. If anything's changed since the earlier reported increases in local Al Qaeda activity, I have nothing to compare it to, unless my requisition for the archived videos gets approved. And nothing's going to happen without approval from Washington. Need I say more?"

"Since when did you let a little bureaucracy get in your way?"

Pauling gave his daughter a long stare. "Next, as you know, the embassy is located well within the outer perimeter-guarded entrances of the Diplomatic Enclave which serves as the primary level of security for most of the foreign embassies here in Islamabad. And as you can probably guess, I have no access to the protocols followed for this area since it is under the direct control of the Pakistani police, their military, and some of their private security firms. Our government is not involved in its operations, only in paying huge sums of extortion fees for its less than stellar services. So, there's no easy way for us to know if anything unusual has been allowed to go unnoticed."

Edie interrupted again. "Any chance you can get a look at those reports?"

He shook his head. "The State Department officials could pressure the Pakistani government to let the security people at our embassy review the data, but they've refused to take a serious look at any of this. I've been told that they don't want to embarrass our supposed allies in Pakistan or do anything to upset the upcoming election process back in the states by raising any danger flags to the possibility of actual terrorist threats. And to tell the truth, I'm not familiar enough with this damned computer program to interpret any of the data. That's why they pay all those geeks to sit on their asses and play video games."

Not for the first time, Edie could feel the toll this job was taking on her father. He was a warrior and had no use for long meaningless discussions that never led to any real action.

"At this point," Pauling sighed, shaking his head, "I don't see anything concrete to take to the security guys at the embassy. I guess there's not much else to do until the real experts on the development team can pry anything of substance out of RESURCON. Maybe then I'll have something to make them stand up and listen."

In a final burst of wasted energy, he said, "But hell, the bureaucratic assholes in the State Department don't even listen to their own intelligence reports."

"You always say, Dad, what you don't see comes back to bite you in the ass."

Pauling looked away from his daughter and stared out the window.

******

Shaking himself back to the present, Pauling was considering slipping back to the embassy for one final walk-through of the perimeter when Edie burst back into the room. Without a word, she got to work packing for the trip home. Hell, he was getting anxious to get out of here, too.

But instead, he said, "I just need to check up on a few last-minute things at the embassy. You should stay here and finish packing. We certainly don't want to miss our flight. I'd say it's about time we get the hell outta here and catch up with the rest of the family to celebrate the Fourth. Even though we'll probably be a little late."

He walked out the door.

Pauling walked down the hall lugging his laptop case. It contained all the data, as well as the written notes he'd been reviewing minutes before. When he got to the elevator, he paused after pushing the button. Did he need to carry all this shit with him? He was about to turn back to the room when the elevator doors swung open, so instead he slid into the tiny compartment. Shrugging, Pauling thought, better than getting the shaft.

He stepped out of the lobby entrance into the hot, steamy afternoon elements, and muttered, "This fucking weather makes New Jersey seem like a goddamned meteorological paradise."

Pauling looked up. He figured the daily monsoons would be arriving just in time to add another level of enjoyment to his final day here.

Sweat was already trickling down his spine and plastering his shirt to his body, making him think of a wet T-shirt contest. He walked the two blocks northwest along Khayaban-e-Suhrawardy and approached the south gate guard post of the Diplomatic Enclave. His embassy credentials allowed him to pass through the security barrier with a minimal amount of problems, unlike the usual fifty-to-sixty-minute wait for the ordinary civilian visitors.

He glanced at the advertisements plastered on the various jersey barriers flanking the security checkpoint and chuckled. "Good to see capitalism is alive and well, even in this God forsaken part of the world."

He imagined seeing a 'Meet Christian Singles' sign on one of those cement ground level billboards. He shook his head as a small smile spread across his sweaty face.

Pauling toyed with the idea of climbing into the air-conditioned shuttle for the one-kilometer trek to the American embassy but decided he needed one more boots-on-the-ground reconnaissance effort. He had to either shake this foreboding cloud consuming him or clear his conscience of any negligence with regards to his final conclusions.

As he walked toward the American embassy, he glanced to his left. The French embassy.

"Why does this make me feel uneasy? Probably being so close to the French in general." He shrugged, looking around to see if anyone was listening.

After several minutes of walking, Pauling neared the grounds of the American embassy. He repositioned the heavy case slung over his shoulder and assumed a heightened level of alertness, scrutinizing his surroundings and dividing his field of vision into distinct sectors—replaying everything he had reviewed in the surveillance videos. He took note of camera angles, positions of security personnel, procedures in place at the access gates to lower the barriers to allow cleared vehicles to enter, and so on, and so on. These images flashed through his mind as he tried one last time to analyze what he could not comprehend.

It hit him again. Something about the damn French flickered across his synapses as if a disco mirror was rotating in his brain.

Pauling turned onto Street Four heading toward the main civilian entry gate to the American embassy. It was located near the west end of the walled compound. He noticed an unusually high level of vehicular traffic heading toward the embassy. And then he remembered the embassy was hosting its annual Fourth of July celebration party for the staff and family members. It must be getting underway. He found himself again thinking about apologies to his own family for missing another holiday.

Pauling proceeded, walking on the side of the street opposite the American embassy. He wanted to get a broader perspective of the procedures in place at the gate. About two-thirds down the street on his left he passed the main access road to Club Twenty-One, a popular French night club. He must have a real problem with the French he thought again, because his hackles ratcheted up another notch.

Almost to the end of the street, Pauling paused next to the service entrance to Club Twenty-One. He stood across from the civilian entry gate to the American embassy, staring at his surroundings.

Large delivery trucks were not allowed access to their routes within the Diplomatic Enclave during the day. Minivan type cargo vehicles, permitted during the daylight hours, were often seen making their regular stops on their routes. For some damn reason these regulations popped into his brain.

He shook his head. "What the hell does any of this have to do with why I'm parading around in this God-awful weather, sweating like a pig?"

He turned his attention back to the embassy gate and observed the center section of the retractable drum barrier system fixed in the lowered position, presumably to expedite the flow of party-going traffic inside the walled compound. The outer side drums remained locked in the raised position so nothing larger than an automobile would have immediate access.

In his peripheral vision Pauling caught a glimpse of a white Toyota Sienna minivan creeping past the service entrance to Club Twenty-One. His body stiffened. For a moment, the minivan stopped, and then reversed, backing onto the service entrance access road to the club.

In that instant everything crystallized in his mind.

Time stood still for Pauling.

He visualized a single still image of the surveillance video merge with the analytical output of the RESURCON software. In less than a heartbeat, a series of freeze-frame pictures bubbled to the surface of his consciousness.

Nothing unusual about a minivan headed for the Club Twenty-One service road—Except the usual protocol was to drive forward.

Large delivery trucks needed to back down the road—No room to turn around at the loading dock.

A RESURCON flagged pattern exception—
On three prior occasions, minivans backed onto
the service road. On those occasions, large public
events were taking place at the American
embassy.

His brain translated this into one frightening conclusion.

"Jesus Christ. Those were fucking dry runs."

The minivan had stopped backing toward the loading dock and began to inch forward. The vehicle picked up momentum, heading right for the open gate to the embassy. Pauling's eyes locked on the face of the driver. He'd seen that blank expression before. There was no doubt in his mind what this fanatical asshole intended to do.

In the background, Pauling heard the faint sounds of a military band playing patriotic songs from inside the embassy grounds. Closer, came the laughter and voices of children romping in the embassy's playground. He remembered seeing the slides, the swings, and the monkey bars. It made him think of his own childhood and the park across the street from his house. The children's play area in the embassy sat adjacent to the perimeter wall, within yards of the access gate. What bureaucratic moron approved that little detail?

Pauling weighed his options. No time for the guards to react and raise the barriers. The cars still flowed onto the embassy grounds. He could see families inside the vehicles, faces relaxed, but excited at the upcoming festivities. Pauling's world shrank, but the children's laughter floating above the concrete walls jammed harder into his brain.

At the wheel of the minivan, Abdul Ali Qadir Ahmed focused on his mission. His entire life centered on this one task. If he heard or saw any of the things that Pauling did, there was no indication. None of that would have mattered. Or if it did, it would serve to strengthen his resolve. The lives of the infidels meant nothing to him. And as he had been taught, neither did his own life matter. The deaths today had a purpose, and Abdul Ali Qadir Ahmed was the messenger.

Without hesitating, he thread his deadly vehicle into the line of cars turning into the embassy gate.

Pauling's body kicked into action.

Abdul's schedule today consisted of a single delivery. Four beer kegs loaded with ammonium nitrate explosives. His face remained expressionless; his eyes locked on his target. The distance to the gate contracted.

Abdul's brain never registered the charging black man heading straight for the driver's side door.

Pauling's laptop case tumbled off his shoulder, crashing to the ground. Sweat streamed down his racing body. He reached the Sienna and ripped open the door. Pauling grabbed the steering wheel and the minivan veered to the left as Abdul's foot pressed the accelerator to the floor.

Their eyes locked, but Pauling knew the fanatic saw nothing but what waited for him in Paradise.

Pauling fought for the wheel as his feet scraped along the pavement. He could now hear the shouts of the embassy guards waving the closer vehicles past the open gates in a frantic effort to clear the area and raise the barriers.

The minivan rebounded off one of the outer jersey barriers. It careened out of control, but in a direction away from the open gate to the embassy. Pauling fought hard to keep a grip on the wheel. Still dangling from the open door, his upper body pressed against the driver, arms grappling for the steering wheel. He could smell the fetid breath of the filthy son of a bitch. His ears picked up words, but they had no meaning to Pauling.

Abdul realized he had failed in his jihad to avenge the killing of Osama Bin Laden. He moved his right foot from the accelerator. Too late, Pauling's eyes registered the movement. In an act of frustration, Abdul crushed his foot down on the brake pedal.

This activated the detonator, and Abdul shouted, "Allah Hu Akbar!"

Pauling replied, "Fuck you and the rest of those putrid shits you're gonna meet in Hell."

Pauling prayed for Edie waiting back at the hotel. And the rest of his family in New Jersey. And Maggie, he thought, we sure have a lotta stuff to catch up on.

Edie barely sensed the muffled rumble on the fourth floor of the Serena Hotel as she struggled to close her overstuffed American Tourister upright carry-on.

CHAPTER 13

Sonoma, California
(present day)

EDIE SHIFTED HER GAZE INTO Steve's intense blue eyes and did what she does best. She spoke in a deliberate voice and never wavered until she trembled at the recollection of the sound and the vibration of the distant bomb blast and the eventual appearance of the American ambassador at the door to her hotel room. In her heart she already knew her father would be returning to America in a sealed casket.

Steve swallowed hard, his face drawn and helpless. "I didn't know you were right there when it happened. I— I'm sorry. I'm sorry for what happened. But don't you see? None of your story changes the words recorded by my father. His hateful ranting played a decisive role in precipitating the actions of this Islamic jihadist. You said everything your father was working on was destroyed in the blast. Besides, you don't know if he ever came up with anything concrete before he… he… well, maybe he was in the wrong place at the wrong time."

"I've been struggling since the day it happened." With an exasperated sigh, Edie kept talking. "But I wasn't there for a vacation. I was by his side whenever possible. For two weeks I listened to everything he said. And I didn't pretend to be some good little girl following her daddy around. I constantly tried to pry everything I could from him. I knew he needed a sounding board. He suspected an attack would happen. He showed me copies of intelligence reports dated back to May—months before the attack. The software program for analyzing surveillance routines he was testing rang alarm bells in his head. The stuff he struggled over started way before the WildFlix video went viral. I was so close to him when he died. But I still feel a million miles away from resolving his death."

Not knowing what to do, Steve bit his lip, his voice a whisper. "What'd you do after you got back from Pakistan?"

"Well, after things... well after I began to think straight again, I tried to contact the people he worked with at the embassy in Islamabad. It was as if they didn't exist anymore. Sure, the officials at the State Department appeared cordial, but you could tell they were going through the motions, trying to buy time for me to lose interest and go away. They kept on repeating stuff about not interfering with ongoing investigations and bringing the culprits to justice. I wasn't allowed anywhere near anybody from the BIR."

"The what?" Steve asked.

"It's the State Department's operational security group back in Washington," Edie explained. "Somebody from that department had given classified security reports to my dad. Wanna guess where those people are now?"

Steve could see Edie's anger and frustration building.

She shrugged. "Being a hotshot journalist, I clawed through the necessary channels to request whatever I could under the Freedom of Information Act. Let me tell ya though, I'll be long dead before they ever act to give out information answering anything not in the best interests of preserving the status quo for certain people in the State Department. The hell with doing what's right for the country."

As she spoke, Edie leaned toward Steve, eyes wide open, lips quivering.

"So why the hell did I come all the way out here?" Edie asked defiantly. "After all this time? And not finding any answers? What could be so important about this video you've been trying to distance yourself from? You think this has nothing to do with you anymore? You've put all this behind you? I think you and I—we both need to understand what the hell happened back then. The problem is you don't know it yet."

Edie paused and gulped down the remains of her iced tea.

"Bottom line is this," she said.

She reached into her laptop case and pulled out a single sheet of paper.

"And this email didn't come through any official channels I know about." She slapped down the paper in front of Steve.

CHAPTER 14

YOUR FATHER DIED A HERO, saving lives on that day, in the same manner he had dedicated his entire life. Just as the sunken heroes of WWII inspired the path he chose, your father's courage will rouse future generations.

Although nothing would have changed his actions on that last day, the circumstances leading up to it should not have happened. State Department intelligence reports routinely get screened by the OTPA. Events were twisted and manipulated. The overall goal was to destroy the RGA. My sources suggest direct communications between the OCCP and a local PUG in Washington state. The timing of the anti-Muslim video was too coincidental and was likely orchestrated. Tom Casella might be another victim in this perverted strategy.

Be strong like your father and follow your instincts.

An Old Friend

Steve looked back up; his expression as closed as a shuttered window attempting to block an approaching storm. Before speaking, he placed the sheet of paper back on the table. He rose and walked to the rustic wood railing separating him from the precipitous terrain dropping to the valley floor. Placing both hands on the top rail, he started-stopped his jaw several times as if testing the words in his head before uttering anything out loud.

And then abruptly turning to Edie, he spoke.

"Maybe I sound like a broken record, but nothing in that email changes my opinion about what happened two years ago. What makes you think this person is not some right-wing nutcase with a stupid conspiracy theory? Or some bureaucratic moron in one of the agencies you were pestering to get information? Maybe he's messing around with you. Some cruel joke. How is it even possible for these ignored security reports about an embassy in Pakistan to have any links to my father's video made on the other side of the world?"

With a frustrated expression Steve threw open his hands and strode back to the table, tapping his finger on the paper.

"And what the hell is with all this alphabet soup crap in there? I don't even know who, or what the hell this person's talking about."

To break the increasing tension, Edie shrugged and started with the easy stuff first, allowing a small smile to spread across her face. "As even any low information voter could figure out, we'll first start with the initials, W... W... I... I.... I believe it's the abbreviation for—"

"Okay. Let's cut the crap. I think I get your point. And I guess I've come across the Restraint in Government Alliance before, too. The RGA was one of the main influences helping my father to unravel and become so fanatical in his beliefs."

Steve took another quick glance at the paper.

"And I'll admit," he shrugged, "I'm even more familiar with the People United Group. I've done a lot of volunteer work with the local PUG people in San Francisco as part of my union responsibilities. And, by the way, you may recall I also helped them out with some campaigning during the last presidential election. So that leaves…"

"Right," Edie said with a smile. "The two four-letter words remaining refer to specific units in the executive offices of the president. The OTPA refers to the Office of Threat Perception Assessment. This is one of the new offices formed by President Connor to make sure the information gathered by the different intelligence agencies doesn't result in any negative impacts on the administration."

Looking up at Steve, Edie raised her eyebrows.

"I'm surprised you don't know what the OCCP is— being such a faithful union leader and all. It's the Office of Commitment to Community Progress. They're kinda the PUG's big brother. You wanna hear my definition of what they do? Nah. Probably not," Edie chided, placing her hands on her hips and leaning forward.

"Anyway, all this leads up to my next point. Didn't it seem a little extreme for those black helicopters to swoop in and drag your father off to some isolated holding cell at a Homeland Security facility for questioning? For what? National security? You can go online anytime you want and find the same rhetoric expressed in that video."

Steve was at a loss for how to respond. His face paled and he had trouble breathing.

"And," Edie said, "aren't you the least bit interested in what happened to your father after he was in the friendly helping hands of our federal government? Protective custody? Seriously? Maybe this resembles a conspiracy theory-like feeling, but how many people die of natural causes under the circumstances to which your father was subjected?"

Edie paused, dropped her arms, and lowered her voice. "Steve. You gotta think this through from the beginning. I never met your father, so I know nothing about him. But what was the point of him making such a video? Could he have been threatened? Did someone force him to do this? Why do you think he was willing or even capable of taking part in any of this? Was he used? Or was he naïve?"

She stared into Steve's eyes. Reaching out, she touched his arm. "More to the point, Steve. Who the hell do you think stood to gain the most from this video?"

Keyed up with a backlog of frustration and pent-up energy, Edie couldn't sit still.

CHAPTER 15

Washington, D.C.
(two years ago)

BEN COURTNEY STRUGGLED TO REARRANGE his lanky frame. Dressed in his customary linen tan Hugo Boss double-breasted suit, now unbuttoned, a rare but necessary evil, he sank deeper into the plush wine-colored velvet seat cushion in the elegant booth tucked against the southeast wall of the Old Ebbitt Grill. With a nervous gesture he glanced at the antique Victorian clock perched above the imposing revolving door entrance to the historic restaurant. The venue chosen due to its proximity to the White House. As the director of the Office of Commitment to Community Progress, or OCCP, Courtney didn't tolerate waiting for many people. This was especially true when he was the one who had arranged for this meeting to take place.

Courtney's gaze returned to the intense dark olive face of the younger man seated across the mahogany table on the other side of the booth. His companion, David Reilly, was the head of one of the pacific northwest branches of the People United Group, or PUG, located in the Spokane and Coeur d'Alene area of eastern Washington and the Idaho panhandle. Although dressed in a cream-colored lightweight sweater, his posture belied the underlying edginess of an animal sensing crosshairs moving into position across his back.

Before either man realized, the third and final participant in their rendezvous arrived. Bursting through the revolving doors, a sea of patrons and servers parted in his path. Ralph Matthews sighted his quarry and headed straight to his destination. The president's chief of staff looked impeccable, attired in a three-piece navy-blue suit, crisp white shirt, and his signature red, white, and blue tie. As he approached the booth, Courtney made an attempt to button his jacket. An impossible task at the moment. Reilly looked ready to crawl under the table.

At forty-seven, Matthews, with his closely cropped hair, remained as fit and imposing as he did when he was fighting his way out of the ghettos of East Saint Louis over twenty-five years ago. He was still using some of the more crucial tactics he learned back then in his current position in the White House.

"Good morning, gentlemen," Matthews said with a smile, revealing an expanse of perfectly aligned teeth as he slid into the booth across from Courtney.

The better to eat you with. That was his adversaries usual reaction to this opening look from Matthews.

As if in response, he turned toward Reilly, extending his hand. "It's been a while since I've had the pleasure of seeing you. I understand you're here in D.C. to help coordinate and reinforce our plans to link our leading opponents to the supposed ideologies of this Casella person. The unwitting star of our featured cinema."

Not expecting an answer, Matthews pushed forward. "I want to commend you in person for the outstanding work you did in getting your man to infiltrate the local chapter of the Restraint in Government Alliance. Not to mention manipulating some of the other local reactionaries to perform like a bunch of trained seals. With a little help from our dependable friends, it took little effort for that video to spread across the internet and every other major media outlet. As I recall, we gave you the go-ahead last week, so you didn't get much notice to make the final preparations. Besides from the need to get in front of the upcoming election cycle, I believe the breaking news from Pakistan this morning gives you an idea of why we needed to move on it right away. A lot faster than any of us could have imagined."

Matthews leaned a bit closer to Reilly but kept Courtney in his peripheral vision. "Without going into too many details, we've known for some time there was a credible potential for violent activity to be directed against our embassy personnel in Pakistan. As you know, we decided it was necessary to downplay any perception of organized terrorist plots in the region. It would be inconsistent with the administration's view of having eviscerated our enemies."

Reilly nodded after a quick glance at Courtney.

"What happened last week," Matthews said, "when WildFlix distributed the video, will pale when the media runs with this morning's story out of Pakistan. You'll see what I mean after the president gives his address later today and we get the appropriate talking points out in front of the American people."

Matthews kept his voice low. He maintained a somber look on his face despite the satisfaction he was experiencing in being a step ahead of this crisis. Or opportunity as he liked to think of it. After all, it's not every Fourth of July the American embassy in Pakistan is bombed.

A shocked expression spread across Reilly's face. His hand reached for a pack of cigarettes. But this was a smoke-free environment and Reilly couldn't excuse himself to rush outside for a smoke. His eyes landed on his coffee cup. At least he was smart enough to have asked for a cup of the house decaffeinated brand. But a slight tremor was still evident as he picked up the delicate cup and sipped the expensive brew.

Realizing both men at the table had been mute, Matthews paused and signaled a passing server for his own cup of coffee. Not decaffeinated.

"Gentlemen," he said, "you don't appear interested in listening to me congratulate you for your accomplishments. So, Ben. Why don't we get to the real reason you wanted to meet me here this morning? I assumed you wanted to see how we could capitalize on the news reports of this embassy bombing to tweak our upcoming plans. But looking at your faces, I'm sensing there's more to it."

As Reilly withered into the overstuffed cushion, Courtney began, trying to keep his voice steady. "We appreciate your comments. And yes, we can talk about the next phase of our plans. We do have some good news to report. But something just came up, and I think it needs to be brought to your attention."

"Well then," Matthews said, "why don't you get to it?"

"Our inside man at the RGA," Courtney said. "Peter Fenton? The one who put this video together for us?"

"Of course," said Matthews.

"Well, after the video went viral," Courtney said, "Tom Casella barged right up to Fenton's house in Coeur d'Alene and made some pretty strong accusations. He ranted on about this video being a bullshit set-up, and he and his local pals were used as—"

"Hold on, Ben," Matthews said. "I thought we expected there would be some backlash and finger pointing. After all, you chose Casella deliberately because he wasn't one of the local rednecks. It was a brilliant idea to use a misplaced college professor. One who might even have the capacity for some independent thoughts. That's why Fenton mentored him and facilitated the process of his gaining access to the inner sanctum of the Restraint in Government Alliance. We needed this link to the RGA to be with a credible individual."

Matthews took a sip of his coffee. Placing his cup back on the table, he spread his open palms out.

"So, who the fuck cares if he thinks Fenton was using him?" he asked. "In fact, it makes everything more believable. I consider this Fenton character expendable. He knew the risks going in. If anything, we now have two prominent members of the RGA linked to the video."

Matthews stared at Courtney.

"Let's make sure Fenton is still on board with us," Matthews emphasized. "As far as I can recall, we have made all this worth his while. He should be more than ready to take the hit for us. You disagree?"

"That was the plan," Courtney said, "but first, why don't I give you the… ah… good news?"

Matthews waited for Courtney to continue.

"Fenton impressed the RGA with his success in bringing their conservative agenda to the public. And his organizational skills in coordinating most of the political activities at their local offices in Coeur d'Alene. They've asked him to participate in the team being put together in New Jersey for the special senatorial election. The RGA thinks this race presents an excellent opportunity to bring Tyler Griffin to the national spotlight. And as you know, they've already made some important investments in linking his political future with the success of their movement."

"Well, well. A most unfortunate event. The untimely death of our good democrat colleague, Senator Hardy," Matthews said in a disingenuous tone. Fine white teeth again exposed. "If Fenton can entrench himself this early in the campaign staff for Tyler Griffin's political ambitions, it would give us the opportunity to keep tabs on what they're up to. Not to mention the ability to deliver some serious damage to someone on the verge of becoming one of our most dangerous opponents. And needless to say, we would strike at the time of our choosing. As you know, I can be a patient man. On rare occasions."

Already the wheels in Matthews' head were churning away at how this might be used as part of his incipient plans for the complete control of congress after the next mid-term elections. In his mind, he considered the outcome of this fall's presidential elections a foregone conclusion.

Looking over at Reilly, who had failed at trying to make himself invisible, Matthews prompted, "What say you about all this, David?"

Unable to avoid the impending train wreck any longer, Reilly said, "Well, when Tom Casella confronted Fenton, he made some blatant statements concerning Fenton's real alliances. Accusing him of ties to the PUG. And well, me in particular. Claimed he would prove Fenton was on the PUG payroll. He would expose him and his left-wing friends for the dissident acts they were trying to lay at the feet of the conservative organizations."

That got the chief of staff's full attention.

"This all happened on Saturday," Reilly said, "and then Casella stormed off. It was the last time anyone has seen Tom Casella. And believe me, since the media hounds arrived on Monday, they've been in a feeding frenzy to get at him. The news today of the embassy bombing is going to intensify their desire to talk to him. It's important we either find out where he is or be the first ones to reach him when he resurfaces."

Leaning back, Matthews assumed his accustomed air of authority and fired back.

"I think we can all agree Fenton is too valuable an asset to throw to the wolves," he said, ignoring his prior readiness to do that very thing. "David, I think you need to get back to Spokane. Be ready to manage this situation up close and personal. Let me know the second you get a handle on locating Casella. I can assure you he will not have the opportunity to cause us any further problems. I do not tolerate loose ends."

Matthews paused, and said, "Good day, gentlemen."

Checking his watch, he shook his head, realizing he would be late for his next meeting. Never a good way to treat your official boss. Especially one who always seemed to forget who ran the show.

Matthews left the restaurant in the same way he had arrived. He jumped into the waiting car outside the restaurant and headed for the next meeting of the morning. This was promising to be a busy day. And if he was as good at his job as he knew he was, it could represent the major turning point needed for the upcoming elections.

******

Matthews' car stopped under the West Wing portico to the White House. He exited and walked around to the West Basement entrance. Security ushered him down a short flight of stairs and through the heavily guarded entrance to the Situation Room.

As expected, the briefing in the main conference room had already begun. President Connor scowled as his tardy chief of staff slipped into a vacant chair between Secretary of State Gerald Singleton and Vice President Alice Andersen.

After the interruption, the secretary of state cleared his throat and continued with his briefing. "We have now confirmed the total number of casualties at the embassy was five. Four American citizens and the perpetrator. Included were three members of the same family: An embassy staff associate, Jonathan Sawyer, his wife, Carolyn, and their four-year-old daughter, Amanda. The fourth casualty was an independent civilian security consultant for the State Department: Name of Chuck Pauling."

"Gerald," Matthews said, "you're telling me we had a civilian contractor snooping around the embassy during this attack?"

The secretary of state glanced sideways at Matthews. "Excuse me?"

"No one," Matthews said, eyes narrowing, "informed this office we were still interfering with the Pakistani security forces and bringing undue attention to any unrest in the area. We informed your people months ago to defer to the local authorities as a show of good faith on the progress we've made regarding their handling any spontaneous outbursts or demonstrations."

"You do know," the secretary of state said, "the State Department follows certain guidelines? And this contractor was performing a routine audit of our internal security procedures. We scheduled the audit at least six months in advance."

"Well," Matthews muttered, writing something on his notepad, "perhaps it's time to review these so-called guidelines again. Maybe make things a little more clear for you folks down the street."

"Gentlemen," President Connor intervened. "Can we move along here? We can worry about those kinds of details at a later time. I've got a speech to prepare."

The secretary of state glanced around the table, eyes finally resting on Matthews. "As I was about to say, we have the initial reports coming in from eyewitnesses at the scene. Members of the security detail who were on duty at the civilian entry gate to the embassy. They confirm at around one o'clock in the afternoon, local time in Islamabad, guards were clearing civilian vehicles into the embassy for the planned Fourth of July celebration. They noticed a man, who they recognized as Pauling..." He paused long enough to see if Matthews would take the bait. "... the consultant they had been working with for the last two weeks. He wrenched open the driver's side door of a small delivery van as it accelerated toward the embassy gate. The vehicle swerved away from the gate, bouncing off one of the security barriers. An explosion followed. The Sawyer family was arriving at the gate in their car at the time of the blast. Regrettably, it was in proximity to the delivery van and bore the brunt of the explosion. It appears Pauling died while preventing the apparent suicide bomber from penetrating the open access gate to our embassy."

With a rueful smile aimed at Matthews, he added, "His bravery saved numerous American lives. And as a footnote, Pauling was a retired Navy SEAL."

Matthews remained silent but considered themselves lucky this Pauling character would not be around to testify at any potential hearings or any other such nonsense resulting from this incident. Who the hell knows what kind of stuff he could've stumbled upon while investigating threat potentials and security lapses at the embassy.

The assembled members of the president's senior staff and cabinet worked over the next thirty minutes in a concerted effort to prepare a series of talking points for President Connor's address to the nation. This was scheduled for twelve noon from the Oval Office. The president was adamant about not missing the opportunity to reinforce the public's attention on the media fervor surrounding the anti-Muslim video released last week. The timing of the embassy bombing couldn't be better. Everything was falling into place. They could continue to emphasize the RGA connection to the video and minimize the potential exposure of any intelligence information regarding possible pre-planned Al Qaeda attacks.

As the elite participants filed out of the room, President Connor turned to Matthews. "Nice of you to make yourself available on such a short notice."

Ignoring the president's sarcastic remark, Matthews whispered, "Mr. President, may I please have a word with you?"

On the brink of exploding, the president reined in his anger. His complexion paled. He understood Matthews reserved that phrase for when a major crisis was about to unfold. He realized Matthews wouldn't be bothering him if it wasn't important. They both knew he needed to prepare for one of his best song and dance numbers in less than thirty minutes.

Exiting the elevator on the first floor of the West Wing, the president entered the chief of staff's office and closed the door. The two men stood facing each other. President John Connor was approximately the same height as his chief of staff, but of a slightly trimmer build with thinning, premature gray hair. He possessed a rugged handsome face with wide-set hazel eyes and a prominent square jawline.

Twenty minutes later President Connor was sitting in the Oval Office amidst a cavalcade of cameras. Matthews was finishing up his last phone call.

"Right," Matthews said in his customary dictatorial voice. "Everything's approved and will be in place within the hour. Be ready to make this happen. We get one chance at this before the media takes over."

Compressed lips veiled his teeth.

CHAPTER 16

Sonoma, California
(present day)

EDIE PACED BACK AND FORTH across Steve's deck like a frustrated caged animal. Her momentum drained; she slid back down onto the patio chair.

Steve pushed away from the railing and returned to the table. He sat down across from her in the same positions they had assumed in what seemed like ages ago but was actually a few intense minutes earlier.

In contrast to Edie's spent expression, Steve's eyes were bright and fixated. "Contrary to your opinion of me, I'm not completely ignorant of the possibility others could've had a hand in this."

"Steve, I—"

"I know those right-wing groups," he said, overriding Edie, "probably got into his head and twisted his fractured view of reality. Dad was vulnerable, and an easy target. I was pissed and hurt. He abandoned what I thought we had going for us here and took off to start a new life. Maybe I could've done more to understand what was happening to him, but I needed someone to blame. I suppose he did too."

In an instant the passion ceased and Steve's face mirrored Edie's. "When Mom died... I... I don't know... I don't..."

Reaching out across the table, Edie placed her hand softly on his. They both sat motionless, as if frozen in the past.

Steve broke the silence and spoke first. "Most of these memories have been tucked away for a while. I don't do well talking about these things. I suppose I'm gonna need time to reflect on all this."

"Perhaps we both do. I'm staying in town at the Sonoma Valley Inn for the next couple of days. Why don't you give me a call when you're ready to talk?"

Edie slid a card with her number on it across the table.

Steve glanced at the card and looked up with a quirky smile, but serious eyes. "Edith *ROSA* Pauling? Well. I guess you might agree with the words someone also named Rosa once said, and I quote, 'Knowing what must be done does away with fear', unquote."

With a distant smile, Edie got in her car and drove away. Except for reinforcing her previous expectations of observing the rugged good looks of his classic Mediterranean features, Steve was a complete surprise. While she remembered using that exact same quote in a civil rights essay for an English Lit class as a freshman, she was also thinking about another Rosa, besides the one Steve just quoted. One from which she drew her strength. If only Nana knew what she was really up to.

As he turned away from the receding vehicle, Steve whistled and called out, "Whaddaya ya say we go for a walk, Amber?"

After starting off with Amber on a leash, Steve lost the battle of the pulling, lunging, digging, more lunging, growling, pulling, snarling, more lunging, and more growling. And this all occurred before he reached the end of his short driveway. He released Amber from her lead and began the next phase of the 'walk' rubbing his aching arm and trying to keep a darting and charging Amber in sight. Amber had some control issues when it came to spotting birds. Squirrels. Rabbits. Chipmunks. Neighbor's cat. Neighbor's dog. Neighbor. Amber was fine with the neighbor once properly introduced and the neighbor's dog and cat were out of the equation. Steve sensed a pattern here. Two legs; acceptable. Four legs or wings; not so good.

This gave Steve a chance to recall a different scene. Two legs. Two legs in tan shorts atop a pair of white slip-ons. That memory looked pretty good to him as he further replayed the image of the stunning and intense young lady who had shaken his world. His face transformed into the kind of smile that had been rare in the last few years.

Steve felt proud of himself. He was beginning to figure out all this dog stuff on his own. Without the help of any smart-assed dog trainer. Figuring out this Edie thing, however, might take a little more work. After a final struggle to get Amber's leash attached, they headed home. Straining and stumbling behind Amber, Steve admitted a little guidance for this dog obedience work wouldn't be a bad idea.

He paused before going back inside and looked at the house he had been living in for about two and a half years. It was a typical mountain-styled A-frame home, perched on a rugged hillside. Level ground edged the front of the house, allowing for a small front yard and a place to park his car. His property continued on the other side of the road and was mostly flat. Room for a barn and maybe a larger garden. Someday in the future.

Four concrete columns supported the cantilevered back side of the house above the sloped terrain. His favorite part of the house was the wraparound deck surrounding the structure, forming a rustic picture frame. The house was small, with one good-sized bedroom, a single bath, and an open living area encompassing the kitchen, living room, and dining room under an exposed beam cathedral ceiling. In Steve's mind this was all incidental to the stunning views out the back of his house.

He'd not been idle since making this his home and had become handy in renovating the interior. Proud of his accomplishments, he sometimes felt cheated. He regretted his dad wasn't alive to see the work he'd done. His dad's sole visit came several months after Steve had purchased the place, so he never got a chance to see the end result. Soon after that visit, his dad was dead.

Once inside Steve busied himself into making an expanded list of needed pet supplies. Then he jumped in with some housecleaning chores. He gave Amber a bath. The pet supplies list grew larger. He made dinner. Hamburger on the grill for Steve. Hamburger on the grill for Amber. Last of the kibble for Amber. More dog food added to the pet supplies list.

The endless list of procrastinations came to an end. Steve forced himself to press the digits on his phone's keypad, making the call he'd put off for almost two years.

The call to Edie would come later.

CHAPTER 17

THE NEXT MORNING EDIE WAS awakened by a bright glare of sunshine intruding through the narrow gap between the closed drapes of her motel room window. Squinting from the sharp rays of light penetrating deep inside her head, she groaned and turned herself away from this unsolicited California wake-up call.

Although a light sleeper, she picked up her phone and checked for any missed calls or messages. What had she expected to happen after meeting with Steve Casella? Maybe still a little groggy from sleep, but Edie couldn't figure out how things went yesterday.

She snugged the covers up to her chin for security. Thank God it wasn't a blind date, because she'd be feeling worse. She never even saw the inside of Steve's house, let alone dinner and a movie.

A sly smile appeared on Edie's face. She peered at the evidence encrusted on her T-shirt heaped next to the bed. But Amber did kinda get a little fresh with her. Continuing down this path, she considered it time to draw the line at an interspecies relationship.

Oh God. She dragged herself into the shower and tried to scrub away any more ridiculous fantasies. At least most of them anyway. One or two found hiding places in the unused crevasses of her subconsciousness.

Dripping wet, corner of the bath towel catching on the big toe of her left foot and yanking free, Edie's naked body slid across the bed to grab the ringing phone.

Without preamble, Steve asked, "When did you say you needed to get back home?"

At least he didn't ask what she was wearing. But Edie felt a hint of disappointment when she answered. "I'm my own boss. I make all the rules. Why?"

"You wanna go meet my Uncle Bob?"

CHAPTER 18

EIGHT HECTIC, BUT PRODUCTIVE HOURS later, Steve and Edie sat across from each other. They were nibbling on the remains of their Tuscan Sun pizza in the bustling pizza establishment adjacent to the Sonoma Plaza. One block from the motel where Edie was staying.

Edie looked around at the red brick oven, the wine collection framing the bar, and the granite fountain babbling in the outside patio dining area. She shook her head.

"Only in California," she mumbled.

"Huh?"

"Nothing, but ya know it doesn't seem right without Sal or Alfonso standing by the pizza ovens yelling to either hurry up and order or get the hell out of the way for the paying customers. And I'll tell you one thing."

Eyes sparkling, pointing at the remains on her plate and gulping down the rest of her locally brewed beer, Edie blurted out the rest. "Somebody in the kitchen has gotta be from back east. And I don't mean Ohio. This is the genuine New York thin-crusted stuff. The real deal."

Steve glanced back from the fountain. He'd lost her about two bites and three sentences ago. What the hell was she babbling about?

"Right," he said. "Exactly what I was thinking. But anyway, I think we're about ready to go for tomorrow morning. You said the motel would take care of returning your rental car. Anything else you need to do?"

"Nope."

In double-time, Edie spoke again, making Steve's head spin some more. "You said your Uncle Bob is a retired cop from San Francisco? And he lives in some place called Hayden Lake in north Idaho? It's near where your dad lived. Right? Why does the name sound so familiar to me?"

Hoping she wasn't thinking of the Aryan Nation's old stomping grounds, Steve conveniently ignored the last part of her question. He moved on to explain Uncle Bob had been a K9 training instructor for the San Francisco Police Department. He was now doing dog training consultations with the local law enforcement K9 units in Idaho, as well as teaching civilian dog classes in obedience and personal protection.

Steve's expression turned serious. "Let me get this out before we go any further. Just because we're going up there doesn't mean I agree with your version of what happened. Or there's some sort of conspiracy going on. I think you've convinced me though. I can't move on without at least trying to understand why my dad left and did all those things after my mom was killed."

Leaning back and exhaling, Steve's body relaxed. "Besides, while we're there maybe Uncle Bob can give me a few pointers on how to handle Amber." Steve hoped his uncle might spot any potential behavior issues and maybe explain this protection dog training too.

"So," he said, "let's try to get an early start in the morning and see if we can drive straight through. We can make it in less than twenty hours if we share the driving. How about I pick you up around eight?"

"I'll be ready," Edie said, but wondered if either one of them could be prepared for what was to come. Regardless, she knew she needed to keep Steve talking, or it would all remain locked in his past.

CHAPTER 19

THE LONG JOURNEY PROGRESSED ON schedule after making a few minor seating arrangement changes. They found it necessary to stop at a pet store in Redding and purchase a vehicle pet barrier to make sure Amber didn't violate any of the established boundaries.

The Metallic Mineral Gray Dodge Durango was cruising north along Interstate 5 in southern Oregon near the Siskiyou Summit. As they descended into the Ashland area, Steve and Edie ran out of small talk.

Edie drove most of the way up the interstate corridor toward Portland while Steve was dozing next to her in the front passenger seat. Tired of trying to find a decent radio station that didn't fade in and out at every hill and valley they traversed, she glanced over at Steve. He still had his eyes closed.

"You sleeping?" she said with an intentional bump to his shoulder.

If that didn't wake him, Amber's barking in response to Edie's raised voice did the trick.

"What? Huh? Is it my turn to drive?" Steve mumbled.

"No, I'm still good to go for a while. Sorry. I didn't mean to wake you," she said without much conviction.

"But since you're already awake, there is something I've been trying to understand."

Edie waited to make sure Steve was roused enough to listen.

"You know," she said, "there were tons of media coverage about your dad after the video came out. And then when he died, you became the focus of the story. You granted interviews with all the different news channels. At the time I didn't give it much thought. But me, I tried to avoid any outside intrusions on my own life. I needed to stay away from the limelight so I could figure things out for myself. I'm not criticizing you for how you handled the media and all the attention you got. But…

"A couple of days ago when I showed up at your house, you thought I was a reporter. And you exploded. Well… I guess what I'm trying to figure out is if you have all this hatred toward the media, why'd you agree to do all those interviews back then?"

Steve let out a deep sigh and remained quiet for several moments, glancing out the side window. "See the sign for the rest area? Pull off. I think Amber needs a potty break."

Edie stared straight ahead. Maybe she should've stuck with the small talk a little bit longer.

A short while later, with a couple of cold sodas in hand, Amber and her water bowl between her paws, Steve and Edie each sat at opposite ends of one of four metal picnic tables at the rest area. Facing out at the interstate. A noticeable gap between them. A couple of cars were parked nearby, but they seemed to have the entire pet area to themselves.

Edie bit her lower lip. "I can withdraw the question."

Staring ahead at the traffic speeding by, Steve ignored Edie's offer, and said, "I could give you a dozen answers or excuses, but I'm still not sure if I can convince myself how to separate the truths from the lies."

Body still facing forward, Steve turned his head slightly toward Edie. "You said you remembered me giving all those interviews. But do you recall what I talked about?"

From the look on his face, Edie knew he didn't expect an answer.

"I became the poster child for fighting intolerance. I felt compelled to erase the hatred I saw spewing from the man who was my father. The man I always looked up to. The man I thought I knew. I needed to tell the world I was not my father."

Steve corrected himself. "No, I needed to *show* the world. So, I became involved in working toward exposing those people he got caught up with for the divisiveness and violence they were advocating. I embraced the progressive community groups working with our leaders in Washington to make sure everybody got their fair share of the American dream."

Steve's body arched closer toward Edie. "And although I didn't recognize it at the time, I looked for someone to blame. But blame for what? My mother's death? My father running away from me? Me, for not understanding what my father needed? My father dying before anything could be resolved? And then I finally blamed every reporter who ever knocked on my door and listened to what I had to say. Or to be more exact, *used* what I had to say.

"But in the end, it was easiest to blame the people who I believed influenced my father's life and twisted his head into thinking the social progressives were responsible for destroying our country."

Looking at Edie, he stretched and clasped his hands behind his neck. "And we're headed there right now. Maybe coming face-to-face with the ideological zealots who sucked my father into their fascist beliefs, I'll come to grips with what the hell happened to make him do the things he did.

"I know you have your own personal idea of who to blame for your part of this nightmare. And given the circumstances, you were closer to the horror of the situation than I ever was. I know you think the big bad government leaders are trying to squelch the voices of the people who represent the teachings of our forefathers. But maybe the people who you think are being demonized are the ones who already got what they want and are afraid the government will rock the boat."

"Steve, I—"

He held up his hand. "I hope to hell whatever happens, whatever we find out, we can finally find some good to come out of this whole mess. Sooner or later we better get something right, because I have a bad feeling if we don't, this country is gonna be a lot worse off than anyone can imagine."

Edie closed the gap between them, momentarily placing a hand on his shoulder.

She whispered, "For you, this whole thing started long before your father died. He was on some kind of a crash course. I want you to tell me about how your mother died."

For a long time, Steve sat staring out across the interstate. "It was their wedding anniversary. Dad took the day off and drove Mom to work at her school. After he dropped her off, he planned to spend the day at the Oakland Library catching up on reviewing some research grant proposals."

"He was a college professor, wasn't he?" Edie interrupted, regretting it and swearing not to let her journalistic curiosity get in the way again. She knew she'd have to let Steve get it all out in the open. On his own.

"Right. Dad had a doctorate degree in human physiology and was a tenured professor in the Biology Department at the University of California in Davis," he answered, glancing at the strange expression on Edie's face.

"They were going to drive into San Francisco later in the afternoon for dinner. They also had tickets to see *Cats* at the Orpheum Theatre. I remember being a little worried about them going to such a dangerous area of the city after dark.

"Mom was a guidance counselor at the Oakland Cultural Center School. The school was founded for the purpose of helping kids who were recent immigrants become assimilated into our country by focusing on our language and our cultural customs as the main part of the school program."

Steve took a sip of his soda.

"According to Dad, Mom had become frustrated with two Muslim students she was trying to help. One of the students, who was from Pakistan, was gay. The other student, from Iran, was somehow against his particular lifestyle.

"A real shocker." Steve interrupted himself.

"They were showing increased signs of hostility toward each other. Mom had been counseling them separately, but she was getting nowhere. On that last morning, Dad said she decided to bring them together, trying to have them confront the issue. She underestimated the vehemence the Iranian student held toward the gay Pakistani. She didn't know he carried a concealed knife taped to his ankle. I guess the school considered metal detectors to be inconsistent with their philosophy of cultural mergence."

Steve paused, looking into the afternoon sky as if waiting for answers. "When it was over, the Iranian student bragged to the cops as he was taken into custody. His actual words were 'the infidel whore got in my way, and I slit the bitch's throat'. He believed killing her was an added bonus to his original intent of, again, in his own words, 'sending the gay pig to the devil'. Don't think Mom could've done much in the way of counseling him."

Steve focused on something across the interstate, shaking his head. "Talking to Dad after Mom died never worked. I think we both succeeded in making a painful situation worse. Dad became consumed about how the media coverage of the story was preoccupied with the injustices and intolerances toward minorities. He said they were fixated on how right-wing zealots were to blame. He thought they ignored the fact the assailant was a Muslim, not even in this country very long, and angered by his own religious views on homosexuality.

"Dad was infuriated because Mom died trying to save the gay student, a victim of Muslim intolerance, but her bravery in trying to save the boy was presented by the media as secondary to their hate crime agenda. Dad convinced himself there were some people in the media who were relieved she died. It got her out of the picture. Then they could accuse her of being insensitive to minority issues. And blame her for deliberately bringing the two students together to cause the confrontation."

Edie couldn't think of a single thing to say. About his mother's death or the emotional turmoil tearing at the heart of his dilemma. This was not a situation she found herself in very often. She felt disconcerted by her own reaction.

Any words would be empty. And nothing was going to sway either Steve or her from their pre-existing perceptions. His understanding of her beliefs was way off the mark, but this wasn't the time to express those opinions. They were headed into the devil's backyard. She was sure of this but didn't know who would answer when they went knocking on his door. Edie was beginning to feel, at last, after all this time, she wouldn't be facing the devil alone.

She stood and pulled Steve to his feet. After a quick embrace, she shrugged. "I'll get us to Portland, then you can buy me dinner. I'll accept a rain check for the movie."

CHAPTER 20

TAKING TURNS AT THE WHEEL, they drove through the remainder of the night in a comfortable silence. On occasion, Amber barked at approaching headlights, breaking the monotony of the rhythm of the tires humming endlessly over the pavement.

They had journeyed through the barren basalt outcroppings of the Columbia Plateau and were descending into the fertile valleys of the Spokane area in eastern Washington when the first signs of the approaching dawn began to transform the darkness beyond their windshield. Before the sun could fully emerge, Washington was in their rearview mirror.

They had begun the final lap of their trip into the Idaho panhandle and the populated Kootenai County. Up ahead were the northern shores of Lake Coeur d'Alene located at the southern terminus of a picturesque open prairie. Pulling off the Interstate onto US 95, they grabbed a quick breakfast and drove the last several miles to Uncle Bob's house.

They drove past the Hayden Lake Country Club and turned right onto a narrow, winding road. The houses were terraced along the hillside overlooking the northern projection of the lake. Within a minute the Durango came to a welcome halt on the asphalt driveway in front of Uncle Bob's archetypal Pacific Northwest A-frame. It turned out to be similar in style to Steve's house, but on a grander scale. It was also surrounded by a large and level front yard with an extensive lawn and garden area to the back.

As Steve turned off the engine, a tall man in his early sixties with a trim goatee and a receding silver hairline approached the car. He wore a dark gray polo shirt outlining a well-defined pair of muscular arms and shoulders. A series of barks from the rear compartment of the Durango greeted the broad smile fixed across his face.

Glancing at the occupants of the car, Uncle Bob said, "Well, Steve. You're traveling with two interesting companions. Which one should I be more cautious of?"

Edie answered for him. "So far as I know, the white girl in the back is all bark. But the black one up front has been known to bite."

Uncle Bob ignored Amber and circled around to open Edie's door.

Taking a step back, he said, "I find it best to keep the more dangerous ones in my direct line of sight. I'm Bob Casella. Welcome to Hayden Lake. Where the word of the day is to embrace our differences." Uncle Bob winked and Steve bumped his head against the steering wheel.

Although tired from their non-stop road trip from California, neither Steve nor Edie took Uncle Bob up on his offer to crash for a few hours. They did, however, spend the next half hour shedding their travel-soiled clothes and showering off the effects of their day-long journey.

Steve and Edie, feeling somewhat human again, walked through the sliding glass doors to the backyard. They both stopped short at the sight before them.

CHAPTER 21

Hayden Lake, Idaho

UNCLE BOB ZIGZAGGED ABOUT THE yard, changing speeds and directions in a random fashion, while stopping and starting dozens of times. And without a single command, Amber followed his every move. She was doing so with the attached lead swaying loosely between the dog and the handler. To Edie's amazement, two additional, though standard-colored German Shepherds, played close by in the same yard. And Amber showed no interest in their presence.

Uncle Bob walked over to Steve, handed him Amber's lead, and faded into the background. As if on cue, Amber barked and lunged at the two other dogs. A crazed and anxious Amber pulled Steve all over the yard.

After watching him struggle for several minutes, Uncle Bob signaled the other two dogs and sent them inside the house. Steve still had problems trying to control Amber. Uncle Bob took the lead back from him. Within a few seconds Amber's behavior returned to her former relaxed and submissive state. A few quick pops on the lead reasserted Uncle Bob as the leader, and Amber followed him, loose lead swaying between the handler and the dog.

"I can see you're feeling helpless," Uncle Bob said, "but I have a confession. The first few minutes I spent with Amber weren't much different than what you experienced. It did take a little time to establish our relationship. Come here a second and let me show you something."

Uncle Bob grasped Amber's collar. "See this? I changed Amber's collar. I'm using what we call a prong collar. Don't worry, it's not going to hurt her. It mimics what the mother does to discipline her pups when she grabs hold of their necks. Take a look. When you give a momentary tug on the lead, it applies an equal pressure around the neck, letting her know you disagree with her actions. You need to demonstrate to Amber that you are the leader of the pack."

Glancing over at Edie, Uncle Bob smiled and made a minor correction to his statement. "Well, at least you're higher up than Amber regarding pack order."

Nodding, Steve asked, "Uncle Bob? Amber's vet mentioned her owner had started protection work training with Amber. What do you think about that?"

"Well," Uncle Bob said, "unless you've got a substantial amount of time and energy on your hands, you should stick to basic obedience training for now. I did notice Amber possesses most of the temperament traits we look for in our K9 training sessions. No doubt you've seen this too. At times she can be sharp."

"Sharp?" Steve asked. "I don't understand."

"Well, I'd say you've already experienced this behavior," Uncle Bob said. "You see how quick she is to react to anything close by? She's got a high prey drive instinct. These are the things we would work with and make sure the handler can control and release those drives on command. Without the proper restraint you'd be relying on Amber's instincts to determine if the situation was a threat. And let me tell you, Steve, this could present quite a problem if you disagree with her analysis. Ask your favorite FedEx agent next time he or she tries to deliver a package."

Steve turned away with a faraway look in his eyes.

"Oh," Uncle Bob said, "on a different note, there's one other point I want to make. You ever hear of something called opposition reflex?"

Confused, Steve and Edie shook their heads in unison, with Edie adding, "I only met this guy a couple of days ago, and I don't do those kinds of things until at least the third date."

"Yeah?" Steve said with a crooked grin. "What does riding in my Durango for almost twenty-four hours count for?"

"In case you've forgotten, you had another girl with you, and I don't do that kind of thing until the sixth date."

"Anyway," Uncle Bob said before he lost complete control, "opposition reflex is something instinctive. And don't either of you even think about saying anything…

"When you apply this type of pressure," he said, pressing down on Amber's back while she was standing by his side. "You see, she automatically resists the pressure and stands more firmly in position. It's critical you don't ever keep Amber's lead pulled tight. Because her reflex is to pull away in the opposite direction. You use a short pop of the lead. See. And then relax it again. She understands this as a correction. A steady pull reinforces her to continue the unwanted behavior. So used in the right way, opposition reflex can be an important training tool to shape the appropriate behavior."

Edie thought, all innuendos aside, how difficult would it be to transfer this particular instinct to a specific human subject?

She was about to comment when Uncle Bob said, "Okay, Steve. Give it a shot for a couple of minutes. But let's save the bite work for another time. Remember, until you can control her instincts, with the proper training to attack on command, things could get ugly.

"Me and Edie are going inside to put together a little something to eat."

As they walked through the door, he turned to Edie and said, "Do either one of you know what the hell you're doing here?"

PART TWO

CHAPTER 22

Hayden Lake, Idaho

UNCLE BOB AND EDIE WORKED together preparing a light lunch for the three of them. Their muted conversation, sometimes serious, sometimes amusing, could not be overheard by anyone not in the same room.

Working outside with Amber, Steve's concentration faltered with images of the journalist and the retired cop inside the house. Through the window over the kitchen sink, Uncle Bob shouted, "You can't train your dog if you don't give her your full attention."

Having achieved a relative degree of success with Amber, Steve joined Edie and Uncle Bob in the house. The other two German Shepherds, Greta and Luka, were sent out to keep an eye on Amber in the backyard.

After lunch they moved into the spacious family room beneath a lofty tongue and groove knotty pine cathedral ceiling. Steve and Edie sat on the chocolate brown leather sofa with a view overlooking Hayden Lake. Across from them Uncle Bob relaxed in one of the two matching leather armchairs facing the sofa.

Uncle Bob raised his eyebrows, and said, "Edie tells me you're here to clear up a few things. Set the record straight. Maybe try to piss off a few people."

Steve squirmed a bit on the sofa and chanced a quick glance at Edie. He then cleared his throat and looked at his uncle. "I'm not sure where to start or why I'm even here. Once getting over the media hype, I thought I could go on with my life and try to forget everything that happened.

"But recently these ideas have been, how should I put it? Challenged?"

This was said while catching another glimpse of Edie and thinking what the hell did she say to Uncle Bob?

"Steve," Uncle Bob said, "I think it's been going on a lot longer. Starting from when your mom died. You guys could never deal with each other's reactions. And maybe not even what was going on in your own heads.

"At first your dad came up here to get away from a life he felt spinning out of control. He questioned everything he believed in and saw no way out."

"Every time Dad and I got together, we'd wind up in a fight. Always wounded by each other's words. I felt betrayed and abandoned when Dad headed up here after resigning from U.C. Davis. Nothing between us ever seemed to work again."

"I'm not condoning his actions," Uncle Bob said. "But too much has happened since then. As you know, the men in the Casella family can sometimes be closed-lipped. And dare I say, maybe even a little pig-headed? I don't know what was going on in your dad's head. Even though I was his big brother, he never felt comfortable opening up to me. I guess neither of us were any good with expressing emotions."

Edie decided to give the Casella men a little privacy and moved outside.

"Did Dad ever talk about how he got involved with those reactionary assholes in the local extremist movements up here?" Steve asked.

"When I came to Idaho ten years ago, it was to get away from all the political crap going on in the SFPD. So no, your dad and I had an understanding. We never discussed politics."

In a more conspiratorial tone, Uncle Bob added. "By the way. A word of advice. You may not want to use those particular political labels when speaking to any of the local residents. In particular, those involved with the RGA. Or any of the other right-wing groups. I think the correct narrative would be citizens for a conservative and accountable government."

Uncle Bob snapped his fingers and pointed at Steve. "Your dad stopped by with a friend once. Someone from his community club. Quirky little guy named Jimmy... something. I think he'd take offense to being characterized by your colorful descriptions."

"What? They expect political correctness around here?" Steve said, shaking his head. "What a load of shit after orchestrating that video with Dad and some of his so-called friends."

"I don't think, Jimmy, who happened to be one of your dad's friends, or some of the others around here, use the same definition of political correctness you're used to. And the RGA has always denied any responsibility for the video and whatever drove your dad to take part in making it."

"Well of course they did. What the hell else could they say? But you know what? Those bastards didn't get away with any of those excuses. Did they?"

"And if I remember, you were an outspoken opponent of the RGA during the last elections. Look, if all you want to do is talk politics, you should've stayed in San Francisco and revisited the talk show circuits again. Your dad and I discussed more mutually acceptable topics, such as his property renovation projects, his job as a rental property manager in town, his love life—"

"Whoa, back up there. His love life?"

"Thought that would get your attention. But no, we didn't have those kinds of talks either. Remember, you're not in San Francisco anymore." Uncle Bob chuckled at his own joke.

"Do you know if Dad ever got involved with any women up here?"

"Well, a couple of months before the video came out, I think he might've mentioned meeting someone. If I'm remembering right, it was while he worked at one of those RGA functions. But he wasn't one to make a big deal about those kinds of things."

Steve shrugged.

Uncle Bob's expression turned more serious, and he said, "But let's talk about something I do know about. And you've ignored this issue for too long. I've been taking care of your dad's estate. I was the executor of his will and tried to keep you up to date on all the finances and—"

"We didn't come up here to—"

"Please keep quiet and let me finish. Pretty much all his investment holdings have been liquidated, but your dad insisted the house he lived in was not to be sold. I don't know if you remember, but it's situated on a thirty-acre parcel east of Coeur d'Alene. He always held out that someday things would improve between the two of you. He thought you might want to build a house for yourself and your family on the same property. Even if you only wanted to use it as a vacation place from time to time. He also talked about if he died—I guess he wanted there to be something left of himself for you to come... ah... home to."

Steve sat there stunned, and then responded in a quiet voice. "I've been to the house. I guess it was a few years before he died. But those thoughts were nowhere near the surface. We could never get beyond our differences."

Probably trying to deflect any more emotional baggage from bubbling up to the surface, Uncle Bob pulled out a set of keys from his shirt pocket and tossed them to Steve.

"The old place is still there," he said. "In one of the spare bedrooms you'll also find all your dad's personal items. I boxed up as much as I could. I had planned to send it all down to you, but for some reason never did. And here you are. When you called and told me you were coming, I had the house cleaned. Don't get me wrong, you're welcome to stay with me for as long as you want, but I don't think I can give you the answers you're looking for. Christ. I'm not even sure what the question is."

The sliding door opened, and three animated dogs followed by a worn-out Edie stepped inside.

CHAPTER 23

Coeur d'Alene, Idaho

TEN MILES EAST OF COEUR d'Alene, Steve pushed up the turn signal stalk and guided the Durango onto the exit lane from Interstate 90. He came to the end of the ramp and turned left.

Edie, arms crossed, turned to him and said, "I meant it when I said I wouldn't mind if you left me in town somewhere. You know, if you wanted to spend some time alone at your dad's house."

Steve stared over at her.

"You could drop me off anywhere." Her chin pointing up and out the side window.

Steve swung the wheel right and stopped in a paved clearing on the side of the frontage road.

Glancing out her window at the long row of green dumpsters, Edie said, "Yeah, this would be fine. I could hang out here for a while. Although I thought Idaho was famous for its potatoes, not its garbage."

A slight smile played on Steve's face. "Look, we're in this together. Right? I wouldn't have gotten this far if it weren't for you."

Knowing those were the words she wanted to hear. Sometimes even a Casella could get it right.

Edie sat up a little straighter, the same slight smile mirrored on her face. "Well, if you're sure…

"So then, tell me again why you didn't ask for Uncle Bob's help to find the house?"

"My dad drove us here when I came to visit a couple of years before he died. I'm sure I can find it by myself." But he was thinking it was in the dark. About five or six years ago.

"Well, at least you took the address from him," Edie said as she unfolded the piece of paper and plugged the information into her smartphone's GPS app.

"Here we go…" she said.

All she got was the computer voice. "You are traveling in an area where turn-by-turn directions cannot be provided. Use the map and the directional arrows to guide you."

"No problem. I told you I know where I'm going. I remember passing these dumpsters the last time I was here."

"All this beautiful scenery surrounding us and you pick out a row of big green dumpsters to key in on. Oops. Never mind. I see your point. Much more recognizable than sorting through all those tall, look-alike trees. No wonder you're the number one alpha male in the car. Right, Amber?"

Amber was learning when to remain quiet, and it had nothing to do with Steve being in charge.

Steve pulled out of the lot and drove down the frontage road. About five minutes later he made a U-turn at the graveled entrance to a campground where the road dead ended.

"Thought I should've turned left at the big rock pile, but I wanted to be sure," Steve said, smiling and lifting his shoulders. He made a quick right turn onto the road.

The narrow, winding road took them through gorgeous pasturelands dotted with cattle and horses to the right. This contrasted with the steep, rugged slopes to the left. After emerging from a sharp left curve in the road, they noticed a hollowed out bowl-shaped clearing with a stand of willow trees. Incongruent to this image they saw at least a hundred cars parked in the field adjacent to the trees. A log cabin with a rustic looking pavilion completed the picture.

"Wow. Look at this," Edie said.

"I think they're having a hoedown," Steve said.

"A hoedown? Christ. Do you even know what a hoedown is?"

"Well, no. But it's probably something they do around here. When they're not shooting at each other."

"What the hell is wrong with you? Look. Under the trees. See? All those people sitting in the chairs. Oh, look. There's a bride and a groom. It's a wedding."

As she finished, Edie looked over at Steve and noticed a big grin spreading across his face. He had an even better comeback to her description of the scene but decided not to use it.

The road narrowed as they climbed out of the valley and pasturelands. They soon became engulfed in a densely wooded mountainside closing in on both sides of the road. Edie scrolled around the GPS map on the small screen while Steve slowed down the pace of the Durango.

"Ah, I think we missed a turn back there," Steve said as he gazed out into the tall evergreen backdrop.

"So now it's we?" Edie chided.

"You're the one with the GPS."

"I've heard these things are better suited for the civilized parts of the country. But if anything on this screen is half-way accurate, I think we should've turned left at the last fork. About a half mile back."

"Okay. But I can't turn around on this damn road. It's too narrow."

Edie pointed at her screen. "Looks like a side road up ahead. Let's try it."

Less than a minute later they saw a narrow road on the left. Looking up at the crest of the dirt road, about a hundred yards ahead on the right, they saw a beautiful sprawling two-story white clapboard house. It had green shutters and was set behind a manicured lawn.

As Steve turned up the narrow lane, he said, "Let's give it a try. Whadda we got to lose? Can you read that sign, Edie?"

"Sure can. It says, 'Neighborhood Crime Watch. If I Don't Shoot You My Neighbor Will'."

Steve stopped the car. "Maybe it's like a welcoming home sign around here."

"I think we're gonna find out. What the hell does that guy got in his hand? And why's it pointing in this direction?"

As Edie blurted this out, Steve also noticed the older man. He wore a sweat-drenched white T-shirt and soiled blue jeans. The solidly built man, sporting a crown of white hair, approached the Durango. Drawing near, the man paused to turn off the black and bronze nozzle in his hand. He dropped the hose to the ground and continued walking as he wiped his hands on the seat of his pants. He jumped off the railroad tie retaining wall and ambled around to Steve's side of the Durango, leaning down to gaze inside.

After glancing for a moment or two at Edie and ignoring the barking dog, he turned back to Steve and said, "You don't look like you're from around here. Is there something I can help you with?"

Before she could stop herself, Edie leaned around Steve and said, "Did you put up the sign?"

The man tilted his head to the side and placed two fingers behind his earlobe. "Say it again."

Pointing, Edie said, "Did you put up the sign? The one on the street post."

The man stood back and smiled. "Oh, no. I had nothing to do with it."

Both Steve and Edie breathed a collective sigh of relief.

"No. The sign was Connie's doin'. Connie's my wife. She's the one with all those damn guns. No. You won't find me shooting at anyone. Wouldn't want to piss her off for getting in the way. See the tractor over there? The one with the backhoe? Connie lets me clean up her messes after she's done. And it seems I'm always having to remind her not to shoot anyone when it's raining out. The damn clay soil we have out here is such a bitch to work with when it's wet."

Seeing the shocked expressions on the two visitors' faces, the man raised both hands out in front and laughed. "Sorry guys. I'm kidding. My name's Joe Wilton. So. What can I help you with?"

As Steve's face relaxed, he said, "We're looking for a private driveway close to the Wolf Bay Community Club. But I think we missed a turn somewhere."

"You sure did. I'll tell you what. If you have something for me to write on, I can give you a quick sketch of where you'll find the community club building. A lot easier than remembering some descriptions, and you won't find many street signs back there."

As he began writing on the provided notepad, Joe said in a casual tone, "I'm a member of the community club. Who are you trying to find, if I might ask?"

Steve and Edie looked at each other, and Steve said, "We're trying to find the house where my dad used to live. His name was Tom Casella. I'm Steve Casella and this is Edie Pauling. Did you happen to know him?"

For a second the pen in Joe's hand froze above the pad. "No, not personally. My wife and I moved to the area about a year ago. But I can't imagine anyone around here not knowing the name, Tom Casella. Seeing what happened and all. It was about two years ago if I recall."

Joe handed Steve back the pad and pen and stood back from the car.

Steve's eyes darted toward the house, half expecting to catch a glimpse of a rifle barrel in the hands of Joe Wilton's wife sighting in on his forehead.

"Well. Thanks for your help, sir. I guess we'll be on our way."

"You can turn around in that little clearing up ahead. Right next to the sign reading 'Caution. Guard Dogs On Duty'."

As Joe Wilton disappeared in the Durango's rearview mirror, Steve said, "And this guy is new to the area? Only been here a year. Can't wait to meet somebody who's lived here their whole life. Edie, you should work on trying to blend in a little better."

"Yessa, masta Steve. Mebbe I should ged back wit da dawg. I's sure lookin' fowawd to geddin to da plantation."

Amber whimpered in the back of the Durango.

"On the other hand," Edie said, raising her chin up high and folding her arms across her chest, "at least my last name's not Casella."

CHAPTER 24

WITH A MINIMAL NUMBER OF false turns and the help of Joe Wilton's notes, they soon drove by a steel-framed building. A decorative handmade sign fastened to the gable end announced the Wolf Bay Community Club. And right where it was supposed to be, about a hundred yards west of the building, they found the half-hidden driveway.

After turning onto the narrow road, Steve navigated the Durango up the steep incline for about a mile. This led to a clearing at the summit with a dwelling perched right in the middle. It was a single-story cape cod home with a right-gabled front. A roofed porch spanned the side-gabled extension. Steve approved of the metal roofing materials from the perspective of woodland fire safety. Having spent two summers rappelling from forest service helicopters into isolated terrains to fight wildfires, he instinctively tried to remain alert to his surroundings.

"Uncle Bob has done a great job taking care of the place. It's almost as if my dad still lives here," Steve said, as he closed the door of his SUV behind him and gazed around the immediate grounds.

Edie opened the rear hatch. She watched Amber scamper about, checking out this new terrain and making sure she staked her claim. Amber didn't waste any time in finding some local resident creatures to harass. Once satisfied with her new environs she scampered back to Steve and Edie.

Looking at the panoramic view of Lake Coeur d'Alene and the distant mountains, Edie said, "You Casella boys do share the genes for finding the killer views."

"I almost forgot how beautiful this place is," Steve said, walking up the steps of the wide wooden porch. He inserted one of the keys into the lock on the back door.

As he opened the door and motioned for Edie to step inside, she felt an unexpected wave of shyness overcome her. Biting her lower lip, she looked up at Steve. She felt things closing in on her. Amber interrupted the moment as she plunged between the two of them, heading straight into the house.

Several minutes later the same awkward sensation returned. Edie was sitting on the edge of the sofa. She watched Steve dump the remainder of the luggage on the living room floor. Troubling thoughts streamed through her head. How did she wind up in this remote, isolated spot with someone she met a few days ago? How well did she know Steve Casella? Usually, she could rely on her own instincts, but…

"Steve," she said, feeling the heat rise up in her face. "Can we talk about the… ah… the arrangements while we're staying here at your father's house?"

He looked at Edie and tracked her gaze shifting from their belongings on the floor to a brief moment of eye contact. She settled on a more neutral direction out the large window.

Steve nodded. "If it wasn't for you and your wild and adventurous spirit? We would've never gotten to this point. In fact, I think I've already said that to you. And now here we are. All by ourselves. Only the two of us. And there's nobody else around for miles."

Edie felt herself stiffen as she turned back toward Steve.

He proceeded in rapid fire. "So, I'll cook breakfast. You're in charge of dinner. And we'll each get our own lunch. I'll vacuum and dust. But you can clean the bathrooms."

As Edie opened her mouth, Steve said, "Why don't you take the master bedroom? I'll go put my stuff in the front guest room. Amber can figure out for herself where she wants to sleep."

Edie couldn't hide the grin settling on her face.

"I believe it's now called the owner's suite. Not the master bedroom. In deference to us pooh slave folks," she said, arching up on her tippy toes and planting a quick peck on his cheek. She grabbed some of her things and walked through the door to the bedroom, swinging it shut with her toe.

Steve stared at the closed door, shook his head, and made his own exit to the front guest room.

Amber at first barked in the direction of the master bedroom, then the guest room. She ambled up onto the plush oversized black suede sofa, plunking herself down with a loud extended grunt.

From inside the master bedroom, Edie was saying, "Hi, Nana. I'm doing great. How are you? No. I'm not on my way back. Change of plans. Yeah. I've decided to take a little side trip with ah...a few friends I met up with in San Francisco. No. I wouldn't be doing this with someone... ah... some people I didn't trust. Anyway, guess where I..."

Chapter 25

A short time later Edie walked back into the living room as she punched the screen to end her call. She was amazed at getting a cell signal way out here away from any visible signs of civilization. She strode around the living room and kitchen to get her bearings and began mentally making a few notes about some things they might need. Not knowing how long they would be here, they hadn't taken the time to stop for any supplies.

Uncle Bob was true to his word when he said the place had been cleaned. The refrigerator hummed in the background, packed with a good supply of all the basics and a tasty selection of choice menu items. She checked the pantry cabinet and noticed some additional welcome items. She picked up the bottle of Blue Ice Idaho potato vodka and deposited it in the freezer. After all, they might need the ice for something else.

Edie thought there may be a chance, with a little bit of work, these Casella men could be domesticated.

She worked her way to the rear bedroom where Uncle Bob had placed Steve's dad's belongings. There she found Steve gazing at stacks and stacks of packing boxes. And there didn't appear to be any labels or markings on the boxes.

"Holy crap, Steve."

Startled by her entrance, he turned and said, "Good thing Uncle Bob didn't send me all this stuff. I'd need to build an addition to my house."

"Well, before we get started, let's go grab a quick bite to eat."

Steve trailed along behind Edie. She filled him in on all the goodies Uncle Bob provided. Amber joined in on the procession, sensing the opportunity for an unplanned meal.

******

"Who the hell puts labels on the bottom of the boxes?" Steve asked after returning to the storage room.

"Must be another one of those Casella genetic traits," Edie responded with a shrug. "Reminds me. I saw a picture hanging up in the living room with Uncle Bob standing next to who I assume are your mom and dad— and I'll take a wild guess—you, kneeling in front? They're all fair-skinned with light colored hair. If that's your family, how do you explain your olive skin and dark brown hair?"

"The Aryan gene sometimes skips a generation?"

"You might wanna disclose this information to your future spouse. For the record."

After upending a random sampling of the boxes, they determined the labeling system was not specific or even accurate. Tom Casella's belongings appeared to be arranged according to how something fit into the box rather than into any meaningful category. So they dug in and tried to sort everything out as they went along. It was an inefficient and distracting method for Steve.

The process afforded him a lot of unsolicited trips down memory lane. Along with the surprising discovery his father not only had held on to memorabilia from their early family life, but he had taken the time to catalogue photos and clippings in several albums. This suggested these items weren't neglected but may have been a source of solace for his dad.

Then Steve came upon something that blew him away. Spread out before him in a thick album, he saw a running chronicle of his own life. Their last years together at home. The time he was in college. His escapades at the volunteer fire department in Glen Ellen. Wildfire experiences. The academy training program. His first year as a rookie. And his subsequent achievements in the department. An unwelcome feeling of guilt hit him hard. Steve wished he could erase any records of the public dissertations and political dialogs he'd engaged in following his dad's death.

All this time Edie had also been foraging and sorting. However, unbeknownst to Steve, she kept a watchful and sympathetic eye on his efforts to swim through a past with both pleasant and painful episodes unfurling before him. When she sensed the time for unobtrusiveness was over, she slipped out of the room and returned with two shot glasses and the bottle of chilled Blue Ice Idaho potato vodka. Edie poured, and without a word they both drained their glasses.

While he had been submerged in his past, Edie made good progress in sorting through the remaining boxes. Settling himself on one of the few unopened boxes, he was about to ask her what she had found when Edie came over and sat down on the floor in front of him.

She looked into his eyes. "All this can wait. You're white as a ghost."

With an agonizing grunt, he mumbled, "Well, what difference does it make now? He's dead. We could never get beyond the stupid anger. We could never talk about what happened. We couldn't even be in the same room without fighting over something. No matter how ridiculous or unimportant it was. He was supposed to be the adult. I know I was twenty-seven, but I acted like a spoiled, rotten little kid. We both should've known better."

Steve swallowed hard, taking a quick glance at the vodka bottle. "What am I supposed to do now? About any of this. Maybe if we didn't shut each other out, he wouldn't have become so obsessed with these reactionary assholes around here. You know he came to see me in Sonoma. A couple of weeks before the video was released. He said he was down in the Bay Area to attend a retirement party for one of his former colleagues at U.C. Davis. As usual, we didn't spend much time together. And in between the bickering? I don't know. He seemed more distracted than usual. Subdued. Maybe something on his mind other than the typical demagoguery he always preached. Of course, we never got to it. I never prodded him. And then he went home. The next time I saw him. It was in the video. But I never got a chance to talk to him. And then he was dead."

He looked down at Edie and shrugged. "I'm undoubtedly injecting a lot of second-guessing into my real memories. At the time I don't think I noticed a damn thing. I don't know where the hell you got the vodka from, but you better hide the bottle. It's tempting, but I think I need to concentrate on something a little more tangible. So before you try to change my mind, please tell me you've found something to make this trip worthwhile."

Thinking this might be the best medicine, she pulled back her instinctual desire to coddle for the moment.

"If you're sure."

Lips compressed, he nodded.

"So there's a ton of stuff from U.C. Davis here. Lots and lots of textbooks, manuscripts, notes. I didn't think any of those things were relevant to what he was doing here, so I pushed it over there in the corner. The rest of what could be useful is piled right here."

Steve looked over at the small stack located in the direction of Edie's pointed finger. "Let's see what we've got."

Over a number of hours, they succeeded in looking through almost everything in the pile they thought was relevant to his dad's lifestyle and activities since moving to Idaho. Edie prepared dinner, giving them a break from their searching. They boosted their energy with pots of coffee, not vodka. By mutual agreement Steve concentrated mainly on the information pertaining to his dad's business and investment affairs. Edie worked on anything hinting of political relevance.

There were two reasons for this division. One, Edie was much more adept at the political aspects. Two, it pissed Steve off to look at any of the ideological crap his dad got himself into after moving to Idaho.

Outside, the night sky had taken over. The moon peeked above the mountains and reflected on the surface of Lake Coeur d'Alene. Inside, the exhausted pair retreated to the living room sofa. Bracketing the peacefully slumbering Amber. Steve dropped a pile of papers on the coffee table.

He glanced down, and said, "How about we re-negotiate the house cleaning chores? Look at all this white fur already covering the sofa."

Amber moaned in contentment.

Edie ignored his comment, but Steve noticed her glancing down at her black slacks. They were also sprinkled with white fur. Edie pushed ahead. "So let's go over what you found."

"Okay. Dad owned two houses in the downtown area of Coeur d'Alene. I remember his original plan was to fix them up and sell. But he kinda got stuck the way everybody else did a couple of years ago when the housing market crumbled. So after completing the renovations, he became a reluctant landlord. Uncle Bob sold those properties last year to settle his estate."

Steve had a vague recollection of Uncle Bob sending him the paperwork on the completed deals.

"He also worked as a property manager for a company called Shepherd Hill Investments. At the time the company owned about twenty houses, all scattered around the downtown Coeur d'Alene area. Here's a map showing the locations. I'd say most of them are close to the lake or the main business areas. Probably still some valuable investments. According to the paperwork I found, he kept himself busy taking care of all these properties. All the accounting stuff for the income and expenses for every house is right here in this ledger book. It all looks straight forward, but I'm not an accountant. My dad was anal, so it's not too difficult to follow."

Edie asked, "You think this company is linked to his political activities?"

Steve shook his head. "No. I can't imagine his working for this Shepherd Hill Investments had anything to do with his political affiliations. But I found one thing that was interesting."

Steve tapped his finger on some items on the coffee table. "Look at this. I found these invoices in the same packet with all the Shepherd Hill papers, but they were stapled separately from the others. At first, I didn't think it meant anything, but when I went through the accounting ledger, I didn't see any of these items specifically listed. I'm not sure what to make of it. Probably doesn't mean anything."

Edie leaned over to pick up the invoices and began shuffling through them. She then paged through the accounting ledger and pulled out the invoices attached to it. Returning to the separately stapled invoices, she finally turned to Steve, holding them up.

"The billing address is the same on every single invoice," she said, "including the one's you separated out."

"Yeah. It was my dad's post office box number in town. He didn't get mail delivered here. So?"

"Well. When I checked the delivery addresses for the invoices attached to the ledger, they all corresponded to a particular property address in town. But look at these separate invoices. See. The delivery addresses are all the same. The stuff was delivered right here to your dad's house. Why?"

CHAPTER 26

STEVE WAS TEETERING ON EITHER being impressed with what Edie had said, or worried at the possibility his father was involved with something potentially illegal. He smacked the side of his head and let out a long sigh. Rummaging through the remaining stack of papers in front of them, he pulled out the accordion file folder holding all the Shepherd Hill papers. He shook it upside down and a folded piece of paper floated onto the floor.

"This was paper-clipped to the invoices and slipped off when I yanked them out," Steve said. "I didn't pay it much attention."

Unfolding it on top of the other papers and reading the scribbled words, they concluded copies of the invoices had been sent to this person on May 28th of the year his father died.

Edie pointed at the paper. "This name. George Sullivan. It sounds familiar." She picked up the ledger book again and shuffled through it.

"Of course," she said. "Here it is. He's listed as the president of Shepherd Hill Investments."

"Okay. But it still doesn't explain why all the stuff was delivered here."

They found an address and phone number for George Sullivan in the ledger book. They saw he was located in Oahu, a time zone three hours earlier than their present location. Steve decided to make the call right away.

He spent several minutes convincing Sullivan he was not a representative from the Internal Revenue Service about to ask some intrusive questions. Some obligatory small talk followed. Then Steve got to the point.

"Mr. Sullivan, I've been going through some of my dad's papers and found something a little odd I wanted to ask you about. It's about the work he did for you as property manager. Oh. And would you mind if I put you on speakerphone? A friend of mine is here, and I want her to hear this too."

"No problem, Steve. Go right ahead. You know, I never found anyone to be more precise in taking care of all the paperwork, not to mention the painstaking craftsmanship and pride your dad took in the handiwork he did for me. What seems to be bothering you?"

"I see your point about my dad. But I was looking at several invoices. They showed certain construction materials, appliances, and some other items delivered directly to his house instead of going to any of your rental properties. Plus, there were no entries in the ledger for any work done related to these items. Everything else he purchased, or the labor involved, was listed in the ledger. Can you tell me anything about this?"

Sullivan laughed. "I guess you're new to the area. Haven't talked to a lot of the local folks yet? Or tried to hire anyone to get something fixed?"

"I'm not sure what you mean."

"A lot of local tradesmen in the Idaho panhandle have a fondness of bartering for services rendered. When I'm out there, I guess I kind of get with the program. So, while your dad and I had a legitimate working contract for managing my investment properties, we also had a gentleman's agreement on a piece of personal land I own. A handshake, no contracts. Anyway, I own several hundred acres of land with a small cabin a few miles from where your dad lived. I don't ever use it, but I have plans of maybe using it someday as a summer getaway in the mountains, or even one day building a retirement retreat. So your dad and I worked out an agreement. He'd work on the cabin, making repairs, getting it livable, and making sure everything was maintained. I'd reimburse him for all his expenses, including building supplies. In exchange, your dad was free to use the cabin until I decided if I was going to occupy it myself. I didn't care if he rented it out, logged the property, or used the cabin for himself, either fulltime or as a getaway."

"So, those invoices were for work done on your cabin?" Steve asked.

"Right," Sullivan said. "He had the supplies he needed to do the work delivered to his house and brought the stuff up to the cabin in his pick-up truck. The access isn't suitable for most delivery vehicles."

Steve could only imagine the road leading up to Sullivan's cabin after experiencing the drive to his father's house. He looked out the window into the deserted surroundings lit by a brilliant full moon. He also had the thought: a getaway from what?

"Would you mind if I took a look at your place? I'm not sure if I have the time, but it might be interesting to see some more of my dad's handiwork."

"Not at all. Let me know if you decide to go. I'll give Walter a call and alert him to be on the lookout for you. He's the current caretaker. If he happened to be there and didn't know you were coming, well… he's almost as loyal to me as your dad was."

After getting directions to the cabin and instructions where to find the key, Steve ended the call and turned back to Edie.

"I'm not sure why I asked him about seeing the cabin. I don't know about you, but I think I've seen enough dirt roads and trees for a while. Remind me to call him if we do decide to go up there. No sense getting shot if it can be avoided by a simple phone call. You feel up to talking about anything you found?"

"Sure do. I've been going through a lot of information on the RGA. Your dad was working with their local group in Coeur d'Alene. He was one of their main liaisons who interfaced with the community. He helped to organize rallies, worked at the group's public display booths at other functions, and hosted a bunch of meetings and conferences for the RGA. If we want to understand any more details about his responsibilities with them, we need to go to the RGA office."

Steve wondered how he'd be able to handle that situation.

"But anyway, you might want to look at this," she added. "I found a bunch of invoices for RGA conferences held at the Coeur d'Alene Resort. And stuck in amongst these papers was this business card for the person at the hotel who I assume he worked with to organize the functions."

"So? What's so important about this guy?"

"This guy's name is Cindy Weaver. And look what's on the back of *her* card."

Thanks, Tom. Great idea. Here's my personal cell number. Waiting to hear from you. C.

Steve picked up the card and turned it over. "Cindy Weaver, Meeting Room Coordinator, Convention Center, Coeur d'Alene Resort. You know, I understand the Dockside restaurant in the resort's lobby has an excellent breakfast menu. What say we get an early start tomorrow morning?"

"Trying to get out of your breakfast duties?"

"Yep."

"By the way, how do you know anything about the Dockside?"

"The Casella men have been known to read."

"You read books too?"

"Let's not get crazy here."

CHAPTER 27

Spokane, Washington and Washington, D.C.

"DAVID," BEN COURTNEY'S VOICE REBOUNDED into the handset. "How are things out there in Spokane?"

"Everything's good, Ben," replied David Reilly. "Some information has been brought to my attention, and I wanted pass it along to you executive guys in the White House. Remember you wanted us to keep an eye on some of the locals who were close to Tom Casella? See if anybody ever started questioning what happened? Well, one of the things we did was to keep audio surveillance recordings on Casella's brother's house. You know, he's the retired cop from San Francisco living up in Hayden Lake? His name's Bob Casella."

"Right," Courtney answered, still paging through a stack of memos.

"So after almost two years of reviewing the digital feeds and finding nothing to be concerned about, when I got this week's report, something interesting popped up."

Courtney put aside the papers and focused on the call. "What've you got?"

"Before you get too excited, I don't think there's any need for you to worry. But I wanted to keep you in the loop."

Courtney glanced at his watch, waiting for Reilly to get to the point.

"As you know, the brother never appeared to have any interest in Casella's political affiliations. More to the point, he's never shown any suspicions about the video or his brother's untimely demise."

"Then what the hell are you talking about here?" Courtney said, raising his voice.

"Probably nothing, but I thought you should know that Tom Casella's son, Steve, the firefighter from San Francisco, showed up here for a visit this week."

Courtney considered ending the call, but instead asked, "Why is that so unusual? He has family there. At least this uncle you talked about. And didn't his father own property up there in Coeur d'Alene?"

"True, but for one, as far as we could determine this is the first time the son has ever been up here since Casella's death. He even had his father's body shipped back to California for the funeral. Never even came up to settle any of his dad's affairs. The brother took care of everything."

Courtney went back to looking over the papers on his desk.

"But the second, more compelling reason for calling you is he happened to bring Edie Pauling along with him. And you know who she is, right? The daughter of the retired Navy SEAL guy who was killed in the embassy bombing."

"Sonofabitch. How in the hell did those two ever hook up?" Courtney said, forgetting about the pile of papers.

He rubbed his temple, thinking about what a royal pain in the ass she had been after the bombing. Trying to latch onto classified documents. Marching around the State Department as if she was running an investigation. Trying to get all her stupid articles about government incompetence and corruption published. When they hadn't heard from her in a while, Courtney assumed they had put out the fire and she had disappeared back into the woodwork.

"Don't know how they got together," Reilly was saying, "let alone why. The audio I listened to didn't register anything suggesting they have any new information. In fact, the Pauling girl didn't do much talking at all. She and the uncle had a few words while the son was out in the yard playing with his damn dog, but the sound quality was muffled and unintelligible. In fact, from the other conversations we picked up, the son is still pretty adamant about blaming everything on the RGA. Remember? He was quite helpful in demonizing them during the last elections."

Courtney's head began to buzz. He could feel the beginning of one major migraine swirling around behind his eyeballs.

"Anyway," Reilly's voice droned on, "maybe he decided to put everything behind him and move on. You know, settle any loose ends with his father's estate. When Pauling and Casella's son left the uncle's house they were heading to his father's old place. And at least we know they won't find anything incriminating there. Our guys picked it clean two years ago."

"Well, you may be right."

Courtney was already rummaging through his top desk drawer looking for his medicine.

"But I'm glad to see you're on top of it out there," Courtney said. "You know I don't believe in coincidences. Been drummed into me by Matthews. Also,

I don't trust that little Pauling bitch. Let's see what they're up to."

"You got it, Ben." Reilly reached for the pack of cigarettes on his desk and remembered something else. "Oh, one other thing."

The bottle flipped open, and the pills spilled all over Courtney's desk.

"The uncle mentioned he thought Tom Casella might've been seeing a woman right before this whole thing unfolded," Reilly said. "He had no idea who she was or how serious they might have been but thought they'd met through his RGA activities. I was thinking about giving Fenton a call. He was pretty much glued to Casella back then. If anybody knew anything, he'd be the guy. I don't think there's anything to worry about though. If there is a girl and she knew anything, we would've heard from her by now."

"I'm sure you're right. But it's a good place to start. Keep me informed. Good work, David," Courtney managed to get out.

He hung up the phone and scrambled around picking up pills, losing count of how many he'd already stuck in his mouth as he grabbed for the mug of lukewarm coffee.

Chapter 28

Coeur d'Alene, Idaho

Steve parked the Durango in the multi-level enclosed parking garage attached to the Coeur d'Alene Resort and cracked open the windows for Amber. Steve and Edie walked through the garage passageway into the lobby. They got directions at the concierge desk and headed to Cindy Weaver's office. They didn't need to detour into the Dockside restaurant because Steve had surrendered to his breakfast duties at home.

As Steve raised his fist to knock on the door to Cindy Weaver's office, it swung inward. In its place stood a slight, attractive woman in her early forties. She had shoulder length curly auburn hair and was dressed in a crisp charcoal business suit and an embroidered white blouse. Her original resolute demeanor of one whose destination was set on autopilot, cycled through surprise, her standard service-oriented smile, and then backpedaled to a fixed exclamatory expression.

"Oh! Oh my God! Steve? Steve Casella?"

He could do nothing to mask the exasperation on his face. It was the second time this week a strange woman recognized him. Either his love life was about to pick up, or he'd been recently featured on America's Most Wanted.

Figuring he could play at this game too, Steve replied, "Wow. Cindy? Cindy Weaver? It's great to meet you in person. I've heard so much about you."

Edie attempted to salvage this disorienting conversation. "I assume you're Cindy Weaver?" The woman nodded, and Edie said, "I'm a friend of Steve's. If you have a few moments, could we talk to you about Steve's dad?"

They settled into the two armchairs across from Cindy's cluttered desk and waited for her to make some quick changes to her busy schedule.

"Just wanted to clear my morning so we won't be disturbed." Cindy's face glowed, and she smiled at her two visitors. "I'm sorry if I upset you with my initial response. It was such a shock to see you standing here. After all this time. Your dad had plenty of pictures of you on display. And I remember watching you on the different news stations after he died…"

Her voice softened after seeing the uncomfortable expression on Steve's face, but her rapid delivery didn't falter. "He was always going on about how proud he was of you; showed me all your academy photos and clippings of stories about the awards you received for your firefighting service. And all the old family photos. He never got over what happened to your mom."

Steve struggled to keep up with her quick mannerisms and speech, now and then glancing at Edie to see if she was having any difficulty understanding what Cindy said. Apparently not.

"Is there anything wrong, Steve?" Cindy asked.

"Ah, no. I guess I'm having a little trouble listening to things about my dad."

Cindy's whole body sank, and her eyes welled up. "You two not getting along troubled him. He was such a stubborn man when it came to personal matters. I got more concerned during those last few months. Right before everything came out. I realize I hadn't known him for too long, but he appeared to be even more brooding than usual."

She reached across and touched Steve's hand as old memories intruded on her previous cheerful countenance. "I thought maybe if he spent some time with you in California, you guys might come to terms about things. He wanted me to go with him to a retirement party. I thought it would be best if he went to see you by himself. But, as you know, nothing changed. I began to worry there could be something else eating at him."

"Were you surprised when you saw my dad in the video?" Steve asked.

"Good God. Of course I was surprised. Nothing in the video bared any relation to who your dad was. To this day I stand by those impressions. He wasn't the person portrayed in the video."

"But wasn't he a part of the group who advocated those sentiments?" Steve asked. "He was brainwashed by this RGA movement. When we tried to talk to each other it seemed he had become intolerant of anybody trying to help the poor and disenfranchised people from getting their fair share. He complained about government handouts and entitlements. Blaming the failures in this country on the overreaching powers of the government. He feigned concern about the infringement of people's rights but worked to try and keep the minority classes in their place."

With a resolute expression, Cindy pushed back. "Your speech reminds me of the campaign rhetoric we've been hearing since before the last elections. Those are the exact same labels the opposition used against the RGA. I'm surprised you would even think any of it's true. Your dad would never have been involved with anyone who said those kinds of things. He respected the people he worked with. He believed the RGA platform could restore the nation's values."

Cindy's face softened again. "Look Steve, if you want to label your dad's life based on a comparison of political platforms, you're never going to get over what's separated the two of you."

"I do want to find answers," Steve said after a quick glance at Edie. "Edie has made those same arguments. She says my blame is misplaced. She thinks this video was part of a conspiracy to discredit these people. That's why we're here. To find answers."

He shrugged, trying to find a place to start. "Edie and I have been going through all Dad's stuff at his old house. But I can't find anything to suggest I'm wrong. If somebody set him up, we didn't see any evidence of it."

He looked at Edie. "Right? Of all the papers you went through relating to his political affiliations, did you find anything to suggest he was coerced? Except for his obvious interactions with the RGA?"

Before Edie could respond, Cindy said, "I can only convey my feelings of what was happening to your dad at the time. I never saw him again after the video was released. I did get one call from him though. Right after it happened. He wanted to assure me he played no conscious part in making the video."

Cindy continued; her eyes focused on something outside her window. "He said he needed to get away and do some thinking. He wanted to look over his notes and try to pin down what had been bothering him for the last few months. He was on the verge of asking me about somebody. I think it was someone he'd known for quite a while. Someone he'd worked with at the RGA. When I pressed him for an answer, he refused to say who. He said things were finally beginning to make sense, but he needed to be sure. He was tired of making stupid decisions in his life and wanted to be certain before he said anything else."

Edie's forehead scrunched. "What did you mean when you said he needed time to look over his notes?"

"I assumed he was talking about his journal. What he jokingly called his lab notebook?"

Steve and Edie looked at each other, eyebrows raised, shaking their heads in unison.

"Well, he never showed me the actual notebook," Cindy said, fumbling for words. "But your dad mentioned it a couple of times. I don't know if he was embarrassed by it or not. He said it was his last connection to his former life at the university. As a laboratory research scientist, he always maintained a bound, hard-covered notebook. He used it to record the objective facts and data from the experiments after they were performed. It was signed at the bottom of each page after completing the entries."

Seeing blank expressions on their faces, Cindy forged ahead. "A second function was to provide a platform to record unique ideas and discoveries so they could be documented for the purposes of patent application filings. When he left the research environment, I guess he continued this habit of writing things down on a daily basis. Maybe he was embarrassed if he thought people might view this as a diary. I got the feeling he wasn't in the habit of talking about it."

Still getting no reactions from Steve or Edie, she said, "I'm guessing you didn't come across any notebooks at his house?"

Again, Steve and Edie looked at each other. Steve said, "No. Not so far. Nothing even close."

After they left Cindy's office, Steve and Edie walked down the corridor and back into the lobby. With little warning, Steve took hold of Edie's arm. He led her to one of the leather sofas facing the huge stone fireplace in the lobby lounge. Not knowing what to expect, Edie sat and tried to read the emotional changes playing across his tortured face. She held one of his hands and waited. She didn't prod. Just waited.

As the crowded lobby faded and muted around him, Steve's voice wavered, but he spoke straight into Edie's probing eyes.

"I learned of the video from an email. To this day I don't even remember who sent it. I clicked on the link, and there it was. My father. For all the world to see."

Hesitating, swallowing hard, he resumed. "So what did I do? Did I call him? Did I even question the validity of the video? Try to get his side? No. I guess I was too damn selfish. Expected him to call me and try to explain and justify his antics. I never made the effort to even understand what was going on."

Steve pulled his hand from Edie and covered his face. "And by then he was probably locked up already. All alone. Even if he did those things on the video. It shouldn't have mattered. He was still my father. I should've got the hell up here and tried to talk to him. I can't imagine what he went through during those last hours. All alone. Thinking I still hated him. And then he was dead."

CHAPTER 29

Boise, Idaho

(two years ago)

TOM CASELLA PROPPED HIMSELF UP on the bare cot against the far wall in the cramped holding cell and gave up pretending to be asleep. Fitting his six-foot-four-inch frame onto this worn and tattered mattress was the least of his problems. His thick head of graying light brown, wavy hair was flattened and damp. His light complexion was now a pale shade of white, and his vibrant blue eyes were bloodshot and stung. Tom assumed he was being watched, although he could detect nothing looking remotely like a camera. Not a surprise, since the Department of Homeland Security should have no trouble accomplishing such a simple task. He looked at his left wrist and then laughed at himself again. His watch, along with everything he had been wearing or was in his possession, had been removed after being incarcerated by the two agents flashing badges with DHS and SS etched on the surface. He was surprised secret service agents were involved. He wondered why the hell the Department of Homeland Security was even interested in him in the first place. They had been waiting for him as he got out of his car. Right there in front of his house.

After the confrontation with Peter Fenton on Saturday, Tom realized a little too late there was nothing to gain by shouting accusations and screaming about conspiracy theories. He'd look exactly like the deranged idiot featured in the video. The evidence he was now gathering needed to be more thoroughly evaluated before being brought forward. He thought he could prove to his friends, as well as the media, that this so-called anti-Muslim video was not legitimate. It was made to maliciously attack a movement aimed at getting people to understand how important our traditional values were needed to restore our nation on a path to prosperity. He shuddered to think what it would take to convince Steve. And then yesterday, the embassy bombing occurred. And the rest of his world came tumbling down. The implications of the video being linked to the bombing erased any hope of undoing the damage. The media intensified the vilification of the RGA and anyone associated with their conservative movement. This public flouncing was used as fuel by the administration to demonize their strongest opponents. Tom bristled at the callous use of such a tragic event for political gain. What the hell happened to the country he loved?

Tom's suspicions regarding Fenton's actions were substantially validated before he confronted him at his home on Saturday. Following the release of the video, Tom wound up doing a little investigative snooping on his own. At first, he had every intention of barging into Fenton's house and beating the truth out of him.

Fenton had taken Friday off and had not been returning any phone calls from his colleagues at the RGA office. Late in the afternoon Tom had driven to within a block of Fenton's house. In such an enraged state, he pulled his car to the side of the road. He wanted to give himself a chance to regain his composure before pounding on Fenton's door. After five minutes of wrestling with his emotions, he made the decision to put the car back in gear and drive the remaining distance to Fenton's house. Before his car started moving, he noticed Fenton's garage door starting to open. Fenton backed his late model BMW sedan out of the driveway and headed down the block away from where Tom was waiting. Without thinking he followed Fenton at a discreet distance. After turning onto Sherman Avenue and passing through the heart of downtown Coeur d'Alene, Fenton entered the on ramp to Interstate 90 and merged into the westbound traffic. With Tom following at a safe distance, they crossed over the Spokane River at State Line and entered Washington. Fenton got off the interstate at the Downtown Spokane exit. He headed north for several blocks and pulled inside the parking structure for the River Park Square Mall. After parking his BMW on the top floor, Fenton headed toward the stairs leading to the street exit of the garage. Tom parked his car and shadowed Fenton's footsteps out of the parking garage as he turned left onto West Main Avenue.

Fenton walked at a brisk pace, not paying much attention to his surroundings. Tom felt confident he wouldn't be noticed. Fenton walked left onto North Howard Street and entered a sleazy looking bar with neon invitations flickering in the window. It was about a third of the way down the block. At this juncture Tom wasn't sure what he should do next. After a little consideration he decided to stick around outside for a while and crossed the street to gain some degree of cover. He sheltered himself in the cramped darkened vestibule of a boutique bookstore. He was rewarded with a curious sight. Fenton emerged from the bar with another man close at his side. This new arrival to the scene was slight and light-skinned with wavy blond hair. He looked to be in his early twenties. And that was giving him the benefit of the doubt. Hand-in-hand, they strode back in the direction of the parking garage. The BMW beeped and flashed its lights as the two men climbed into the back seat. They slid down, out of sight. Tom snapped several pictures with his smartphone as they entered the car but did not wish to get any closer to the action. He waited in the shadows. After a shorter interlude than Tom had endured at the bar, both men exited the car. Fenton handed his blond companion an envelope. He pocketed it and strode off toward the mall shop elevators.

To Tom's surprise Fenton didn't climb into the driver's seat of the BMW. Instead, he glanced at his watch and walked back down the stairs to the street. Hoping he didn't have to witness a second tryst this evening, Tom followed Fenton out the door. This time Fenton bypassed the bars and entered nearby Riverfront Park. He strolled over to a bench in front of the Loof Carrousel.

Under his breath, Tom said, "Jesus Christ, don't tell me the little bastard's trolling for kids."

But instead, Fenton sat down on the bench next to a familiar looking figure. The man had a dark olive complexion. He was older than Fenton. Tom wasn't sure, but swore he'd seen this guy someplace before. The two were highlighted under the bright glow of a streetlamp. Tom maintained a safe distance, keeping himself hidden behind a row of vending machines. He snapped off several more pictures using the zoom feature to its maximum capability. After a brief conversation with no intimate interactions or gestures, the man handed Fenton an envelope. Both men stood and shook hands and walked away in different directions. This was a transaction of a very different nature than the one Tom had witnessed earlier. While the first one was telling in its own right, the latter one presented itself as being more important to Tom's immediate predicament.

Tom sat in his car watching the taillights of the BMW disappear down the exit lane from the garage. He was no longer interested in following Fenton tonight. After several more minutes of reflecting on what he had seen, Tom started up his car and drove back to Idaho.

At home he printed out some enlargements of the pictures taken in Riverfront Park. Tom browsed through additional research materials online and printed out several archived newspaper articles with press photos attached. He confirmed the identity of the person sitting next to Peter Fenton as David Reilly, the director of the PUG in Spokane, one of the key political activist groups working on behalf of the current administration in the White House.

When Tom awoke Saturday morning his temper had overridden his waning sense of caution. He stormed out of the house and headed back to confront Fenton. This time he followed through on Fenton's doorstep, making accusations of fraud and collusion, and threatening all kinds of reprisals for Fenton's role in making the video. He should have pummeled the son of a bitch when he had the chance.

Since Saturday night, Tom remained secluded at Sullivan's isolated cabin trying to make sense of what had transpired over the past six months. He spent the time going over his journal entries and trying to assemble the pieces of this frightening puzzle. For an educated man, he had acted naïvely. Although Fenton's presence, and the way he had been acting made Tom uneasy, he never connected the dots and realized what the son of a bitch was up to. It wasn't until Jimmy Martin called a few days ago. Jimmy's voice had been strange and chilling. He told Tom to get online and look at this video on WildFlix.

He watched the video several times before the reality of what had transpired started to develop and emerge from the depths of his memories. At first he almost failed to recognize he was the featured character in the video, speaking with others, in a context of hateful rhetoric.

While viewing the video, Tom imagined how Steve would react to seeing his father on the screen. The editor of the video had succeeded in twisting the truth. Tom was portrayed in the role of a bigoted, reactionary fool. He was sure this video would serve to strengthen Steve's resolve to counter everything he was trying to accomplish. It would sever any last remaining bonds between the estranged father and son.

Since his wife had been killed five years ago, he had not responded maturely in the wake of her death. His actions served to poison his relationship with Steve. He was aware Steve felt betrayed at how he turned his fight inward and withdrew from the previous life they had together. Although neither of them had ever expressed any political inclinations, Tom was convinced our nation was heading in the wrong direction. This concept had hit him like a runaway freight train after his wife was killed.

In the microcosm setting of the university where he worked for a major part of his career, he felt isolated by his belief that this nation could only survive if there was a strong desire to produce rather than consume. He saw a growing lack of cultural integrity, fostered by a government having more to gain by dividing its citizens. It was a government that wanted a single common denominator cementing the people together. And the glue holding them was the understanding that they were entitled to whatever their government promised. To Tom, the goal of this insipient government was clear. To establish an electorate so dependent on entitlements they would be powerless to defend themselves as their individual rights were abrogated to an all-powerful government.

This had been the basis of the building blocks walling off his relationship with Steve. Steve had argued his father was using a newly found sentiment of hatred, focused on gaining revenge for his mother's death. As a result, Steve, fueled by what he took for his father's abandonment of what little remained of their family, fought back opposing his father's reactionary views.

Now, sitting in this cell trying to make sense out of everything, Tom Casella understood the reckless nature of his acts. The events over the last several days had stabbed him with a new sense of reality. He felt trapped and alone. But he was at least thankful his captors found none of the evidence he had been gathering, either with him or in his car. They failed to uncover anything of significance in his house. Again he looked at his wrist to check the time, shaking his head at the gesture.

After being grabbed at his house, Tom was forced into the stereotypical black Suburban and driven down to the dumpster site near the freeway exit. There, believe it or not, a black helicopter sat waiting to fly him to his current location, the Idaho branch office for the DHS in Boise. Under the guise of protective custody for his own personal protection. This whole thing would have made him laugh as being a ridiculous caricature of everyone's worst nightmarish visualization of the federal government, except here he was sitting in this tiny cell. He almost expected someone to walk in and say, 'I'm with the government and I'm here to help'.

Staring at the ceiling, Tom heard the sounds of footsteps increasing in volume until they stopped outside his cell door. The lock clicked and the door swung aside. Tom leaned forward on the edge of his cot. He glared at the two individuals who entered the cramped quarters as the door closed behind them. They were the same two agents who had been waiting for him at his house.

The one standing on the left and a step in front of the other was tall and deeply tanned with thick black hair. The shorter man had a light complexion with clipped sandy blond hair. The taller man introduced himself as Cagney, and his partner as Lacey. Tom wasn't the least bit amused. He was sure they weren't here to apologize for his inconvenience. Or to inform him this was all a big misunderstanding, and he was free to go.

"Casella," Cagney said. "We understand you haven't been cooperating, so we're going to give you a little incentive boost to facilitate your ability to share the truth with us."

"Instead," replied Tom, eyes narrowing, "why don't you take me to a phone so I can get my attorney down here to facilitate things from my perspective. You know? As an American citizen?"

"This is as close to a phone as you're going to get," Cagney hissed through his teeth as he placed the cold barrel of a semi-automatic pistol against Tom's left ear. "Lacey. As you can see, Mr. Casella has granted us permission to proceed. Why don't you oblige him?"

Lacey uncapped the needle from a small syringe he had been holding. He pushed up the right sleeve on Tom's orange jumpsuit. Without hesitating he inserted the needle into the muscle of the upper arm and depressed the plunger on the syringe. He let the sleeve fall back in place and moved away from their prisoner. Cagney placed his weapon back inside his coat and they both turned to leave.

Before the door closed, Tom called out, "I thought you guys came here to ask me some questions?"

"We're done for now," Cagney said and smiled. "Your government thanks you for your cooperation."

The last thing Tom heard was the resounding clank as the lock engaged. He had no idea that before these two agents had appeared, the surveillance camera he'd guessed about had conveniently malfunctioned.

He felt an overwhelming crushing pressure in his chest. The magnitude of his mistakes accentuated by the crippling force working to arrest the muscle fibers in his heart. An agonizing pain spread up to his chin and radiated out to his arms.

At first, he conjured up memories of his wife Penny. Dwelling on the pleasant ones. Trying to extinguish the pain he experienced from her death but still consumed him up to this minute. He thought of Steve. All their failed conversations. The looming certainty of never resolving their differences or restoring what they had once shared. He thought of his last phone call to Cindy and what he neglected to say.

And then there was nothing.

CHAPTER 30

Spokane, Washington and Washington, D.C.
(present day)

"BEN," DAVID REILLY SAID TO Courtney. "I spoke to Peter Fenton this morning."

Reilly crushed out his cigarette in the overfilled ashtray on his desk and reached for another. "Fenton remembers Casella getting close to a woman they worked with at the Coeur d'Alene Resort. Where they held most of the more formal RGA events. Her name is Cindy Weaver. Fenton and Casella worked together on these types of activities. This was how he gained Casella's confidence after the RGA distanced themselves from those more extreme local elements. Where Fenton first identified Casella as a target. As it turned out, Tom Casella maintained his friendships with those people. And that had worked to our advantage. It enabled Fenton to make frequent appearances there as well. Which was how he put together the video. Lucky for us, those redneck idiots never suspected the building had our electronic equipment hidden inside."

Although Reilly was rambling as usual, Ben Courtney noted a decided urgency in his voice. He had this bizarre image of Reilly fumbling around trying to light up a cigarette and singeing his mustache.

"Fenton also reminded me," Reilly said after a brief coughing fit, "that before we selected him to infiltrate into the RGA, he had taken part in a few of our PUG meetings held at the Coeur d'Alene Resort. He recalled Cindy Weaver working there at the time, but he didn't think she remembered him as being a member of the PUG or having anything to do with me."

"Can he be sure?" Courtney asked.

"According to Fenton," Reilly replied, "the three of them worked together for the RGA functions, but she'd never said anything to him."

"Let's not take any chances. I want you to take a closer look at this Cindy Weaver. We need to see if those two showing up have caused her to remember anything or maybe look at things from a different perspective. And do this surveillance real time. I don't want to wait for any recorded updates. Understand?"

"Ah, sure," Reilly stuttered, finally getting his cigarette lit.

"Be ready to move on this, David. Don't let things get out of hand. And I think it's time we keep a better eye on what Casella's son and Pauling are up to. Their snooping around may be enough to get people starting to rethink about how things went down back then."

Reilly remained silent, blowing out a huge plume of smoke.

"I'm going to send out some additional help in case things heat up. And they'll be prepared with the appropriate authorizations from Matthews to implement anything we need. For now, they're not going to interact with you directly. Let's try to keep you out of this part of the mix for as long as we can. You give me the word. I'll initiate the action from here. They should be available by tomorrow. I'll talk to you then."

CHAPTER 31

Coeur d'Alene, Idaho

STEVE AND EDIE RETRIEVED AMBER from the parked Durango. They walked along the concrete boardwalk circumventing the lake's shoreline, processing what they had learned. Neither spoke of what transpired in the lobby. They made their way onto Sherman Avenue and headed north away from the lake. Their next destination, the local RGA headquarters office, was a few blocks up on the right. Edie had made the suggestion to first return Amber to the Durango.

A young woman with long, straight blond hair fixed in a loose ponytail sat at the front desk in the reception area of the building. She wore a pair of tight-fitting jeans and a baggy maroon and gray sweatshirt with the letters *NIC* imprinted across the front. She had been studying from a well-worn textbook perched on her desk, her pretty face wrinkled from concentrating. She looked up with a genuine smile, dropping the pencil she'd been chewing on, in her notebook.

"Hi guys," she said. "Welcome to the Restraint in Government Alliance. What can I do for you?"

Taking the lead, Steve looked down at the name plaque on her desk.

"Thanks, Peggy," he said. "Could we talk to somebody who has worked here for at least two or three years?"

"Oh. Well, I'm pretty new. I came to work here when the spring semester classes got under way over at North Idaho College." She pointed at the letters across her chest. "But let me go get Sarah. She's the director and should be able to help you out. Wait a sec, guys, I'll be right back."

A minute or so after disappearing around the corner, Peggy returned with a solidly built older woman with clipped dark brown hair. She was wearing a no-nonsense light brown business suit and a stark white blouse.

"Hello. I'm Sarah Nelson. Peggy told me you wanted to talk to one the old timers as she put it. What is it I can do for you?"

"Good morning, Ms. Nelson," Steve said. He plunged ahead, thinking it was a good thing no one around here recognized his face. "My name is Steve Casella. And this is Edie Pauling. We were hoping to speak with someone who was working here when my father was involved with the RGA. His name was Tom Casella."

Peggy showed no recognition at the mention of the name and glanced at her boss, whose expression had turned guarded.

Sarah Nelson said with tight lips, "I think you better follow me." Turning to Peggy, she added, "Could you please get Dean and have him come to the conference room?"

Without another word Sarah Nelson spun around and headed back around the same corner she'd come from. Steve and Edie followed her toward the rear of the building. They had barely reached the inside of the conference room when a robust man with graying, once black hair, appearing to be in his late fifties or early sixties, peered into the open doorway. His light blue blazer, tan slacks, and open cream-colored dress shirt served to counter the already tense atmosphere unfolding in the room.

After terse introductions were completed, they all sat down around the large oak table. Steve, squarely in the midst of what he considered to be the prime instigators of his worst nightmare, couldn't find any words. He avoided any desperate glances at Edie, seated on his left. Impatient to figure out what in the hell the point of this unannounced intrusion was all about, Sarah Nelson collected her own thoughts.

"Let's get something straight here for the record," she said. "I was brought to this office two years ago when all the accusations about your father's video put the entire RGA in crisis mode. My job was, and frankly still is, to repair the damage done to our organization by all the unfair propagandizing and demeaning messages linked to us by his ill-advised video."

"I don't think—" Steve tried to say.

"That brief little episode, Mr. Casella," Sarah said, drowning out Steve's interruption, "succeeded in crumbling years of solid work by groups of patriotic people gathered all over the country. They were striving to get their message out to the ordinary citizens of this nation. Their goal was to get people to wake up and see what years of misinformation and ignorance were doing to the basic values of our free enterprise system. Not to mention the deterioration of our traditional cultural values."

Sarah Nelson barreled on without giving Steve any chance to reply. "We have investigated this whole incident and never found anything on the video to link it to the RGA. Besides, the video contained no philosophical basis for any of the fundamental tenets of the RGA. The hateful footage chained together in a series of poorly edited pictures and sound bites was fabricated in an effort to derail our momentum during a vital period of some critical elections. The results of this smear campaign were clear. The media jumped all over it. There was never any truth to the accusations our opponents cast at us. Their deceitful demonizations stuck to us and destroyed our opportunities to restore this nation."

Sarah Nelson's narrowed eyes dug into Steve. "Wouldn't you say so, Mr. Casella? As I recall, you played right into their hands. You called us a bunch of reactionary, homophobic racists who want to oppress the minorities and the poor. Not to mention contaminating our air and water."

Ratcheting up her blazing glare at Steve, she said, "It's got to be clear to anyone with an ounce of intelligence this whole thing was orchestrated by our enemies to marginalize us."

In a losing effort to maintain any degree of composure, Steve, his face burning, got up and walked out of the building.

Edie jumped up and turned to Sarah Nelson. "Please. Let me go and talk to him. There are some important things we need your help with about Steve's dad."

"I don't think I'm in any position to help you," Sarah said. "Look. I never even met the man. Dean Sanders here is one of the few members of the staff who remained after the shit hit the fan."

Sarah looked over at the man seated at her side. "I'm done here. It's up to you. I understand you knew Casella quite well. If you want to discuss any of this with these people, you're free to do so. If you'll excuse me, there are a number of upcoming elections needing my attention. As you know, we're still trying to fight all the negative ads and propaganda that cost us those last key elections. The PUG office in Spokane has already intensified their rhetoric for this time around. Those White House charlatans are still calling the shots. And the flunkies in Spokane lockstep to the tune. Their aim is to finish the job of the last election. Get rid of the RGA for good. And this time they're aiming higher. The goal is to decimate the entire republican party too."

Dean Sanders and Edie watched as Sarah Nelson made a less dramatic exit than Steve.

"Edie. I'll be taking my lunch break in about thirty minutes." With a warm smile Dean wrote down the name and directions to a nearby restaurant on the back of his business card. "If you can convince Steve I'm not a fogey redneck dinosaur, I want the two of you to be my guests for lunch. I knew Tom Casella for a number of years. We were friends, and I had a great deal of respect for him. There's nothing that'd please me more than to answer any questions you two might have."

Edie looked at the card. "Thank you. I'm sure I can talk some sense into Steve."

Dean nodded. "I have some lingering questions about those last few days myself. A lot about what happened back then didn't make a damn bit of sense. Anyway, I'm looking forward to the chance to talk to you and Steve. His dad was always giving me an earful about his firefighting son."

CHAPTER 32

EDIE'S EYES SQUINTED, HER MOUTH set, as she looked up and down the street in front of the RGA office building. She spotted Steve at the far end of an open grassy plot along the bustling Sherman Avenue. He sat on a wooden triangular corner bench leaning back against one side of an attached advertising backboard. As Edie approached, she read the message on the backboard. It was a community reminder for the upcoming Fourth of July Festival featuring the American Heroes Parade to be followed by this year's main attraction of the Vietnam Traveling Memorial Wall exhibit in City Park. Since Steve hadn't noticed her, she took the opportunity to peek at the ads on the remaining backboard sides. One announced next month's schedule for RGA rallies in the immediate area. It was balanced by a similar schedule for PUG rallies. At least Steve was sitting in the neutral zone. While she was trying to come up with a tactic to reveal her presence, he opened his eyes and warded her off with extended arms.

"Don't start on me," he said. "I've reached my limit of being beat up by right-wing ideologues for the day. I guess I should've realized the offices of the RGA would not roll out the welcome mat for another Casella at their doorstep. At least they're consistent with their denial of any responsibility for my dad's actions. So where the hell does this leave us now?"

Ignoring his standoffish attempts, Edie cozied herself up close to Steve. She noticed he didn't try any retreat tactics. A pleasant tingling pressure in her side convinced her he had leaned in a little himself.

"Funny you should ask. But before you say no," Edie said, emphasizing her words using a subtle push with her thigh, "try summoning up a tiny slice of your broad-minded liberal attitude and hear me out."

A short time later they were standing in the reception area of the Lakeside Grill. Before they had a chance to question the hostess, the door opened and in strolled Dean Sanders from the RGA. Dean smiled at Steve and Edie. He stepped up to the hostess and requested seating in the outside patio area.

As they were escorted to their table, Dean said to his companions, "We can stay as long as you want out here; we won't be disturbed until the dinner crowd starts moving in. Oh, and I hope you're not bothered by dogs. This is the one area of the restaurant where pets are allowed by the tables."

Hiding behind their menus and avoiding any eye contact, Steve and Edie remembered Amber abandoned in the Durango as the waitress took their orders. Dean settled on the Cobb salad and a raspberry iced tea while Steve and Edie both got identical Lakeside cheeseburger platters and root beers.

"So," Dean asked, "how long have you guys been married?"

Edie's head tilted. "Married? He still owes me a movie. And so far the only thing we have in common appears to be those cheeseburgers."

"Thanks for taking the time to meet with us," Steve said. "Edie told me you knew my dad pretty well. Sorry about the scene back in your conference room. I should've known being his son wasn't going to win me any friends with the RGA."

"Well, you can't blame Sarah for her attitude," Dean said. "She didn't even know your dad. She was brought in right after the video was released, and it was her job to try and limit the damage to the RGA. Everything went downhill fast. She was fighting a losing battle to dissociate the organization from the video because your dad had been so visible in most of the RGA events in the community. From the outside, the video came across as prejudicial to our cause. She had no one to blame but your dad. It was clear to everyone in our office this had to be a planned sabotage effort on the part of our enemies, but there was no proof. Your dad had been closely linked to the RGA, so our arguments never stood a chance."

Steve looked up from his half-empty glass.

"The minute the story broke," Dean said, "all our opposition groups hammered us, led by the PUG and the full force of the president's re-election committee. The media descended on us like hawks on chickens. This was a perfect storm for them. They couldn't wait to revive all the old stories of every would-be extremist group ever setting foot in Idaho."

Dean's expressions and mannerisms reminded Steve of an old high school English teacher.

"I've been with this organization from the beginning," Dean said. "We've worked hard to make sure the attitudes and rhetoric represented on the video weren't a part of the RGA philosophy. Or any of the people who worked with us."

The waitress hustled in and arranged the dishes around the table and refilled their glasses. For a while they ate in silence, each reflecting on the past events which brought them together on this balmy late June afternoon, sitting on the patio overlooking the tarnished coppery waters of Lake Coeur d'Alene.

Edie's head rose and she broke the silence. "Back in the conference room you said you respected Steve's dad. He was a friend. What do you think happened back then?"

Dean placed his utensils on his empty plate, took a sip of his raspberry iced tea, and wiped his lips with his napkin. He looked first at Edie, and then addressed Steve. "I met your dad about four years ago. The Coeur d'Alene RGA office had been open for less than a year. In fact, the RGA itself was still in its infancy. We were starting to gain a foothold because of growing concerns by many citizens of the rampant and reckless government spending and the overburdening regulatory policies coming out of Washington. Your dad was introduced to us by one of our staff members, Peter Fenton. At the time, Fenton worked with a few of the quasi-established conservative community groups in the area he thought would support the RGA's efforts. He ran into your dad at a nearby community club. They were holding some informal political gatherings."

Steve stole a glance at Edie, thinking of the new steel building down the hill from his dad's house.

"Fenton attended many of these meetings, making an effort to educate their members as to the purpose and philosophy of the RGA movement. But as I said," Dean emphasized, "we've always tried to avoid any associations with the fringe and extremist elements. As you may know, this region has had a notorious past in regard to certain political manifests."

Neither Steve nor Edie took the bait.

"Nonetheless," Dean said, "when your dad came along, he fit right into our new organization. Fenton took it on himself to bring him on board. They functioned as a team on membership drives, rallies, and organizing our district meetings. Fenton was a full-time staff member, and your dad spent as much time working with him as his obligations as a property manager allowed."

Interrupting, Steve said, "Peter Fenton. He might have some good insight as to what motivated my dad's behavior. Is he someone you trusted?"

Dean twisted his head sideways and looked at Steve. His eyes narrowed. "Well, I'll say this about Fenton. He was an energetic worker. Always dedicated to the RGA movement. In the beginning he was our acting head, but a lot of the mundane local activities didn't suit him. He spent a lot of time attending district and national meetings. To some of us local staffers, he could come across as condescending, but on the surface, he was always pleasant. Sometimes a little over the top, if you get my drift."

Dean cleared his throat. "Thinking back, I thought it a bit strange the way he stayed teamed up with your dad. It didn't seem to fit with the rest of his ambitious agenda. At the time I assumed he took a liking to your dad. Maybe it gave him an excuse to still rub noses with some of the locals at the community club. Gave him the opportunity to connect with the real grassroots of the movement. Who knows."

Dean's face scrunched up. "I do remember something your dad talked to me about once. It happened, I recall, when Fenton was away somewhere on one of his little networking escapades. Not too long before the video was released. I thought he was joking at first, but Tom said he was getting annoyed with the way Fenton was always breathing down his neck. He said Fenton had a way of showing up at this community club whenever he was there. Said it was starting to unsettle him. He didn't know what to make of it."

"Do you think Fenton would consider taking me and Steve out to lunch?" Edie joked.

Laughing, Dean replied, "If Fenton thought it might help his career, I'm sure he would. However, it might be a little inconvenient for him."

"Why?" she asked.

"Fenton left the Coeur d'Alene office two years ago. That happened right after the video was released and your dad was picked up for questioning. Or protective custody, depending on who you ask. While everyone else scrambled for cover, Fenton benefited from all this."

"What do you mean?" Steve asked.

"All the networking he did back then? I guess it paid off. He was asked to work on the campaign staff for Tyler Griffin, who at the time was a candidate in a special senatorial election back in New Jersey. Fenton succeeded so well he is currently the senior advisor for the now Senator Tyler Griffin and a key player in Griffin's upcoming campaign for re-election. I don't know if you realize it, or even care, but this is an important election for the RGA. There's a lot riding on the political future of this particular candidate."

They thanked Dean for lunch and his taking the time to give them some insight into Steve's dad. As he walked back to his office, Dean turned back to them and said, "One last word, Steve. I still don't understand what happened and how the video surfaced when it did, but your dad was a good man. I will never believe he could have been responsible for it. The reason for the video has been clear to us at the RGA. We have enemies. We are in a fight to take back our country."

Dean paused with a faraway look on his face.

He shook his head and refocused on Steve. "Can you tell me why your dad was taken into custody? And the next morning, before anyone could've heard his side of the story, he was found dead? Did you know if your dad had a bad heart?"

Dean turned away, still shaking his head and mumbling as he walked down the steps. Steve and Edie stood   in silence, watching as he disappeared around the corner. His unheard words evaporating in the misty wind swirling off the lake.

Chapter 33

Confused by what they'd learned, Steve and Edie decided to rescue Amber from the garaged Durango. Seeing a sign with a trail map describing Tubbs Hill, they strolled up a series of winding paths leading to an expansive overlook of the lake. In a setting such as this, it was difficult to imagine the weighty problems they were facing or the consequences their actions would have on this nation.

They watched as Amber threaded her way through the trees and over the rocks, working her way down and splashing into the cool waters of the lake. Selecting a lone piece of driftwood, Amber returned to her two companions sitting at the top of an outcropping of rock and placed her gift at their feet.

The drive back to Tom Casella's house was subdued. As they passed by the Wolf Bay Community Club, they noticed several cars and a pick-up truck parked out front. Looking at each other and parroting 'what the hell?' kind of shrugs, Steve turned the Durango into the gravel parking lot. He slipped in between a rusting faded red Ford Ranger and a clean, but dusty white Jeep Grand Cherokee.

After a moment of hesitation at the unlocked gray steel door, they stepped inside the community club building. They walked through a deserted small reception area and entered a sizable meeting hall. A few metal folding chairs were scattered around. A number of stained and smelly canvas tarps were piled up in one corner next to several paint-encrusted ladders leaning up against the wall. The smell of fresh paint permeated the air. They heard animated voices coming from an opening on the other side of the room and approached the source. Steve knocked on the side of the open doorway to a good-sized commercial type of kitchen with a large stainless steel table forming an island workstation in the center. The table was flanked by padded bar stools occupied by three men clad in paint spattered work clothes. They were engaged in an animated conversation fed by a healthy number of beer bottles strewn about the table or tilted toward their uplifted heads.

At first Steve's knocking went unnoticed. A more assertive pounding brought the conversation to a halt. All eyes focused on the two outsiders outlined in the doorway. A familiar face peered around the man sitting in front, and said, "Hi there, guys. Welcome to the Wolf Bay Community Club. I hope you're not still driving around trying to find your dad's house, Steve."

Joe Wilton got up and extended his hand, first to Steve, who was closer, and then to Edie. He then turned to his friends. "Guys, this is Steve Casella and his friend, Edie Pauling. Remember I told you about running into them the other day?"

The other two men stood and introduced themselves. Jimmy Martin was of average build with close-set blue eyes and medium length sandy blond hair. Stan Wassermann was short, beer-belly shaped with a ruddy complexion, and buzz-cut hair of indeterminate color. Both men were in their early thirties.

"Pull up a stool and join us," Joe Wilton said. "We're the leftovers from today's painting crew. Cleaning up and solving the world's problems." He slid over a couple of bottles in their direction.

Steve and Edie twisted off the caps. They saluted their hosts with the opened bottles and took hearty gulps of the not so cold brews.

Stan Wassermann spoke up first. "I'm real sorry about your dad." The others nodded and echoed his sentiments. "Your dad, he would have been right here with us. And I don't mean drinking beer and shooting the breeze. Tom played a big role in getting this building up and running. He spent as much time, and maybe more than almost any of our other members did on the construction of this place. He was also active in all the functions we had going on here. This place serves as an assembly hall where local groups can get together and hold their meetings. Whether it's politics, weddings, community events, or whatever. I bet you thought we just have hoedowns here every Saturday night, right?"

Steve looked at Edie, eyebrows raised.

"Your dad fit in here like a glove," Wassermann said. "You wouldn't a thought so, being he was a college professor, but he never flaunted his education. To Tom, we were all equals."

Steve asked if they remembered Peter Fenton.

"Sure," Wassermann responded. "Before we got this place up and running, our club sponsored political meetings wherever we could find a vacant room large enough. Usually in some room above one of the bars downtown."

Jimmy Martin gave Wassermann a quick salute with his bottle and urged him to continue.

"Once in a while Fenton would show up and jump into the discussions," Wassermann said. "Don't recall him ever helping out with any of the work done on this building though. His main interest was getting us involved with this new conservative organization. At the time I don't think it even had a name. Now it's called the RGA."

"It stands for the Restraint in Government Alliance," Jimmy Martin said, smacking his lips together.

Wassermann waited to see if Jimmy Martin had anything more to add, and then moved on. "When your dad became a regular, we began to see more of Fenton. I think he worked real hard to get your dad to join the RGA. You know, he never fit in with us locals. He was different than your dad."

"What do you mean?" Steve asked.

"Oh, don't get me wrong," Wassermann said. "Fenton was okay. Hospitable, too. In fact, he always provided a generous amount of needed refreshments. He'd show up right after the work was done. I don't know how he managed it. You could always find him by your dad's side, as long as Tom wasn't busy working."

Wassermann turned to Jimmy Martin, this time prompting him to talk. "Jimmy, you know a lot more about it than I do. Right? You and Tom were here together at the club a lot."

"Yeah," Jimmy Martin responded. "We sure were. I used to call Fenton the 'coach'. He said we needed to get better at arguing our conservative ideas to the public. I didn't even know I had any conservative ideas. I just spoke the truth. So, he'd set up sides. He'd have one of us take up the position of being some stupid reactionary racist asshole. And Stan—you keep your big mouth shut. Then he'd have the other guy try to counter that position with logical, rational thinking as he called it. On occasion, with all the alcohol he provided, we sometimes lost sight of any rational thought."

Joe Wilton appeared to have a problem swallowing his beer. He was struck with a sudden coughing fit.

Jimmy Martin waited him out, and continued, "We did have some good times and a lot of entertainment though. But some of it was a little foggy the next day. On those days we supplied a good deal of empty bottles to the recycling center. The last winter before your dad died. We had a helluva lot of snow, and so we wound up spending a good deal of time holed up in here. Jesus. I think winter lasted till June. There was a lot of talking and drinking going on back then."

Edie said, "How do you think Steve's dad got involved with the making of the video?"

Steve closed his eyes and braced himself. Jimmy Martin and Stan Wassermann looked at each other. Joe Wilton opened up another bottle and leaned back.

"Well. If I believed in conspiracy theories—" Jimmy Martin said.

"What the hell are you talking about?" Wassermann interrupted. "You think the government's responsible for every damn thing happening to you."

"Just the bad stuff," Jimmy Martin said, eyes wide open. "But damn, if I could figure out how the feds snuck in here and twisted around everything Tom, me, and the others said. Ah… wait… maybe we should be a little more careful here. They might still be listening. And then they're gonna make out like I said something I never even thought about."

"Christ, Jimmy," Wassermann said. "If you could just remember a smidgen of what you or anyone else ever said about anything—"

"Hey, Stan," Jimmy Martin said. "You made me think of something else. I think it happened a little bit before the video showed up. Yeah, listen to this."

He waited to make sure he had everybody's attention.

"Tom. He called me one day. It was right after one of our political discussions with Fenton. At least that's what he was wanting me to remember something about. Anyway, he asked if I felt confused or had any trouble remembering specifics about what happened the night before," Jimmy Martin paused and looked around.

"What did you tell him?" Steve prodded.

"I told him I sure was confused. And I guess I was. 'Cause I didn't even remember being there."

"Now that's a real fucking surprise. Sorry, Miss," Wassermann said, laughing.

"So let me get this straight," Steve said. "You're saying what appeared on the video was true? And some of the stuff with my dad happened right here?"

Wassermann thought he'd better jump in before Jimmy Martin had a chance to remove the beer bottle from his lips. "Let me answer, Steve. I think we, and I mean all the community club members, have looked at the damn video hundreds of times. Personally, I can recognize some of the voices of people I know. Though nobody admits to their voice being on the video. And there were no clear pictures of anyone except your dad. But the way the words came out. You know, the way it sounded so derogatory and so damn hateful? Well, nobody could ever remember it happening. And believe me, I'm not relying solely on Jimmy's recollections. No offense, Jimmy."

Jimmy Martin wasn't sure if he should be offended or not, but he let Wassermann continue.

"It was just, I don't know any other way to s   ay this, but somebody fucked it over real bad. There were lots of other scenes in the video too. It showed Tom working at all those different RGA functions, interacting with the public. Those things looked legit to me. That was the way we all remembered Tom. The thing is, he was the same way here. He was one of the most caring and sympathetic persons I knew. The way the video made him sound was pure and simple bullshit."

Edie asked, "So do you think Fenton was responsible for this? He made recordings and edited them to make it look like Steve's dad and the RGA had some evil alliance with extremist groups?"

"Doesn't make any sense," Wassermann responded. "Why the hell would he do that? He was the one who came here in the first place to convince us the RGA was the conservative wave of the future. He thought it was important for all our local groups to become a part of this movement. So as to not look so radical or extreme. And Fenton. Hell, to everyone here, he *was* the RGA. He had no reason I could think of to try and destroy it."

Jimmy Martin yanked the beer bottle from his lips long enough to blurt out, "I told you all. It's the damn fucking government who's behind this. And I haven't given up looking for those hidden microphones and cameras either. I know they gotta be here someplace. You wait and see."

CHAPTER 34

"I'D SAY IT'S TIME TO go grocery shopping. Or be prepared to take me out to a decent restaurant." Edie smiled. "Because after tonight, all we got left are some bacon, eggs, and a smidgen of vodka. And don't forget. If you're gonna give Cindy Weaver a call, you better do it before it gets too late."

"Just looking for her number now," Steve replied as he punched in her home phone number he'd gotten off the back of her business card.

"Hi, Cindy. This is Steve Casella. Hope it's not too late for you."

"No. Just got home from work. What can I do for you?"

"You sure put in a long day." Steve was struck by her cheerful response. "Got a question for you."

"What's up?"

"We came across a name today of someone who worked with my dad at the RGA. I was wondering if you knew a guy named Peter Fenton."

"Yeah, I do," Cindy said after a slight pause. "Peter and your dad worked together a lot. In fact, they teamed up to organize most of the meetings held here at the Resort."

Cindy hesitated again. "You know after you left today, I kept reliving that last phone call with your dad. The guy I told you he was worried about? I don't know why it didn't click before. But I'm pretty sure he was talking about Peter Fenton."

Steve could almost sense how she was putting the pieces together.

"Something else has been nagging at me too," she said. "I don't even know if it's important. Never mentioned it to anyone before."

"What's that, Cindy?"

"This happened way before Peter and your dad started organizing the RGA meetings. I'm sure I remember Peter Fenton being at some other meetings here. I didn't think much of it. I thought he was kind of an opportunist. Not committed to any cause except what served his own self interests."

"What type of meetings are you talking about?"

"Peter used to attend the local PUG meetings when they were held here in the Coeur d'Alene Resort. Their district office is in Spokane, but they also cover the Coeur d'Alene area. I'm pretty sure he used to be on their staff. Or at least showed up at most of their meetings."

Steve controlled his voice. "Thanks, Cindy. I would guess the RGA wasn't aware of his past activities."

About to end the call, he remembered something else. "Oh. One more thing. Did my dad ever mention anything about a cabin he might have gone to from time to time?"

There was a long pause before Cindy answered. "Oh God. This is embarrassing. I don't know if I can even say this to you, Steve. Tom. Your dad. Well, he took me up to this cabin once. Called it his secret hideaway. Oh God. Please don't ask me where it is. I couldn't tell you. It was kind of a game he wanted to play. I can't believe I'm telling you this. Well, he blindfolded me in the car on the way up there. And going home it was sort of too dark to see anything. And maybe I was a little, well… I had a few glasses of champagne."

CHAPTER 35

"COME AND GET IT. BACON and eggs it is. I'll save the vodka for lunch," Steve called out to Edie from inside his father's house.

She was on the porch with a hot cup of coffee, watching Amber explore the wilds of north Idaho.

"After breakfast I'll give Sullivan a call and make arrangements to go to the cabin," Steve said as Edie came inside and sat down. "As for now, we might as well spend the day going through the remainder of the boxes and look around the rest of the house to make sure we haven't missed anything."

******

Steve contacted Sullivan about their plans for trying to get up to the cabin the next morning. Sullivan said his caretaker was out of town for the next several days, so they didn't have to worry about getting shot. At least not by the caretaker. Sullivan also recalled his caretaker telling him about a large wood and metal trunk at the cabin with a hefty padlock securing the clasps. He assumed it belonged to Tom. He thought it might contain some of Tom's power tools. But so far nobody had gotten around to looking for the key and trying to open it. Steve was entertaining some other ideas about what his dad might've stashed in the trunk.

Edie decided to go through all the books and college-related items she had put aside. There was the off chance she might have missed this journal somewhere stuck in with all the other academic items.

"I think that does it," Edie said.

"Yeah," Steve said, "I've gone over every nook and cranny of the rest of the house but can't find a thing. By the way, you didn't happen to come across any keys, did you? It would make it a lot easier than using a crowbar to open the trunk."

"Nope," she said. "So I guess you didn't find any extra keys on the keychain Uncle Bob gave you before we left his place?"

"Ah shit," Steve said and walked out of the room.

A few moments later a hand appeared through the doorway with a set of keys dangling back and forth. Steve peeked his head in. "You're the brains and I'm the beauty in this operation. There might be a few extra keys attached to this."

"Hey, big boy. It's not necessarily, either… or."

"I can't think of any place else to look around here," Steve said, throwing an open box filled with a nest of wires on the floor next to the TV. "Since we missed lunch, whaddaya say we go into town and grab an early dinner?"

They found a quaint Italian restaurant on a busy one-way street a few blocks north of the center of town. For the next hour they enjoyed a quiet meal in a cozy corner of the restaurant sharing a bottle of Pinot Grigio. Edie looked alluring in her fitted plunging V-neck yellow summer frock, bare legs, and mid high pumps. Then again, Steve recalled he had the same reaction watching her working around the house in her oversized sweats.

After dinner they retrieved Amber from the Durango and strolled about the downtown area. Edie mentioned how impressed she was at the way Steve handled Amber. Nevertheless, she said a few prayers asking they didn't run into any other dogs in the immediate vicinity. Before heading home, they stopped at a nearby Safeway and picked up a few supplies.

CHAPTER 36

THE LATE MODEL MEDIUM GRAY four door sedan went unnoticed as it maneuvered down Northwest Boulevard toward the heart of downtown Coeur d'Alene. Passing the northwestern shoreline of the lake and the city beach, the car stopped for the traffic light at the end of Northwest Boulevard at South First Street. The passenger riding in the back seat glanced out the right side window and noted the time on the clock tower was approximately 8:30 P.M. Looking further out over the expanse of the lake, the passenger observed the dark and threatening clouds rolling in from the south. They were accompanied by lightning flashes on the horizon and the faint rumble of thunder in the distance, heralding in an early summer storm. Dusk promised to be a fleeting event tonight, drawing a smile on the hidden face of the passenger.

The car turned right and crossed over a small section of the Centennial Trail where South First Street merged into the private access road to the Coeur d'Alene Resort. It drove around the curving flower-lined drive and came to a stop underneath the grand entrance portico of the Resort. Before the Resort staff had a chance to assist the new arrival, the passenger emerged from the car and the driver pulled away.

If the arrival of this figure occurred either the day before or several days later, the appearance would have evoked some intense stares from anyone who witnessed the scene. But today, the figure garbed in a flowing blue afghan burqa and an embroidered mesh screen shrouding the head and face went completely unnoticed. If the western styled expandable leather briefcase held in the left hand of the figure was unusual, it too was ignored.

This week the Resort was hosting the annual meeting of the Pacific Northwest Muslim Women's Council. Hundreds of similarly dressed patrons were in constant sight around the grounds and interior of the Resort, so no one gave a second thought to this figure entering the lobby through the revolving doors.

Once inside, the figure strolled purposefully across the polished marble rotunda, past the concierge and reception desks, several lobby shops, and the grand fireplace in the lobby lounge. Not needing any directions, the figure turned down the corridor leading to the administrative offices of the Resort's convention center and stopped in front of an office door. The polished brass plaque identified it as belonging to Cindy Weaver, meeting room coordinator.

Close to the end of a long and busy day, Cindy was filing some last-minute scheduling changes for a breakfast banquet tomorrow morning. She heard the knock on her door as it was opened.

"How can I help you?" she said, still capable of smiling at this time of day.

"Good evening," said a low, raspy and muffled voice. "I need a room to hold a meeting for leaders of the Islamic Council."

Cindy leaned closer so she could better hear what was being said by the veiled person who had entered her office.

"I apologize," the voice said. "I am recovering from laryngitis and cannot speak much louder."

"No problem. My name is Cindy Weaver, and I would be glad to help you with whatever you need."

Cindy rose and extended her hand, not sure if this would be perceived as offensive.

Apparently it was not and the figure returned the gesture, saying, "Thank you. My name is Mysha Nadia Ahkeem. Would it be possible to reserve a room to hold a luncheon meeting the day after tomorrow for approximately fifteen to eighteen people? Preferably a room on an upper-level floor with some nice lake views."

"Of course. I think we have some good choices for you. If you want, I can show them to you now."

"If it is not too much of an imposition."

Cindy turned away and rummaged through one of her file cabinet drawers to find the room plans and specifications. Mishya stealthily removed an opened cushioned manila mailing envelope from the briefcase and slid it out of sight under Cindy's desk. The envelope once contained two identical vinyl banners. Now only one remained inside. It displayed the standard RGA emblem exhibited in a stunning red, white, and blue with American flags surrounding the perimeter.

"Ah. Here we go," Cindy said, turning back to Mishya and placing a brochure on the desk. It showed the floor plans and features of the Twelfth Floor Lakeside Tower Executive Boardrooms.

Cindy pointed to one of the rooms, and said, "I think this room here, Boardroom Nine, could work for you. If you're ready, let's go take a look."

As Cindy guided Mishya out of her office and onto the elevator to take them to the meeting rooms, she absently observed her guest. It was amazing how this traditional Muslim outfit could completely disguise all femininity in the woman who was wearing it. Even her walk and actions didn't look feminine.

It gave her the creeps talking to someone whose face was hidden behind a snug headscarf. Not to mention the loose, flowing robes which obscured any hint of the expected female curves. But she guessed it was the intended purpose of the outfit.

The elevator doors opened onto the corridor leading to a suite of meeting rooms. Cindy exited the elevator and led Mishya to a set of ornate double doors, and they stepped into Boardroom Nine. Cindy started her customary standard speech, citing all the associated amenities and described specifications, options, and the going rate range for the boardroom.

Mishya nodded her approval, and Cindy said, "This door opens to the outside rooftop deck. We should check this out first. The storm's approaching fast. Yikes. Look at how threatening the sky is."

They walked out onto the tiled observation deck and Cindy noticed a maintenance service cart parked up against the glass paneled guard railing which overlooked the lake. Grimacing, she thought this was a little odd. She made a mental note to send an email to the maintenance office first thing in the morning to remind them the carts are not supposed to be left unattended. More than likely, she'd wind up moving it herself. Might as well do it before this storm hits.

"Oh," Mishya exclaimed, "this is beautiful. Ms. Weaver, I have heard the Resort's golf course has a unique and famous floating green. Can you see it from here?"

"You sure can," Cindy responded by walking over to the railing next to the cart.

Just as she placed one hand on the metal top of the glass railing and pointed in the direction of the golf course, something slipped out of Mishya's hand onto the tiled floor. Mishya kneeled down as if to retrieve the fallen object. Instead, both hands clamped forcibly onto Cindy's ankles. With an unfeminine display of strength, Mishya catapulted Cindy up and over the railing. Twelve stories below, a splintering noise resounded on the wooden boardwalk. Cindy Weaver's body landed in front of the entrance platform to the Resort's lake cruise departure point.

A bolt of lightning flashed, followed by a deafening blast of thunder. The floodgates in the sky opened. Mishya tossed the dropped banner over the railing and walked back inside the building.

Mishya disappeared inside a nearby vacant restroom and was never seen again.

Five minutes later a deeply tanned man with thick black hair, dressed in a dark blue business suit, and carrying a western styled expandable leather briefcase emerged from the same restroom. He walked toward the elevators.

During his elevator ride to the lobby, his stroll through the rotunda, and his entrance into the waiting black Suburban SUV, the man pondered the chain of events he had helped unleash. Already entered in Cindy's calendar was the July 4th reservation for an RGA conference. There was the envelope with one banner in her office and the second banner fluttering around somewhere near or in the lake. The maintenance cart, etc., etc., etc. Most of this was not necessary. It was there to provide a little help and misdirection for the local law enforcement agencies. Maybe a little blow-back to the RGA. Of course, if anyone looked too closely, it wouldn't stand up to any serious scrutiny. No matter though. The storm wasn't planned, but nonetheless, it was a nice touch.

CHAPTER 37

IT WAS STILL LIGHT OUT when they reached the house. Edie spent the next half hour romping around outside with Amber. Finally exhausted, Amber headed for the sofa and Edie settled into a steaming hot bath. Steve messed around behind the television, attempting to sort out the tangled nest of wires surrounding him.

A considerable time later Edie emerged relaxed from the bath. She towel-dried her hair as she walked over to the bed. For a while Edie stared at the object positioned on her pillow.

"Humph. Let's see about this," she whispered, foxy expression spreading across her face.

Edie headed for the closet, moving garments aside, and then searching through one of the open storage boxes on the floor. After a brief struggle she glanced in the mirror and nodded with satisfaction at what she saw. She walked out of the bedroom and into the living room, carrying the object found on the bed. Steve was seated on the sofa stroking Amber's neck and ears. In front of him a menu was displayed on the video screen. In an endless loop, it cycled through its options.

Edie tossed the empty DVD case found on her pillow onto the sofa next to Steve, and said, "What in the hell is a Blue Max? And who the hell is George Peppard?"

Without turning, Steve said, "It's a World War I British war film about a German fighter pilot played by Peppard."

"So, this is dinner and a movie? I guess the Casella romantic gene skipped this generation?"

Steve turned to face Edie. He found himself staring at her lost inside of what appeared to be an oversized snowmobile suit.

Sighing, Steve said, "Okay, why don't you sit down, and I'll get the movie going."

As he turned to push the play button on the remote, Edie playfully punched his arm and lumbered back toward the bedroom.

Looking over her shoulder, she said, "You know big boy, this thing has a zipper, and I might need some help if it gets stuck."

With all thoughts of the remote gone from his consciousness, Steve tripped over a yelping Amber and followed Edie into the darkened master bedroom. A few steps into the room he stumbled over a hefty garment heaped on the floor. Edie hadn't encountered any problems with the zipper. Steve fumbled out of his own clothes. He snuggled next to Edie on the bed. Things heated up at a frenzied pace. They became tangled in a knot of sheets, the comforter thrown to the floor. Edie's shrieks and squeals were answered by several grunts from Steve.

Screeches, scrapes, and scratches resounded across the bedroom floor. Steve pushed Amber through the door and slammed it shut.

"Thanks anyway," he grumbled. "I don't need any of your help tonight."

Steve took a deep breath and climbed back into bed. He again snuggled up next to Edie. The gentle caressing became a frantic urging as they both unbridled the building tensions and frustrations from not only the last few days, but from the past events bringing them together. The distant rumblings and lightning show of a passing summer storm surrounded them. Later in the night, when they again made love, the experience was one of sharing and exploring the softer edges of their desires.

Their passions spent, in the darkest hours of the night, they awoke to a medley of snarls, growls, and earsplitting barks. Not targeted at the bedroom door, but from the sounds of the crinkling, crumbling, and crashing of at least two sets of window blinds, probably the dining room windows. By the time Steve unfolded himself from the soft contours of Edie's comforting embrace and peered out into the front yard, the lone figure was long gone.

This time there was no black Suburban parked close by to whisk away the deeply tanned man with thick black hair. Now clad in a black ski mask, black long-sleeved pullover shirt, black jeans, and black hiking boots, he slipped back to the county road where the Suburban was parked.

He climbed into the passenger seat and turned to the driver. "Let's get the hell out of here. I was damn lucky the fucking SUV wasn't parked too close to the house. They got some nasty sounding guard dog. I barely had time to secure the tracking device underneath. If the boss decides he wants the house bugged, we better make damn sure the fucking dog is nowhere around."

"Don't tell me you're turning into a limp dick pussy," the driver said as he started the engine and drove away without turning on the headlights until he was sure they wouldn't be noticed.

Back at the house, Steve had grabbed a flashlight and was about to open the door to do some additional investigations when he heard Edie call out. "Steve, if you take Amber outside with you, maybe you better put a leash on her. You don't know what she might be chasing after in the dark."

Agreeing, he secured a leash on Amber and then headed outside to check things out. After being pulled down the porch steps, Steve was dragged to the parked Durango. Once there, Amber became even more agitated and yanked Steve around the SUV several times. Then with her nose to the ground, she almost succeeded in pulling him down the driveway. There were no immediate threats, and having had enough of Amber's antics, he dragged the barking and growling dog back inside the house. With a final grunt, Steve re-deposited Amber on the outside of the bedroom door.

As he cuddled back up against Edie, he thought, what the hell. Never let a good crisis go to waste. She turned into him as his body responded to the heat of her touch.

CHAPTER 38

Washington, D.C.

A FIRE WAS CRACKLING FROM BEHIND the ornate white marbled hearth. From above, General George Washington stared off into the distance as if trying to escape the scene below. On most occasions this room was the picture of symmetry, but today one of the high-backed Victorian armchairs flanking the fireplace had been yanked out of its stately repose. With its back to the fire, it sat at one end of the glass coffee table. It faced the two opposing sofas, which formed the conversational focal point of the Oval Office. The air conditioning system strained to maintain a comfortable temperature, but today the fireplace was not the main source of the heat emanating from the room.

With her back to the fire, her hawk-like beautiful brown eyes peeked below her trademark bangs, darting back and forth between the two men seated across from each other. Although she was looking at the two most powerful figures in the world, the heat radiating from her body alone made the fire appear cold in comparison. Some may have argued, or even feared, her own power out-shadowed the other occupants in the room.

At thirty-nine, Maria Santiago was a stunningly gorgeous woman with full breasts complementing the remaining assets of her curvaceous body. Her five-foot-six figure started with statuesque legs. It was completed by a tangled mane of thick black hair cascading over her shoulders. What made her a dangerous woman, however, was not the way she exuded sexuality. She possessed one of the nation's most daring political minds. She had the uncanny capability of analyzing every event in terms of the voting public's perception. The facts were irrelevant.

Maria was a top senior advisor to President John Connor. Her political proclivity had guided him first into the governorship of California, and then a series of successful campaigns leading to the leader of the free world sitting on her right. The man on her left, Ralph Matthews, the president's chief of staff, might have debated over who the real leader was, but never in the presence of Maria Santiago.

Her immigrant parents moved to the Central Valley of California from Argentina when Maria was four years old. Although poor, they worked hard and instilled in the young Maria the mindset to achieve what was beyond her grasp. She graduated from the University of California at Berkeley with a master's degree in political science and a minor in psychology. After those accomplishments were behind her, she jumped onto the political carousel and never looked back.

As her voice got louder, her faint Hispanic accent became more pronounced and menacing.

"Matthews. Are you fucking out of your mind?" Maria said. "You've been secretly investigating the vice president of the United States? Do you have any concept of what the hell would happen to this administration if any of this got out? There's no fucking way this is possible to do legally. Or at least without getting caught. How does the fact she happens to have a few friends in the State Department lead you to send some of your goddamned goons snooping around? You do remember she is the former secretary of state? Or is that beyond your capability? And for God's sake, how long has this shit been going on?"

Matthews tried to gauge if she was calm enough to respond to. "Maria, you look even sexier when you talk dirty."

"If you don't want one of my designer stilettos stuck up your fat ass you better start explaining what the hell you're up to."

Good, he thought. She's not as angry as he had expected. Putting on one of his best fake smiles, he started from the beginning. "As you recall, a few months prior to the last elections we were required to interject a diverting event to lessen the potential impact of, for lack of a better phrase, decisions to downplay the threats to our embassy in Pakistan."

Matthews turned his fake smile into a frown. "I've always been troubled by the fact we didn't have complete control of how certain communications were handled by the State Department back then. At the time we relied on our own resources to generate a different story for the world."

The president and Maria exchanged glances. Catching this, Matthews assumed a more conspiratorial tone.

"Look," he said. "We're all big boys and girls here, so we need to get beyond any of your childish deniability claims. No disrespect, John, but we all know what we had to do back then to get through the election. Until now we've been able to keep things under control. But I think you are both aware of recent events. At least we've discussed these in general terms."

"For God's sake, Ralph," the president said. "What the hell does this have to do with you investigating the vice president?"

"To be honest, at this point I'm not sure—"

Maria interrupted. "Fucking great, Matthews. So you take it on yourself to violate every possible—"

"For Christ's sake. Would you let me finish?" Matthews said. "As you reminded me, before Alice Andersen became John's running mate, she was the secretary of state. So, let me back up to where you guys started panicking. Okay?"

Maria raised her hands in mock surrender, allowing Matthews to explain. "We've been looking into the communications of State Department personnel around the time of the embassy bombing in Pakistan. Before the attack, a few key memos were leaked. They addressed security issues at the embassy and reports of heightened terrorist threats intercepted by the State Department's intelligence offices. During our investigation we stumbled across the names of three employees, all from different departments. At this point there's no evidence they even know or are aware of each other. But in the last three months they have been independently, we think, communicating with the vice president by email. Nothing specific revealed. On several occasions the vice president has also met with these people for lunch. Individually, I might add. And again, there doesn't appear to be any direct links between any of these people. As far as we know it doesn't look like they have shared any information amongst themselves."

"What departments do these people work in?" Maria asked.

"One works in Intelligence and Research, the other in Diplomatic Security, and the last in the South and Central Asian Division of Political Affairs. Now you may want to believe the vice president was just having lunch with some former colleagues, but I for one don't believe in coincidences. Besides, these people are mid-level workers. Not the kind of positions the former secretary of state would interact with."

Matthews was milking this for all it was worth, knowing how it got Maria annoyed.

"Now this is where things get interesting," he said. "I decided to dig a little deeper and checked out the vice president's personal email accounts and other activities."

"And who the fuck did you get to do this without any legal authority? To do this appropriately you would have to go through the National Security Agency. Please tell me you weren't stupid enough to do that," Maria said through gritted teeth.

"I've been working with Homeland Security. With the Special Assignment Detail for Counterterrorism, Information Sharing, and Cybersecurity."

The president looked bewildered. "What are you talking about? Who the hell do you have doing this?"

"Relax, John," Matthews said. "I'm in charge of this Special Assignment Detail. On the surface, there are two, let's call them secret service agents, which happen to be their formal job titles. They have worked with me on all aspects of this, and several other investigations."

At last, any lingering pretense of plausible deniability was thrown out the window.

"What we found," Matthews said, "is something disturbing, but helps make sense about the latest series of events I've been trying to deal with."

"I'm sure congress and the American people will be glad to hear that," Maria said.

"Just look at this." Matthews pulled out two sheets of paper and handed one to each of them.

As the president and Maria read, Matthews said, "This is a copy of an email the vice president sent from what she believed to be one of her private, anonymous accounts." He laughed at that thought. "It was sent to Edie Pauling a couple of months ago. To remind you, Edie Pauling is the daughter of the retired Navy SEAL guy killed in the embassy bombing in Pakistan. Remember?"

Maria looked to the president and back to Matthews, her face scrunched in bewilderment. "But what could possibly be this Pauling girl's connection to the vice president?"

CHAPTER 39

Coeur d'Alene, Idaho

THE NEXT MORNING STEVE AND Edie lingered in each other's arms. Afraid if the moment was broken, they would lose the precious gift they had unwrapped in the midst of all their confusion. As the sun rose in the morning sky, they accepted a new day had begun. And they had unfinished work to do. Amber had already realized the day had begun some time ago and had been whining and scratching on the door as a reminder.

Steve was again working on his culinary masterpiece of bacon and eggs, as well as trying to come up with a few spontaneous thoughtful phrases to say to Edie. Nothing he could think of seemed to cut it.

Curled up on the sofa and watching a local news station, Edie called out, "Hey there, Mr. Casella. You know you can still talk to me. Right?"

Ah shit, Steve thought. What the hell should he call her? Again, nothing seemed right. Maybe he should stick with Edie.

"I'm sorry," Steve said. "I didn't get what you said. I'll be right there. Ah… Edie."

Steve walked into the living room, and at the last second decided on cozying up on the sofa next to her.

"Well. Hi there. Ah… Steve," she said with curled lips and an upturned nose.

Just as he was thinking how deep he was digging himself, their attention was diverted to the news anchor's voice and the picture of a familiar face emblazoned on the screen. Edie grabbed the remote and punched up the volume.

>*"This just in. We are now getting in more details from Coeur d'Alene, Idaho, of a terrible accident that occurred last evening at the world-famous Coeur d'Alene Resort. The woman, Cindy Weaver, whose picture you're now looking at, died after falling over the railing from a twelfth-floor open air pavilion area outside the Lakeside Tower Boardroom complex. Authorities speculate Ms. Weaver, age forty-five, was attempting to attach a banner to the outside of the glass railing and lost her balance while leaning over the top. A banner was found entangled on the mooring lines of a nearby lake cruiser. Thus far, no witnesses to the accident have come forward. The approximate time of death, around nine or nine-thirty last evening, corresponds to the arrival of a severe thunderstorm with heavy winds and torrential downpours. The conditions would have made the tiled flooring and metal topped glass railing slippery, leading to a hazardous condition, and a contributing factor to the accident. Ms. Weaver had been employed at the Resort for fifteen years and currently held the position of meeting room coordinator. The authorities report another banner, identical to the one found near the body of Ms. Weaver, was discovered in her office. The banner carried the insignia for the Restraint in Government Alliance. Pending further developments, the authorities are ruling the death of Cindy Weaver an accident.*

When we return…"

Edie muted the sound. "Oh my God. This is terrible. She was such a nice lady. How awful." The dark look on Steve's face made her stop. "What's the matter?"

Catching his breath, Steve said, "Why in the hell would she be standing out in the rain? A damn thunderstorm no less. Leaning over a slippery railing to put out a sign that would blow away in the storm? I doubt this would even be in her job description. You saw the way she was dressed the other day. Would you be bending over a twelfth-floor railing in that kind of outfit?"

"Well." Edie hesitated. "We don't know what she was wearing yesterday. What? You're not buying this was an accident?"

"Me? What the hell do I know? I thought you were the conspiracy theory advocate of our team."

Edie cuddled up closer to Steve. "I guess I'm too upset to think clearly right now. But I feel a little bit better by the way you called us a team."

He would have never figured 'team' was the word she was looking for. Maybe this sensitivity stuff was easier to grasp than he thought.

"Come on," Steve said, looking away. "Breakfast is getting cold. Let's finish up here so we can head up to the cabin."

As Steve got up to walk back into the kitchen, Edie grabbed him by the arm. "Steve," she said. "Wanna tell me what's going on in your head?"

"After talking to Cindy again the other night, I felt a kind of connection to my dad. And now she's dead. A coincidence?" He stopped and shook his head, a pained expression on his face. "God. This could be all our fault. What the hell is going on? I guess we need to be careful—take it slow and see where all this leads."

He took Edie's hand as she wiped a tear from her face. He helped her off the sofa, unaware of the understatement of those last remarks. Or it would be quite some time, if ever, before they held each other in this house again.

CHAPTER 40

STEVE FOLLOWED SULLIVAN'S DIRECTIONS TO the cabin. Although only three or four miles from his dad's house, the trip took almost half an hour. They spotted the cabin as they snaked along the edge of a rutted dirt road with steep, narrow switchbacks. It sat on a level knoll which had been cleared of trees and heavy brush. Several rocky retaining walls stabilized the soil around the cabin. The knoll stood about two-thirds up to the summit of an expansive wooded terrain. As far as one could see lay a countless array of peaks, valleys, ravines, and draws, all densely timbered, making for a rugged and dangerous environment.

The tires of the Durango crunched to a halt near the cabin. Edie released Amber from the cargo area and watched her run off chasing nearby birds. Steve double-checked his notes as to where the key was hidden. He found it right above the door frame as instructed.

As he unlocked and opened up the door, Edie said, "Maybe a little late for this, but you did bring your dad's key ring. Didn't you?"

Dangling the keys in her face, Steve said, "You think you're sleeping with an idiot?"

"Whaddaya mean sleeping?" Edie said. "I can hardly walk."

Holy crap. He could be the sensitive one in this relationship.

Edie watched Steve return Sullivan's key to its hiding place, and said, "You might've found that same door key on the key ring you dangled in my face. Don't ya think?"

Steve didn't bother to reply.

The modest cabin built with heavy logs had a front-facing, U-shaped design with a covered porch extending between the two front wings. The roof was covered with dark forest green metal panels. The interior was well-appointed with hand-crafted finishes and cabinetry. Custom made roughhewn plank flooring dominated the inside. Tucked away in the far corner of the main living area they spotted a wood and metal trunk.

Steve selected different keys until the correct one unclasped the lock. Opening the lid, he thought of Geraldo Rivera, except this treasure chest held some tangible objects. Including a locked portable fire safe box. He handed the box to Edie and sifted through the remaining contents of the trunk. It turned out to be a collection of what he assumed were his dad's tools.

Steve closed the lid and Edie placed the fire safe box on the trunk. He selected another key from the ring. He inserted it and opened the box. A black bound laboratory styled notebook sat on top. The box also contained photos, newspaper clippings, and a few sheets of paper with handwritten notes scribbled on them. Several canvas pouches found inside were filled with a sizable amount of cash.

"Jeez," Steve said. "There must be at least twenty thousand dollars in here. If these are all hundred-dollar bills there could be a helluva lot more."

From outside the cabin they heard frantic barks, and then paws clattering across the porch. Amber bolted inside, barking and whining. She circled a few times, nipping at Steve's ankles and dashed back out. Still barking, Amber returned, bolting through the door and scratching her paw on Steve's knee. She jumped up as he stood, pushing her nose into his chin and neck. This time Steve and Edie followed her outside.

At first, he didn't see anything unusual. A faint scent reached his nasal passages. A slight flare of his nostrils drew in the invisible particles floating in the morning breeze. He spotted the first spidery wisps of smoke rising from the woods below the cabin. Steve swallowed, and a dry acrid taste clung to his throat. He pointed in the direction they'd driven through, where the road disappeared into the thick trees. Thick smoke plumes and ash masked the clear blue skies. He watched the isolated clusters of smoke and flames merge. The growing fire spread and edged up the hillside below him.

And the cabin stood directly in its path.

"Come on, Steve," Edie screamed. "Get Amber in the Durango and let's get the hell outta here. Let's go. What's the matter with you? Why're you standing there?"

Steve took a couple of deep breaths and scanned the entire scene. He looked at the lay of the land between the fire and the cabin. Then the distant terrain, and their immediate surroundings. Gauging weather conditions, existing dead fuel and ground moisture levels, and live fuel elements in the fire's trajectory, Steve arrived at the only possible decision.

He grasped Edie by her shoulders, steadied her, and said, "Edie, listen to me. We can't drive out of here. The road we drove up isn't safe. Everything below us will be consumed by the fire. The road ends here. And there's no way we can outrun this thing on foot. The safest place for us is where we are right now."

Edie stared at him.

"Edie. Do you trust me?"

Nothing.

"Edie. Listen to me. I need to know if you trust me."

She nodded.

"Good," Steve said. "We've still got a little bit of time to prepare. I'm gonna get some things we need out of the Durango. Can you go into the cabin and bring out the fire safe box?"

She nodded again, and after a slight hesitation, ran off. Steve jogged to the Durango and retrieved a number of items stowed in the cargo area. Finding the most suitable place in the clearing, he picked up the folding shovel and scraped away any remnants of lingering vegetation from an already barren section of earth. Close to this spot was a retaining wall section built of rocks protruding at least several feet above ground level. It was situated between them and the rapidly approaching firestorm.

Edie returned with the fire safe box cradled in her arms. He took it from her and placed it in front of the rock wall near where he had cleared the ground. He then ran back to the Durango and drove it to the boundary of the knoll. Placing it as far as he could from the spot where Edie was standing.

"Steve," Edie cried out as he returned. "I can't find Amber. I've been calling her. But she's not coming. She must've run off. We've gotta go get her. She must be scared. Come on, let's try to find her. Hurry."

Coughing, Edie wiped the palm of her hand across her eyes, trying to clear the stinging of the smoke from the approaching fire and the tears for the missing dog.

"You said you trust me," Steve said, eyes riveted on Edie. "Right?"

He got a tiny nod from Edie.

"Now listen to me," Steve said. "Please. Amber knows what to do. Her instincts will get her out of danger. After the fire passes over, we'll go and find her. Okay?"

Edie nodded, biting her lip. Her eyes widened. "What the hell do you mean by 'after the fire passes over'? Passes over what?"

Steve bent over and grabbed some of the stuff he'd thrown on the ground. "Put on these gloves."

Opening up the storage case, he removed the sealed package and pulled the ring tabs to tear away the vinyl bag, exposing its contents. Steve then flipped it out in front of him and unfolded the aluminized tent-like structure. He put on the remaining pair of gloves and motioned for Edie to stand next to him.

The neighboring air pulsated with the heat of the approaching flames. The fire born winds rattled the fire shelter Steve struggled to assemble. Smoke particles and ash assaulted their lungs. A cacophony of crackling, snapping, and popping was accompanied by an ever-growing roar. It sounded like they were in the path of a gigantic runaway locomotive.

Steve threw down a folded towel in front of them. "This is what we're gonna do." He positioned them facing away from the oncoming inferno. Centered within the area he had scraped clean. Edie was to his right.

"See these straps?" Steve said. "I need you to loop the bottom one around your right shoe. Then grab the upper one in your right hand. I'll do the same with mine. When I say so, we're gonna lay down on our stomachs. As flat as you can, with your face buried in the towel. I want you to keep yourself close to me. Breathe through the towel, keeping yourself as low as possible to the ground. Don't take deep breaths. Remember to take nice shallow breaths. Any questions?"

The air around them became almost unbearable. Their eyes stinging, lungs coughing in protest. They fought to hang on to the shelter's straps. The entire shelter strained against the increasing force of the winds.

"Steve? Is this thing big enough for two people?"

"Of course it is," he lied. "Ready? Let's do it."

They maneuvered themselves onto the ground with the A-framed shelter above them.

"It's gonna get deafening in here, and the wind will be brutal," Steve said, voice straining against the approaching firestorm. "And it might get a little toasty. Make sure you don't let go of those straps. And keep your body away from the sides of the shelter. Here we go. Remember. Shallow breathing. Face the ground. Into the towel."

Edie's brain overloaded as the skin-searing heat, the ear-splitting shock waves, and the thickening particulates and acrid gases all competed to terrorize everything in its path.

Steve coughed from the thickening smoke but tried to keep his voice steady. "This may be the one time I want to hear you say, 'talk to me, Steve'. So, Edie. Did you know when I was nine years old, I already knew I wanted to be a fireman? Excuse me, firefighter. I was at a supermarket in Santa Rosa with my mom and this giant shiny red fire truck pulled up and…"

Bodies tight together, buried inside the thin rattling shelter, Steve felt Edie trembling, but she never let go of the straps. He heard the muffled, lung clearing coughs racking her body. Sensing her terror, he understood the steady breaths she took helped fight off an immobilizing panic.

In between his own shallow breaths and continued hacking, in an attempt to lessen Edie's anxieties, Steve rambled on about his childhood, how much he enjoyed his early school years, some funny stories about his job, and the first girl he had sex with in high school. Well, thank God the firestorm had passed before he got to that last story.

It seemed hours had gone by, but in reality it was considerably less time when Steve gave the nod to remove themselves from their little cocoon. With an exhausted sigh of relief, Edie stood up and looked around at the devastation. Flames engulfed the cabin. The Durango was a heap of twisted steel and melted plastic and rubber. Their senses assaulted by the caustic smells. They had heard the gas tank explode while still inside the shelter.

Edie leaned into Steve, placing her arm around his waist. They both stood motionless for several minutes. He could feel the tension drain from her body.

"I bet this made you think of the first time you screwed a girl in your little boy scout tent."

He never said that out loud. Did he? What? Now he had to think sensitive thoughts?

"Why do you have such a funny look on your face, Mr. Firefighter?" Edie said. Before Steve could respond, Edie crashed back to reality. "What about Amber? Do you think she's okay? I wish we could hear her barking."

"I'm sure she's fine. But she won't be anywhere around here. She'll find us when we get ourselves clear of this mess." Steve prayed he was right.

"Edie? Listen to me," he said. "I'm almost certain this fire was deliberately set. I think they used some powerful accelerants too. These conditions aren't favorable for a wildfire. Not even one started by a careless camper."

"What're you saying?"

"Somebody didn't want us to find whatever was in the cabin, and they wanted to make sure we're not around to talk to anyone else."

"Oh my God," Edie said, absorbing the devastation. "They probably think we're dead. I guess that's helpful—at least for now."

Edie picked up the cooling fire safe box and looked inside.

"Everything looks okay," she said, shuddering as she glanced at the wrinkled-up fire shelter.

"Good work, Dad," Steve mumbled, patting the metal box.

He checked his pockets. "Oh crap. I left my phone in the car. You got yours?"

Edie reached into her pocket. "Yep. And it looks intact too."

"Wait," Steve said, "it might be better to shut it off for now. I don't know if they're capable of tracking us with it, but let's not chance it. Somebody knew we were here."

He stole a quick glance at the remains of the Durango, biting his lower lip.

"I don't think they knew anything about the cabin until we led them to it. Or this stuff wouldn't have been here. We need to find another way out."

"I thought you said there wasn't any other way out?" Edie said.

"We need to try. And make sure we avoid the way we came in. The longer they think we're dead, the better off we'll be. It should be safe to use your phone to check our GPS coordinates once in a while, as long as it's not turned on for too long. I think I remember that from a movie."

"Can't wait until the next date night to see that one," Edie said. "By the way. Before I turned my phone off. I checked. No cell signal here anyway."

"Well, let's hope we don't get lost. With any luck we'll pick up a signal as we get closer to civilization. Let's go."

Steve collected the shovel and the remnants of the fire shelter to carry out with them. He didn't want anything left to alert anyone they had survived the inferno. He inwardly shivered while handling the crumpled aluminum and reflected on what one of his instructors had said about never wanting to put yourself in the position to be forced into that damn roasting pan. Because by then, you have exhausted all reasonable options.

Edie pulled Steve into a tight embrace and kissed him on the lips. "Thanks for saving my life," she whispered in his ear and pulled back.

"Only one kiss? I've gotten more for pulling some sexy lady's kitten out of a drainpipe."

"You had your chance in the tent you're holding."

CHAPTER 41

FOR SEVERAL HOURS STEVE AND Edie worked to distance themselves from the scene of the smoldering cabin and ruined Durango. They took a circuitous path away from the road leading to the cabin and the suspected origin of the fire. Every so often Edie switched on her phone and checked the GPS coordinates.

Not long after the fire had blown over, the skies were disrupted by the distinctive sounds of a couple of Blackhawk helicopters. The former US Army air assault choppers had been converted into air tactical support vehicles for firefighting crews. They delivered a progression of water buckets from nearby Lake Coeur d'Alene to douse the flames of the leading edge of the fire. Ground crews handled the accessible portions in the valley areas closer to the road. Steve noticed that the spreading flames were quickly suppressed. A tribute to the rapid deployment and diligence of the firefighting crews. He knew even though the fire danger level was low, the spreading fire could have gotten out of control and caused serious damage. Hidden in the trees below, as the last Blackhawk screamed by on its return flight to base following a final drop, he gave a silent salute to his firefighting comrades.

Exhausted, grimy, and in desperate need of water, they emerged from a dense slice of forest onto a rutted off-road vehicle trail. A quick check on the GPS failed to register this as anything of note. But it appeared to intersect with something more promising. A lane connecting to the county road within a mile.

Amber never responded to any of their frantic calls. More burning than their parched and aching throats was the stabbing pain in their guts that Steve may have overestimated Amber's instinct for survival. They trudged across a deadfall of tangled branches and stepped onto a gravel road.

"There's something damn familiar about this," Steve said. "Don't ya think?"

Before Edie had a chance to answer, they both spun around to the sudden outburst of barks, and the sight of an excited white German Shepherd running toward them.

Amber leaped onto Steve, knocking the shovel and the remnants of the fire shelter to the ground. She then turned her attention to Edie. Amber knocked her on her ass and washed off her dirt-streaked face with wet kisses. Steve gathered up the fire safe box which was shaken from Edie's hands and helped her back onto her feet.

"You're damned lucky nothing happened to Amber," Edie said, and then paused as her eyes looked over the dog.

Edie leaned in closer and wrinkled her nose, looking up at Steve. "Hey," she said. "Why is it you look and smell like shit, and Amber looks and smells like she just won Best in Show at the Westminster Kennel Club Dog Show?"

"I have no idea. But she does feel a little damp. And if I might add, you also look like... ah... well, you could use a bit of freshening up yourself. Besides, what the hell do you know about a dog show?"

"My journalistic talents have no boundaries. I've covered a few important ones in my time," Edie said smartly.

"Wow. You're right up there with Connie Chung."

"Thank you. But I do feel the need to correct myself on one minor point. Amber could not be Best in Show. She would've been disqualified for being white."

"I think I'll pass on that one."

"Don't be stupid. It's an AKC standard for the breed. AKC stands for American Kennel Club. She could be entered into an obedience trial though."

"An obedience trial?" Steve said, raising his eyebrows. "Are you out of your f—"

Before Steve could finish, the piercing grinds of an approaching bright red vehicle shattered the silence. As the off-road Kawasaki Mule rolled closer, Amber rushed toward it and jumped into the rear cargo box, sitting on her haunches.

Joe Wilton sat in the driver's seat.

"I'll be damned," Joe said. "I've been looking out for you guys ever since this dog showed up at my place this morning. Wasn't sure it was yours, at least until now. No more doubts at all, I'd say. And if I might comment on something. Jesus, Steve. You look like shit. What the hell happened to you?"

Steve pointed to Edie. "Thanks for noticing, Joe, but what about her?"

"Hey, do I look stupid enough to answer that?" He tipped his cap to Edie. "Jump in guys. There're some water bottles in here someplace. Let's get you back to the house and cleaned up. Then you can fill Connie and me in on what's going on. All hell's broken loose since the fire started this morning."

CHAPTER 42

AFTER A THOROUGH SCRUBBING, STEVE and Edie felt almost human again. They were seated on a cozy French country floral patterned sofa in the family room of Joe and Connie Wilton's home. They stared out the multi-paned picture window at the same manicured lawn they'd noticed several days ago, albeit from the opposite direction.

Connie Wilton, a slight woman in her late sixties, had a full mane of long red hair framing her smiling face and accenting the twinkle in her keen green eyes. She wore a flowered house coat that would have made her magically disappear if she had chosen to sit on the sofa. Best of all, she carried no weapons.

"I hope those clothes fit okay," Connie said. "I'm afraid the things you were wearing earlier are well beyond cleaning. My oldest granddaughter's close to your size Edie, but sorry Steve, I think Joe has a few inches in the waist on you. Plus he's a tad bit shorter, so you won't be winning any fashion contests."

Steve and Edie told their story of being trapped in the path of the wildfire, trying to make it seem as harmless as possible, but some expert grilling by their hosts prodded out too many of the suspicious details. Steve was getting nervous about hanging around and involving the Wiltons in their problems.

Joe said, "You must be thinking we're pretty stupid around here. And I'd have to agree. In the short time since you guys have arrived, you've shaken up a hornet's nest. I should've seen the writing on the wall when I came here too. Damn. Maybe some of the boys at the club can be naïve, but I should've realized they weren't capable of being party to such an outrage. The first rule is never ask a client if he's guilty. I should've asked tougher questions. Maybe listened a little more to what they were saying."

Joe saw the surprised look on their faces. "Guilty. I'm a retired attorney. Practiced criminal law in Seattle for over thirty years."

When Joe had driven the Mule loaded with his passengers back into his shop earlier, Steve had noticed an assortment of antique and classic cars in various stages of restoration.

"Guys," Steve said. "We appreciate what you've done for us. And Amber, too. She's never looked or smelled better. We can't thank you enough. But I'm afraid it might not be safe for you if someone finds us hanging around here. Sooner or later somebody's gonna show up looking for us."

"Just bigger targets," Connie said. She had a distinct twinkle in her eyes. "Should be no problem at all."

"At this point," Steve said, "I'm sure they think we died in the fire, but eventually they'll begin to question the lack of any bodies being found."

"We want to help. So keep us in mind," Joe said. "You know you can't do this alone. I'm guessing there's a lot more going on than what you can see right now."

Joe snapped his fingers. "Let me lend you one of my cars. You can have whichever one you want, except for my fire engine red Corvette. I'm putting the finishing touches on it, and the black leather upholstery is brand spanking new. No offense, Amber," he said, looking sideways at the dog resting next to his leather recliner. "Of course, you're welcome to stay here if you choose, but it might be wise to put some distance between you and whatever you stirred up. Until things cool off a bit. Give you time to come up with some kind of plan."

"No deal, Joe," Steve said, shaking his head. "We do this as paying customers or not at all. We don't even know where we're headed. Or when we can get back. Besides, our last vehicle didn't fare so well."

Steve's mind flashed to the bags of new-found money. "We apparently are in a reasonable position, cash-wise at least. Not so much to want to spend it all on your prize Corvette, but maybe you have something else in mind out there to suit our needs. Whadda ya say?"

Joe sat back in his recliner and mentally checked his inventory. "I brought home a big old Ambassador a couple of days ago."

"An Ambassador?" Edie said. "I thought they were cigars."

Steve's jaw dropped. "I guess I've got a lot to learn about you. I didn't know you smoked."

"Not me. My dad was a Navy SEAL," Edie said. "Remember? But a couple more of these kinda days, I might be contemplating a new habit."

Joe shook his head. "Just finished checking out the mechanics on it. It runs damn good. The engine and transmission were rebuilt last year. Not much body work done, but it's not in terrible shape."

For Edie's benefit, and maybe Steve's as well, he filled in the rest of the details. "It's a 1966 American Motors Ambassador four door sedan. It has an automatic transmission and one of the biggest V8 engines available at the time. I think it was one of the last models before the emission control gadgets began to gum up the works. As long as you don't expect good gas mileage by today's standards, you shouldn't be disappointed in its performance. You can sign the paperwork and take it off the lot today for what I paid for it. Three thousand dollars. And I don't negotiate."

Before Steve could react, Joe added, "By the way, when we're done with this deal, we can talk about something else I'd like to interest you in."

Chapter 43

Washington, D.C.

Ralph Matthews watched from behind his desk. The clicking of Maria Santiago's heels silenced as her footsteps transitioned from the polished hardwood floor onto the plush carpet in the chief of staff's office. Wouldn't it be great having her covering his back? His thoughts drifted to more explicit images as Maria pressed her voluptuous body into the chair in front of him. She seemed to take a little more time than necessary arranging her skirt as it slipped higher up her thighs. Most of this vision was speculation as his direct line of sight was blocked by the untidy stacks of papers on his desk.

Maria got right down to the problem at hand. "John's too busy to be bothered by a lot of these annoying details."

Which Matthews took to mean there were some things she wasn't ready to tell the president. She couldn't get away from that plausible deniability crap. They both knew the president was in as much deep shit as the rest of them.

There was a knock on the door and Ben Courtney was ushered into the office, the heavy door slamming shut behind him. Matthews paid no attention to Courtney as he struggled to get his long legs positioned in the seat next to Maria.

Matthews picked up a paper on his desk and got to work. "This is what we know so far regarding earlier activities of the vice president. Most of it is public knowledge, but we're now looking at it from a different angle. Back in the day when Alice Andersen was a prosecutor, she lived in Hackensack, New Jersey. For a couple of years, she leased a duplex apartment on Clay Street. The Pauling family, we now know, lived in the other half of the duplex during that same timeframe. Chuck Pauling, the future Navy SEAL, later to become our so-called hero in Pakistan, lived there until he enlisted in the Navy."

"So? What the hell does this mean?" Maria asked. "She lives next door to this family thirty years ago, and now after becoming vice president she decides to avenge this guy's death? Besides, a damn suicide bomber killed him."

"I don't know what her motive is," Matthews countered. "Does it make a difference as to why she's doing it? She has succeeded in re-igniting Edie Pauling's quest to uncover some version of the truth by steering her out west to connect with Casella's son. And with what's been developing out there right now, they might've already linked some of these events together."

Matthews stopped and looked at Courtney. "But before I go on, Ben, I want you to fill us in on the latest from Reilly and our Special Assignment boys."

Ben Courtney smiled. "Turns out Tom Casella mentioned a few disturbing facts to a girlfriend of his around the time the video was released. She never made the connection until our two friends showed up asking a whole bunch of questions. She started connecting the dots. We were privy to one of her recent, or should I say, last phone conversations. I've been informed that this former girlfriend, Cindy Weaver, had an unfortunate accident and no longer presents a problem."

Maria looked at Matthews who nodded and indicated for Courtney to go on.

"Our guys," Courtney said, pausing for emphasis, "have also been keeping an eye on those two troublemakers since they met with the girlfriend. And guess what? Pauling and Casella appear to have perished in the path of a horrendous forest fire. A cabin they were visiting burned to the ground along with the vehicle the two were known to be driving. Due to the inaccessible terrain in the burned-out area, it could be quite some time before the bodies are found."

Matthews sat up straighter, and asked, "There were no bodies found at this cabin?"

Courtney shrugged. "If the wolves and coyotes get there first, they may never be recovered. The local authorities don't think there's much of a chance they could've escaped, being how fast the fire erupted. The fire marshal, however, is investigating the fire as being suspicious. They do suspect arson. Can you imagine?"

"I shouldn't have to even say this, Ben," Matthews said, "but I assume we're not going to rely on the locals here? Anyway, let's move on."

"Ah, as you suggested," Courtney said, squirming a bit in his chair, "the time has come to wrap up our plans with Peter Fenton and Senator Tyler Griffin. This should be taken care of very soon, but not in the way Fenton would have anticipated. Didn't you once say he was dispensable?"

CHAPTER 44

Coeur d'Alene, Idaho

STEVE AND EDIE HEADED TOWARD the interstate in their new Ambassador. They took Joe Wilton's advice and drove up the county road in the opposite direction from Coeur d'Alene, the Wolf Bay Community Club, and the place they'd called home this morning. Steve imagined navigating an ocean liner down a narrow winding stream might've been easier. After several miles of dense trees, enduring the dusty and bumpy dirt road, they emerged into daylight at the summit of the Fourth of July Pass, gazing at the welcoming signs for the interstate. They moved onto the entrance ramp for eastbound Interstate 90 and headed down the mountain toward the Silver Valley where they hoped to sequester themselves and sift through what they salvaged from the cabin. They needed time to decide on their next move.

At the first signs of civilization, they spotted a Walmart and exited the interstate. Judging by what they had with them, only the clothes on their backs, it was time to replenish supplies. At the last minute they grabbed a couple of prepaid cell phones. As they returned to the interstate and headed toward their destination, Amber was enjoying her new rear seat passenger status, chewing on a jumbo dog treat.

With barely enough time to bring the Ambassador up to cruising speed, their exit came into view. Their destination was the ski village of Kellogg, home of the Silver Mountain Resort and the world's longest single-staged gondola.

According to Joe Wilton, Kellogg, once a bustling mining town, cycled through times of feast and famine. Joe had asked them not to repeat the fact it was also the home of the Environmental Protection Agency's largest Superfund site. Although remediated and deemed safe, as a local investor, Joe considered this information was not something to be publicized.

The tourism boom got under way in the early nineties with the city funded building of the gondola, allowing better access to the Silver Mountain slopes. Things spiraled up when large investment groups descended on the town with plans for world-class attractions and amenities aimed at turning the obscure ski village into a four-season resort destination. The Silver Valley region was hit hard by the prolonged recession and bursting of the real estate bubble. The big investors abandoned ship, leaving the locals to bide their time until the cycle started its next upturn.

Joe made his move when the prices were low and purchased a renovated vacation home in Kellogg. The house was situated on a slight knoll overlooking the base ski lodge. It sat under the path of the gondola. In an earlier life the classical colonial was probably home to a mining company executive or one of the company's staff physicians. The silver mining industry in this region was even more fickle than the recent tourism market.

More germane to Steve and Edie's predicament, the house's current rendition boasted an attached garage to keep their Ambassador out of sight, and a fenced-in yard to keep Amber in sight. It stood isolated from the surrounding properties, unless you considered possible prying eyes from the overhead gondola cars. This being the low season, the gondolas only ran on the weekends to carry bikers up to the mountain trails and spectators to the summer concerts at the Summit Pavilion on top of Silver Mountain. Joe insisted they were renting this place at a rock bottom price. In addition, Edie convinced Joe to forego the usual pet deposit requirement, seeing how clean and fresh Amber appeared.

Edie handed Steve the garage door remote controller found in Joe's rental pouch. He pressed the button and backed the Ambassador into the garage. He closed the door with only inches to spare in front of the huge classic car. No big deal. He'd done it hundreds of times with a variety of fire fighting vehicles in his historic fire station back in San Francisco.

They grabbed their bundles from the trunk and stepped into a spacious laundry room. This house was a bit large for their needs, but there were no complaints from the new guests. At 3500 square feet on two levels, the house boasted four bedrooms, three bathrooms, a gourmet kitchen, a formal dining room, and a family room with a large flat screen television set up with the best in premium satellite channels.

Darkness settled in around them as they landed in the dining room to wolf down the fast-food take-out collected from a local McDonald's. The impact of the ordeal they had endured over this endless day sank into their consciousness.

Exhausted, Steve and Edie stripped off their clothes and crashed into the comfy king-sized bed in the first-floor master bedroom suite. At this point Edie didn't care what the hell they called the bedroom. Amber took advantage of Steve's negligent behavior and secured a prime location at the foot of the bed.

Sometime in the dead of night Edie awoke with a stifled cry. Shedding off the remnants of a disturbing nightmarish reflection of being scorched in a blanket of tin foil, she turned into Steve's reassuring embrace. Her ebbing sobs swallowed by Steve's gentle kisses and caresses. They came together with a tenderness that soothed their troubled bodies, and a rhythm that drowned their fears. With a final quiet moan, Edie fell into a deep and dreamless sleep.

Amber remained at the foot of the bed and waited for a belly rub.

CHAPTER 45

Washington, D.C.

THE MEETING HADN'T CONCLUDED, BUT Ben Courtney excused himself from the chief of staff's office to check on the final arrangements for Senator Tyler Griffin and the senator's campaign advisor, Peter Fenton. Ralph Matthews sat behind the desk staring at his remaining guest, Maria Santiago.

Maria continued to tap the heel of her stiletto on the front rail of the chair. She rose and paced back and forth from the window to the credenza on the opposite wall. Matthews had witnessed this unfolding drama on several occasions and was wise enough not to make any moves to interrupt the process. He understood Maria wouldn't tolerate the disturbance without severe repercussions. He remained seated in his chair and fantasized about her slinking movements.

When several beads of sweat formed in the narrow space above his mustache, Matthews decided he had tortured himself enough for one day. He slipped over to the bar cabinet in the corner of his office and pulled out two glasses, filling each with several ice cubes from the mini refrigerator under the bar. Trying not to clank the bottles, he came up with the prize. A bottle of Don Julio Real Tequila. Maria's drink of choice. On the rocks. Maybe he wasn't done torturing himself.

Maria turned to him with a smile on her face.

"I'm glad the two of us are finally alone," she said. "We must be careful in handling this next step. It's important that we both agree to what we'll be doing. If we do this, there can be no possibility of discovery."

Matthews misunderstood the meaning of those words. With his back still to Maria, his hand shook as he filled the glasses with the expensive tequila. He turned to face her. Some of the tequila spilled down the sides of the glasses and dripped onto the cuffs of his shirtsleeves. With an awkward smile, he held out a glass to Maria.

"I think," Matthews said, "a toast would be in order to get things rolling. I can't tell you how long I've been waiting to hear those words."

Without thinking, Maria accepted the glass and they both took a sip.

Maria choked as the liquid hit her throat. "Wait a minute you fucking moron. What the hell do you think I'm talking about? Keep it in your pants or you're going to need these ice cubes for something else."

Matthews gagged on his drink, listening to her Hispanic accent override the tenor of her voice like a freight train bearing down on some helpless victim tied to the tracks.

"Maria… Maria… Calm down. Can't two friends enjoy a drink together on a friendly basis without you taking every word as a sexual advancement? You should know me better than that." He prayed to God she didn't. And forgot about those other times. "A toast to our success for the final phase of our plan."

Maria cocked her head to the side and stared at Matthews. "Don't think I believe you, Matthews, not for a goddamned minute. But we need to get serious here."

"Nobody's more serious about this than me," Matthews said.

"You damned well better be. We've got a major fucking problem. The vice president is becoming a threat to what we're trying to accomplish. She could break this thing wide open, and the president would be caught right in the middle along with the rest of us. I know you've been dealing with these so-called loose ends and coincidences which you don't want to hear about, but from where I'm standing, Alice Andersen holds the key to putting the pieces of the puzzle together. The bitch has been slinking in the shadows gathering all this shit together from the start. Who the fuck does she think she is to undermine our work?"

"Well, some might call her the vice president of the United States," Matthews said dryly. "Do you think she could be turned? Maybe we can bring her on board. Convince her into thinking that what we're doing is in the best interests of our country. We could create a key role for her."

Maria shook her head. "Matthews. Have you forgotten who you're talking to? I've been dealing with this woman throughout our whole first term. Before we began advocating these game-changing policies. It's my job to read people and predict how they'll react to any situation. Shit, I know what they will do even before they do. There is no way in hell Alice Andersen can be persuaded or bought to see things our way. I've advised Connor to be careful about what gets discussed in her presence, and we've diverted her energies in other directions. I still can't believe the bitch found out any of this. Everything has been so compartmentalized it should've been impossible for her to put it all together. Those assholes in the State Department usually have trouble finding their own offices."

Matthews could see where this was going but held his tongue.

"You and your not-so-smart asshole associates probably fucked up somewhere," Maria said. "Special Assignment Detail. Right. Now we've got us one special fucking headache to deal with."

"You think you got a way to salvage this mess?"

"Jesus, Matthews. What the hell do you think? I like to parade my sweet ass around your pitiful office to give you a hard-on?"

Matthews had no intention of answering.

"It's clear to me," Maria said, "and if you could think with your head, it should be clear to you as well. We need to eliminate the vice president. Permanently."

Matthews added more tequila to his glass and downed it before answering.

"And you said I was out of my fucking mind for investigating her?" Matthews gasped. "Besides, that's not even a plan. And how in hell could we get away with this?"

"Do you even have to ask?" Maria said, pursing her lips. "Anyway. I'm still thinking about this in general terms. I've got some ideas clicking in my head. Let's think this through. I'll depend on you to come up with the more mundane details."

Maria's eyes shifted down Matthews' body. "I think you've got lots of experience handling the little things." She turned and walked out the door.

CHAPTER 46

Kellogg, Idaho

EDIE AWOKE TO THE SMELL of hot coffee and the crinkling sounds of the paper bag from McDonalds Steve carried with him into the bedroom. She sat up and reached for the covers.

"We may have wasted some of your cash on buying me new clothes if your intent was to keep me bedded and naked the whole time we're here," Edie said.

"I still have the receipts. You wanna bring the clothes back? I'm willing to deal with it."

"Let me at least finish my coffee and Egg McMuffin," she said. "And then I'm taking a shower."

"While you've been regaining your stamina, I've been busy reading the newspapers and scanning the news channels. So far, they've traced the Durango's registration to me. Some of the locals they interviewed speculated I might've been traveling with a female companion but didn't give the authorities a name. They're looking for the remains of two individuals. The authorities don't think anyone could have gotten out alive. And because of the isolated terrain, they're not sure how long it could take to find the bodies. Oh. The fire marshal reports there are definite signs of arson."

Edie sat staring at the far wall.

"And you'll love this little side story on page two," Steve said. "Some reporters stopped by the Wolf Bay Community Club—and guess who they got to talk to? Jimmy Martin. He had some good quotes for the story. He's convinced the government was responsible for setting the fire to punish the local right-wing groups. In this case he might be on to something."

"Well, I'm sure whoever set the fire knows the name of the female. And they aren't going to rely on what the local authorities have to say about finding the bodies." Edie's eyes widened and her hands slapped her cheeks. "Oh my God. What about Uncle Bob? He could be in danger if they found out we talked to him. We should've called him as soon as we heard about Cindy Weaver."

"Already taken care of. I texted him with one of our new phones. I tried to keep it as unidentifiable as possible in case he's being watched. He'll get the gist of the message, but anyone who doesn't know him probably won't think anything of it."

Steve paused, collecting the food wrappers and stuffing them into the bag. "Looks like we've both come to the same conclusion about Cindy's fall not being an accident."

He headed out the bedroom door. "I'm going to sift through the papers and journal we found at the cabin."

After a quick shower Edie joined Steve. He was already deep into his dad's journal. He looked up. "Guess what? This journal goes back to February of the year he died." He pointed to the inside of the front cover. "It says this is book number eight. Where the hell are the other seven books?"

"It's hard to believe we missed anything at your dad's house," Edie said. "Could be he stashed them somewhere else in the cabin, but that doesn't make a whole lot of sense. Not much we can do about it now anyway. Probably not relevant to the video if they're so old. But it's too bad we didn't find them. I'm sure they would've helped you better understand what your dad was going through all those years. By the way. Wait till Mr. Sullivan finds out about his cabin. I feel terrible. He was trying to be nice—and look what he gets."

"Yeah, I was feeling bad about that myself. We still got a lot of cash from the cabin. I'll try to figure a way to compensate him for the rest. Uncle Bob said there's a cash account from settling my dad's estate." He paused and shook his head. "The last few days haven't done much in the way of restoring any goodwill to the Casella family name around here. I hope our new friend, Joe Wilton, doesn't wind up a victim."

"Speaking of Joe. Did you look at this computer desk? And did you notice there's a laptop sitting right on top? I'm gonna see if we're connected to any internet service." She got her answer. "I think Joe is my new best friend. This could come in handy."

Steve shook his head again. "Here I thought having the satellite service was over the top. I bet if I tried a little harder, we could've been driving his Corvette too."

Steve buried himself back in the journal. Edie gathered up the remaining papers and photos and sat down at the computer desk. After several minutes she handed him back a few sheets of paper.

"I think these might go with the journal," she said. "See the page references here? You might want to check this stuff out."

They both got back to work. Outside, Amber was patrolling her new perimeter. She wasn't as impressed as Steve and Edie were with the amenities Joe had provided. She preferred Joe's house and grounds back in the hills around Coeur d'Alene.

Ignoring a potential lunch break, they worked through the remainder of the afternoon when Steve said, "I need something to eat. How about we take a walk downtown and find someplace? I'll fill up Amber's food bowl before we go. She should be fine in the yard. It's a giant kennel."

The walk helped clear their heads after a long, but productive day of sifting through what they had saved from the fire.

"You okay with going through your dad's journal?"

"There doesn't seem to be a lot of personal stuff in there. Most of it is a chronicle of daily events. He reported on the details of everything going on around him."

He said this without much conviction, and then his voice became more animated. "But those papers you gave back to me. Seems my dad had reviewed all the dates when he met with the guys at the community club and compared their discussions and comments to the video. When you look at how things were put together on the video, the information in the journal, and his papers which analyzed the actual discussions—it all suggests this Peter Fenton character deliberately fucked with what was discussed at those meetings."

Edie stopped and stared at Steve. "My God. Things are starting to make sense. With a clever editor, you can distort everything."

"Right. Fenton changed the context and outcome of the original conversations. He juggled discussions from different meetings taking place over a five-month period. It gives credibility to what we heard from those guys at the community club the other night."

Steve shook his head. "Too bad Jimmy Martin didn't look harder for the surveillance equipment at the club. Anyway, Fenton latched onto Dad, and Jimmy too, I guess. It was like he was pulling the strings on a couple of puppets. You could almost believe they were drugged. Maybe that's why Jimmy had problems remembering what the hell was going on back then."

They both started walking again.

"Did you find anything interesting in the rest of the papers and photos?" Steve asked. "You looked pretty busy tapping away on the laptop over there."

"Can't keep your eyes off me?"

"Is that why you came out of the bedroom this morning dressed in an oversized sweatshirt and baggy sweatpants? I can't be deflected so easily."

"Seems to me you couldn't figure out what to do with the zipper on your dad's snowmobile suit."

They reached the heart of Kellogg's downtown area and settled on a funky restaurant with a local wildlife species in its name.

As they ate, Edie picked up the conversation from outside. "Using the information your dad left, plus Cindy's help, I dug deeper online into some of those news clippings and things have started to come together. There's plenty of evidence to link Peter Fenton with PUG, the local political action group in Spokane."

"So, before Fenton joined the conservative groups and the new RGA movement, he was involved with the PUG," Steve said. "I guess Cindy was right about seeing him at those other meetings. That's how he knew the PUG's director, David Reilly."

"No, Steve. Not only from before the RGA formed, but right up to the end when the video was released. The guy with Fenton in those older newspaper pictures is the same one in the photo your dad took of Fenton in the park right before they incarcerated him. So Fenton was linked to the PUG right up to the end. Fenton worked for Reilly. The RGA had nothing to do with this. They were the victims. Like your dad."

Steve poured the remaining wine into their glasses.

"This thing had to be set up way in advance—to discredit the RGA," Edie said. "Fenton was a plant from the beginning. And from what you've found, your dad's journal documents how the video was made. If your dad confronted Fenton with any of this, it would've put him in a dangerous position. Fenton couldn't let him expose what had happened."

She paused and looked into Steve's eyes. "Do you think he would've been reckless enough to confront Fenton?"

"Believe it or not, there've been times when the Casella men have been known to pull some stupid stunts. But those days are gone," Steve said, eyes diverted from Edie. "Besides, it was people from the federal government who picked him up. Agents from Homeland Security whisked him away to Boise."

"And?" Edie said. She leaned forward, elbow on the table, chin resting on her closed fist.

"Whoa," Steve said raising his hands. "I know the PUG has strong links to the political aspects of the party and campaign strategies, but are you saying people in the federal government were involved in a conspiracy to eliminate the competition? After the embassy bombing, with all the media attention and radical statements escalating out of control around the country, it made sense for Homeland Security to step in and investigate. Didn't it?"

Edie shook her head. "First of all. I already told you it made absolutely no sense for your dad to be picked up by Homeland Security or anyone else from the government."

Steve tried to interject, but Edie was on a roll and needed to get it all out.

"Listen, Steve. Right now, all we have is this evidence to implicate the PUG. And they had motive to stop your dad from blowing the whistle. I think that's clear. But we don't have anything tangible to link this to anybody else. Somebody a lot bigger has got to be calling the shots. I don't think a local political activist group from Spokane could've orchestrated all this. And don't forget. This damn thing ain't over. We're smack in the middle of something that might've begun with the video, but whoever is running the show may have even bigger plans in the works. And we were getting a little too close."

Edie took a breath and gulped down her wine. "Right now, we have a little breathing room to try and connect more of the dots. Least until they figure out we're still alive. Come on, let's get back to the house."

Edie thought back to what triggered her journey to San Francisco in the first place. Something was troubling her about the anonymous email, but she couldn't put her finger on the problem.

PART THREE

CHAPTER 47

Morristown, New Jersey

IT'S BEEN SAID THAT TYLER Griffin emerged from his mother's womb carrying the Bible in one hand and a copy of the Constitution of United States in the other. A point of contention was whether his Smith & Wesson came strapped to his ankle or held between the gums in his toothless mouth.

His closest friends argued it depended on whether the birth was normal or breech. Everyone agreed Tyler Griffin was always prepared. The truth had never been revealed. His friends knew and respected Tyler's views regarding medical records. They were private and should not be available to the public. Especially not to anyone with a government passcode.

Tyler Griffin, the first born of five siblings, had equal pairs of brothers and sisters. His father owned a small but prospering lumber mill and retail operation in Morristown, New Jersey. His mother managed the more important family business of nurturing their expanding household.

Although his father made a good living for the family, due to its size, they were considered more middle than upper class. Both parents taught Tyler the necessity of living within one's means, and that resources were limited. As the oldest child in the expanding brew, Tyler learned from an early age that redistribution and dependency always came at the expense of others. Raised in a nurturing environment, his family provided him with a loving and caring background. They taught him to work hard, be responsible for his own actions, but to never disregard the needs of the less fortunate.

Tyler Griffin's values were put to the test at the age of seventeen. He had just finished high school and was preparing to trade a life at home for a new adventure on college campus. Then his father died from a coronary episode while seated at his desk in the tiny office overlooking the millworks.

With the help of his mother, Tyler stepped up to take over the family business. As his siblings came of age, all worked together to turn the small operation into an expanding business. Today it boasted twenty-six stores in New Jersey, New York, and Pennsylvania. The Griffin Millworks and Home Centers were becoming the most lucrative do-it-yourself establishments throughout the northeast.

Tyler Griffin had also found time to continue his education on a part-time basis and completed a bachelor's degree in arts and a master's degree in business administration from Rutgers University. He also married Alison Crawford, his high school sweetheart, and they were busy raising children of their own.

Tyler Griffin did not become involved in politics until one day about seven or eight years ago when he and Alison had been seated at the breakfast table. Tyler slammed down the newspaper he was reading in a gesture of disgust. The article was about an ill-advised plan of several corrupt local politicians who were promoting, in the name of progress, the bulldozing of a popular community park and ball field complex. They wanted to replace this with an overpriced underground parking structure for the benefit of a few political cronies at the expense of an apathetic public.

Alison put on her best smile, turned to him, and patted his arm. "Instead of sitting here in the kitchen and complaining to me, why don't you get out there and show all those incompetent losers that Tyler Griffin knows better and can put Morristown, the state, and maybe even the entire nation back on the right track."

Tyler never considered Alison was being facetious in her advice. He nodded in response, picked the newspaper back up, and began to read it from a different perspective. He might not have been the inventor of the Restraint in Government Alliance, but he was the embodiment of the RGA's basic principles. He completely embraced its values, becoming an important advocate for their goals of revitalizing his nation and invigorating fellow citizens to rein in what he referred to as the ever-expanding government intrusion.

Tyler Griffin possessed the integrity and a positive boldness for delivering his message to a supportive populace, and his physical presence provided the necessary attributes to be noticed. Griffin was an imposing six-foot-one figure with close trimmed dark brown hair and deep set, virtually black eyes. You could be taken in by his rugged good looks when accompanied by a smile that even transformed those eyes. On the other hand, when the situation called for it, his intense stare could chill an adversary into oblivion.

Earlier today Tyler Griffin met with the key staff members of his new re-election committee at the campaign headquarters in Morristown. This included his senior advisor and associate, Peter Fenton. Fenton had been on Griffin's staff since his first successful bid for the senate during the special elections held two years ago.

Leaders of the RGA tagged Fenton as the new wave of political advocacy. They had persuaded Griffin to give Fenton a key role on the staff being put together following the death of the incumbent democrat senator. They had been impressed with Fenton's ability to know what the opposition was thinking. After joining Griffin's team, Fenton demonstrated this same uncanny trait.

CHAPTER 48

THE BUILDING WAS QUIET AT THIS time of day. It was early evening as the building's sole occupant worked to finish up some reports he would be sending back to his unofficial boss located almost three thousand miles to the west. The Morristown campaign headquarters for the upcoming New Jersey senatorial race for Senator Tyler Griffin was located in an historic building on South Park Place across from the Morristown Green. Up until the early 1920s, it was the site of the Wells Fargo Bank. Its strategic location served as a major junction point in linking the important financial center of Morristown to the untamed west, first via the stagecoach line, and later replaced by rail.

The campaign season was gearing up, and even this early in the game all involved recognized the importance of this race as a defining moment in the future direction of the country. Since the last presidential election, the stature of the republican party had taken a dramatic and some declared fatal hit. John Connor's presidential campaign had surged ahead early in the race, spawned by the media frenzy surrounding the release of the anti-Muslim video and the bombing of the American embassy in Pakistan. These events were followed by a deluge of negative advertisements and slogans citing the reactionary and racist sentiments of the leaders and followers of the RGA movement.

Over the last two years a disorganized republican party pointed fingers and chased their tails in an effort to rebrand the mainstream philosophy that had kicked them in their collective asses. Somehow Tyler Griffin had stayed on target. He dodged the political fallout threatening not only the conservative wing, but the entire republican party as a viable alternative to the democrat party. After winning the special election to replace the deceased incumbent democrat senator from New Jersey two years ago, he forged on to become the lone spokesperson for the republican party who still garnered overwhelming support from the dyed-in-the-wool conservative faction led by the RGA. Winning this latest bid for re-election would galvanize his position as the leading contender for the top spot on his party's ticket for the next presidential race. And this was scaring the hell out of the current administration. The prevailing wisdom was that if there was no Tyler Griffin, the republican party would return to its dysfunctional pattern of destroying itself from within. And this time the republicans might be facing their final struggle to maintain even a failing role as the second major party.

Peter Fenton was anxious to get home for an unofficial anniversary celebration he and his partner had planned over the phone earlier today. Before leaving, he needed to retrieve some campaign materials from the basement storage room. The senator was in town preparing for a campaign speech at a rally in the park across from the county's Fourth of July celebration festival. It was Fenton's role to make certain everything was in order.

Since it was getting late, he decided he would pick up Randy, his long-time steady partner, on his way home. As he descended the final steps into the basement, he remembered there was no cell signal down here, so he would call Randy about the change in plans as soon as he got back upstairs. Still smiling in anticipation of this evening's encounter, he moved some boxes around trying to locate the one he sought. Creaking from the floor above momentarily distracted him. Not unusual in a building this old. He worked until the definite sound of a door clicking shut stopped him cold. Footfalls on the old squeaky staircase followed.

Before Fenton could investigate the intrusion, two figures materialized at the door to the storage room, blocking any notion of exit.

"What the hell do you think—" Fenton stammered.

"Good evening, Mr. Fenton. Why don't you have a seat at the desk?" The taller, deeply tanned man with thick black hair motioned with the Smith & Wesson .357 Magnum revolver. It was pointed directly at Fenton's head. Fenton sat down.

The second man, shorter, with a light complexion and clipped sandy blond hair, walked over to the desk. With gloved hands, he placed a sheet of typed paper on the desk and dropped a pen on top. Next, he withdrew a small tablet device from his coat pocket. Removing one of the gloves, he tapped the screen several times and held the device in front of Fenton's face.

"It's Randy." Fenton cried out. "My God, what have you done—"

He was looking at a photo of his lover. Randy was conscious, but with one eye swollen and blood dripping down his nose and onto the gag fixed over his mouth. His hands and legs were bound with duct tape and his body lay on top of a pile of old blankets crammed into the back of a windowless van.

"Shut up and listen," the taller man said. "You have a simple job to do, Fenton. But it's an important one. It can save your life, as well as the life of your partner. As you can see, we've already had the pleasure of meeting Randy. Right now, he's our guest. So if you would agree to sign your name at the bottom of this page, we can be on our way, and you can be re-united with Randy."

"Why do want me to sign—"

The hand not holding the gun swung across Fenton's face, almost knocking him off the chair. His gloved hand muted the blow, leaving no telltale marks, but it was still powerful enough to get his point across to Fenton.

"You see," the taller man said, "now you're making this more complicated than it has to be. There is no need for you to read anything or ask any pointless questions. The faster you follow my simple instructions, the quicker we can let you see Randy again. I don't think I can make this any clearer. So what'll it be, Fenton? You going to do what I say, or do I need to send my colleague to pay Randy a final visit?"

Without any further prompting, Fenton picked up the pen and signed the document in front of him without any thoughts as to what it contained. The shorter man carefully folded the paper and placed it into an envelope, depositing it inside his coat pocket.

"Where is Randy?" Fenton asked. "I want to go see him now."

"As soon as we finish up here," the taller man said, "I can assure you, we will go and get your friend."

"What do you mean? Finish what? I did exactly what you wanted."

"Yes, Fenton. Your job is finished, but ours is just getting started." He nodded to the shorter man who grabbed Fenton from behind and pushed him down further into the chair. "You've earned the right to hear this. This comes from your real boss in Spokane, David Reilly. He asked me to tell you he has appreciated all the work you've done for the cause. Your video production in the backwoods of Coeur d'Alene was the first volley in getting us started on this mission. And as a matter of fact, your final assignment will do much to assure there will be nothing left to prevent us from reaching our ultimate goal."

He forced the revolver into Fenton's right hand, jamming the polished stainless steel barrel into Fenton's mouth, and pulled the trigger.

"Jesus Christ," the shorter man spit out. "Why am I always the one who gets his coat splattered? Let's go get his little girlfriend out of the van so we can finish up."

The two men hurried out to the van and brought the now unconscious Randy down into the storage room. They removed the duct tape and positioned the body across from Fenton. Keeping the gun wrapped in Fenton's cooling hand, the taller man pulled the trigger three more times. The bullets fatally penetrated Randy's chest.

"Remember. Make it a little sloppy," the taller man said. "It's supposed to look like Griffin was trying to set this up as a murder-suicide scenario."

After completing their task, the two men exited the rear of the building. There was little chance the sounds of the four gunshots could have been heard anywhere outside of the building. The storage room in the basement had been an old bank vault. Before driving away in the van, the shorter man removed the envelope from his coat pocket and tucked it under the rear mat of Fenton's parked blue Geo. The taller man watched the van drive off and walked to the front of the building. When he saw several pedestrians in sight, but not too close, he climbed into the driver's seat of a Black Raven

Cadillac ATS sedan and pulled out into the traffic. Coincidently, Tyler Griffin owned the same make, model, and year vehicle. At this moment it was parked in the garage of his Georgian Colonial home ten minutes south of the Morristown Green, near the Spring Creek Golf Course. There was one minor difference in the two vehicles. The color of Griffin's sedan was Black Diamond Tricoat. The man driving the Black Raven sedan didn't think this was going to be a problem. Smiling, he thought it was close enough for government work.

CHAPTER 49

Kellogg, Idaho

STEVE AND EDIE RETURNED HOME after a relaxing walk back from dinner. Amber was ready for some exercise, so Steve grabbed the lead and took her for a walk while Edie settled back inside to finish unwinding in the jetted bathtub.

As Edie stepped out of the steamy bath and dried herself, Steve and Amber returned from their walk. "You should try it, Steve."

"Any chance of you jumping back in?"

"Nah. I'd shrivel up."

Steve shrugged. "Then I guess I'll stick to the shower for tonight."

Amber took one look at the draining tub and scooted out of the bathroom, cozying up on the bed. She was winning the battle for bedroom rights. By the time Steve finished his shower and entered the bedroom, both girls were sound asleep. One of them snoring contentedly.

******

Finishing up a quick breakfast, they grabbed their coffee mugs and settled onto the sofa to figure out a course of action. Steve flipped on the television and set the channel to one of the twenty-four-hour news stations, keeping the volume lowered to background levels as they discussed their options.

"At this point we've got two names to work with," Steve said. "David Reilly and Peter Fenton. Other than walking into the PUG office in Spokane or heading back to New Jersey to confront either one of these guys, I'm at a loss as to what we can do to find out who else is involved. Let alone what their overall game plan might be. And don't get me wrong, I'm not suggesting we march up to these people and announce we're still alive. Somebody will figure it out soon enough."

After saying this, some dark thoughts crossed Steve's mind, with an unsettling feeling in his gut. At the moment he chose not to share it with Edie.

Edie placed her mug on the coffee table and began shuffling through a mess of papers in front of her. "I'm thinking," she said, "the video must've been planned way in advance of the embassy bombing, and its release a few days before the bombing occurred was probably a coincidence. So that couldn't have been its primary purpose, unless you want to believe our government was involved with the terrorists who planned the attack."

"No," Steve said. "I don't think I'm ready to go that far, but if what you told me last week about the State Department neglecting to provide more security for the embassy is true, then they could've prepared the video in anticipation of a confrontation to deflect from the truth."

Smiling, Edie looked at Steve and nodded. "I can't believe you said that. Last week you believed I was full of crap, and you were hell bent on proving the RGA tricked your dad into making the video."

"Humph. You think I'd be sleeping with someone who didn't share my values?"

"Before I came along you were sleeping with your dog."

"Exactly my point."

"Seriously, Steve. It's a frightening possibility, but more likely they used the embassy bombing to strengthen the impact of the video. They got lucky." Pausing, Edie remembered the last words she heard from her father. "The video was just part of their strategy to undermine the RGA and the conservative candidates in the party, including Connor's republican opponent. I think the embassy bombing jump-started their campaign tactics."

"What you're saying insinuates the president's campaign organization could have been behind this."

"Right," Edie said. "But I wouldn't use the past tense. This mid-term election coming up is crucial for setting the stage for the next presidential race. They're probably going to hammer the opposition even harder this time. And at this juncture they can't let any of the evidence we're looking at come out."

"We don't have anything concrete to prove there's any conspiracy. Only two names. One from a minor political office in Spokane, and the other a key advisor to the leading RGA candidate. And who we happen to think still works for the PUG. They'd just deny and dismiss whatever we say."

"We must be getting damn close to something, or they wouldn't have killed Cindy or be trying to kill us. Would they?"

Steve blinked and twisted his head toward the TV screen. Reaching for the remote, he punched up the volume.

"...over to our FOX news affiliate reporter on scene in Morristown, New Jersey. What have you got for us, Charles?"

"Thank you, Martha. We're standing across the street from the New Jersey campaign headquarters for Senator Tyler Griffin. Local police have reported two bodies discovered in the basement of the campaign headquarters. Early this morning, a staff member entered the building and found the bodies in a storage room located down in the basement. The police have identified one of the victims as Peter Fenton, who is the senior advisor for Senator Griffin. The second body is that of Randy Bachmann, a local businessman here in Morristown. Although still early in the investigation, it appears both victims died from gunshot wounds. Fenton's appears to have been self-inflicted. A statement from the police cautions it is too early to rule this a murder-suicide, and they are still in the process of systematically working the scene. They caution it will take a considerable amount of time to analyze the evidence. Back to you, Martha."

"Thank you, Charles. A spokesperson for Senator Griffin has issued a statement saying the senator was shocked and horrified when he heard the news about the death of his long-time associate and political advisor, citing Fenton's key role in the special election two years ago, and his continued dedication to the senator's campaign efforts. Fenton will be missed by the senator, as well as the entire staff. The senator is confident the authorities will launch a complete in-depth investigation as to what happened."

Steve changed the channel to another news station.

"This just in. MSNBC has received information from an undisclosed source at the Morris County District Attorney's office regarding the discovery of the two bodies early this morning at the campaign headquarters for Senator Tyler Griffin, as we have previously reported. We have now been told there was no suicide note found at the scene and there appears to be conflicting evidence in regard to calling this a murder-suicide. The police are also looking at a document found in Fenton's car. Contained in this document addressed to the Newark Star Ledger was a disclosure regarding a long-term intimate relationship between Peter Fenton and Senator Griffin, and a threat to reveal this relationship and expose the republican senator. We are told the document was signed by Peter Fenton. As you know, Senator Griffin is married and has three children. He has been an adamant opponent to gay marriage and has had numerous run-ins with the LGBT community. We also have word Senator Griffin will be brought in for questioning by the Morristown police."

"Jesus Christ, Edie. Our list has just been cut in half. What the hell do we do now?"

CHAPTER 50

Washington, D.C.

MARIA SANTIAGO WAS BACK IN the chief of staff's office, and Matthews once again envisioned the tequila bottle in the cabinet. As Maria moved toward his desk, he looked up from the laptop screen and a fleeting image sailed across his brain. He shook his head and cleared his throat. "We'll save the tequila for later. Let's get to work."

Maria's smile became the dominant feature under her trademark bangs. "Do you remember we talked about sending someone from the White House out to participate in a local Fourth of July celebration in Coeur d'Alene? The place where this all started? The local PUG director, David Reilly, was the one who suggested this several months ago."

Maria took a seat and attempted to readjust her skirt. She continued as Matthews looked on. "The city of Coeur d'Alene is also hosting a ceremony for the Vietnam Traveling Wall Memorial exhibit. We all thought it made sense to maintain a countering force to the local right-wing organizations in the area. They were hit hard following the release of our video. Opened up a lot of old wounds. Reilly thought this would be a good time to reinforce our presence there again. Kind of stop any momentum before the campaigns get up to speed."

Matthews nodded, watching as Maria gave up fixing her skirt.

"So," she said, "instead of sending the original flunky we picked for the job, I propose we send the vice president. Not only would it strengthen our influence in the region, but we might be able to set up a situation where one of our favorite right-wing extremist supporters decides to assassinate the vice president."

Maria stood up and began to pace. "I can make sure the president insists that Andersen represents the White House."

She waved a hand toward Matthews. "I'll leave it to you to come up with the specific details of how to kill the vice president and blame it on those reactionary racists in Idaho. I knew having a black running mate would come in handy for us someday."

Maria concluded with a big smile. "God. I love this country."

Matthews glanced at the bar cabinet and then replied to Maria. "Why do I get all the easy jobs when pretty little Maria has to work so hard to convince Connor to tell Andersen to do something? Has Connor ever turned you down for anything? Please, don't bother to answer. It's a rhetorical question."

Maria pushed out her lips and tilted her head. This time Matthews didn't confuse her gesture with anything of a sexual nature.

"Meet me back here Wednesday morning around eleven," Matthews said. "I need some time to figure out a few logistical matters and get things in place. In the meantime, please make sure Andersen will be on Air Force Two on the Fourth of July."

With some ideas already forming in his head, he added, "And make sure they land her jet at the Spokane Airport. I don't want them setting foot onto Fairchild Air Force Base. Too many complications. You understand?"

   With one final agonizing gaze at the backside of Maria as she sashayed out of the office, using the toe on her stiletto to swing the door shut, Matthews sighed and reached for the phone.

CHAPTER 51

Kellogg, Idaho

EDIE FINISHED SKIMMING THE PAPERS on the coffee table then rose and walked over to the computer desk. She positioned herself into the office chair, picked up a pad and pencil, and began writing. Steve came up from behind and was about to ask a question, but Edie held up a hand to block any interruption. Steve shrugged and motioned for Amber to go outside with him to play in the yard.

Sometime later, Edie stood at the back door and watched Amber fetching the ball and scampering back to Steve who was seated on the porch steps. After the cycle repeated itself several times, Edie walked across the porch and sat down on the steps next to Steve. She kissed him on the cheek and handed him the paper she was working on.

"I wasn't sure why I had to do this," Edie said, "or if my memory would allow me to, but take my word, I was able to recreate the last remaining copy of the email message destroyed by the wildfire. After deleting it from my email account as a precaution, I guess I should've listened to Nana when she told me never to leave anything valuable in my car. Well, in this case, your SUV. And trust me on this. This letter has been so ingrained in my head, I'm certain I got it word-for-word correct."

Steve read through the email again, as he did over a week ago. Arching his brows, he stared at Edie. He still didn't get it.

"The fact I could recreate this email should convince you how much of an impact it had on me. This little exercise has re-ignited those flames. There has been something in this email sticking in my brain. I've always thought I should know who this person is. This person had to be someone close to my father. Of the hundreds of times I read each and every word, I never saw it until now. The second sentence in the letter. See?"

Steve looked at those words again.

Just as the sunken heroes of WWII inspired the path he chose, your father's courage will rouse future generations.

He wanted to understand but couldn't see why Edie was so energized.

"Edie?" Steve tried. "Why don't you start from the beginning?"

She took a deep breath and nodded. "When I was a little girl, my father took me to the place where he grew up. Hackensack. It's in New Jersey. Not far from where I'm living now. We drove through his old neighborhood and walked around in this park across the street from where he lived. Not the best of neighborhoods, but he was proud of how his family survived and even prospered from the experience. We were sitting on a bench across from his old house when all of a sudden he grabbed my hand and said he had one more place he wanted to show me."

Edie jumped up from the steps, looked up at a passing gondola, and turned back to Steve.

"He drove us over to a nearby river. To this museum for submarines. It actually was inside of a submarine or, I remember him correcting himself, a submersible. It was called the S.S. Ling. Dad became my own personal tour guide through this cramped, and kind of creepy, tiny war machine. I had never seen him so animated before. He said he spent a good deal of his early teenage years volunteering with the upkeep for the museum and helping out with the tours."

Amber barked at the gondola before it disappeared behind some tall pines. Edie kneeled in front of Steve, her voice stronger.

"This experience inspired him to join the Navy and become a SEAL. He was so impressed by the bravery of the men who served on these submersibles. He said they put themselves in a situation where they would probably die. And they volunteered for these missions anyway, because they believed fighting for their country was the most important thing in the world. This class of submersibles was particularly lethal. Almost half of the fleet was sunk during the war. There were over 3500 crew members on board the sunken submersibles, and only six men survived. They were referred to as the sunken heroes of World War II."

Edie took a deep breath and relaxed. She lifted herself up and turned to sit beside Steve. She pointed at the paper, and a smile spread over her face.

"See right here. And it's been sitting in front of me all this time. I'll bet you anything the person who wrote this email knew my father when he was growing up. When he lived in Hackensack. It all fits."

"How old were you when your father took you to this museum?"

"I guess I was about ten. Why?"

"How in the hell could you remember these details after... what? Almost fifteen years?"

"That's what they invented the internet for. Thank you, Mr. Gore." She gave Steve another kiss and added a hug this time. "So. I'm thinking it's about time to give Nana another call. She might remember more specific details from back then. I'll try to approach it in a way so she's not worried. I don't want her to think I might be in any danger or anything."

Edie ran inside to grab one of the prepaid phones.

A couple of minutes later she returned to the porch, eyes watering, mouth open wide, and her face a lighter shade of brown.

"What's the matter?"

"Nana. She hung up on me. I started to ask about Dad's childhood, and she pretended to be someone else. Said she didn't know who I was. She took my name and phone number, asked where I was calling from, and said as soon as Mrs. Pauling returned home, she would give her the message. My God. Do you think she's going senile or something? I should get back home. She needs my help right away. I can't leave her by herself. Why didn't I see this coming?" Edie fell into Steve's arms crying.

"Come on. Let's go inside. I'm sure we can figure out what to do." Knowing he didn't stand a chance in hell of figuring out how to deal with a distraught Edie. As they walked through the door, he looked back helplessly at Amber. Amber decided to stay outside and disappeared under the porch.

Once inside, Steve struggled to come up with something to do. Maybe he could bring Edie a glass of ice water. He thought of adding some vodka to the mix, but it was still a little too early. When he got back to the family room and placed the glass in front of her, he saw Edie was distracted, searching the internet. Must be trying to diagnosis Nana's condition. The phone in Edie's pocket chirped, making her jump. She knocked the glass of water onto her lap and started to fall out of her seat. Steve grabbed her before that happened. So, he was good for something.

Yanking the phone from her pocket, she brought it up to her ear.

"Hello?" she said.

"Edie?"

"Nana. What happened? Are you okay? This is Edie. Do you know who I am?"

"What the hell are you babbling about? Of course, I know who you are. Do you know who I am?"

"What? Of course, I know… Nana… When I called before, why'd you pretend to be someone else? Are you okay?"

"I'm doing fine young lady. I guess it's about time we had a little talk though. But not on the phone. We need to do this in person. So listen up, girl. You weren't lying to me before when you said you were still in Idaho, were you?"

"I'd never lie to you, Nana."

"Right. How was the convention you went to? And those new friends you met out there in San Francisco? Never mind. I need you to pick me up in Montana, at the Missoula International Airport around twelve-thirty tomorrow afternoon. I'll be arriving on the US Airways connecting flight from Denver. Can you be there?"

"Where are you calling from?"

"I'm in New Jersey. Close to my house. I'm at a pay phone at the ShopRite in Newton. When I see you tomorrow, we can all sit down and have a pleasant conversation. I'm looking forward to meeting Steve Casella."

After exchanging a few more details, Edie ended the call. She bit her lower lip, then smiled at Steve.

"I guess it's time you met my Nana. Don't ya think?"

CHAPTER 52

EDIE LOST COUNT OF HOW often she'd used the luxurious jetted tub as a way to calm her frayed nerves. She was getting used to this aspect of their ordeal. The latest excuse came after the exasperating exchange with Nana. Edie eased her way out of the steamy bathroom with a towel wrapped around her still moist body. She called out to Steve, thinking of an even better way to release any remaining tensions hidden deep in her psyche. She got no response after several calls and figured he was out back playing with Amber.

With smiling eyes, Edie dropped the towel to the floor. She reached out to open the door to the patio. Her plan was to see if Amber could stand a little unfair competition for Steve's attention. As she opened the door, Amber barged through, almost knocking her to the floor.

"Not your turn today, sweetie," Edie muttered.

There was no sign of Steve. She turned back into the bedroom and saw the note taped to the mirror above the dresser.

Edie paced back and forth across the carpeted bedroom floor and re-read the note several times before crumpling it up and tossing it against the wall. The message failed to change. Edie tried to call Steve on his prepaid phone but got no answer.

"Shit. Shit. Shit. Fool sonofabitch. He said he wouldn't even consider something like this. Goddamn it. At least we could've done this together. Team, my ass."

Amber whimpered and tried unsuccessfully to scoot herself under the bed. "That's what you get for eating all those big bowls of chow Steve keeps giving you."

******

The Spokane office of the People United Group was located on the second floor of an office building also housing a dentist, a chiropractor, and an insurance broker. The building was located a few blocks north of where Ruby Street turned into North Division near the Garland Business District. Steve had gotten this far but now wasn't sure what the hell he wanted to accomplish.

He had neglected to take any of Edie's calls because he didn't know what to tell her. This was probably a stupid stunt, but he knew he needed to be face-to-face with one of the instigators in this whole damn scheme. He guessed if they were going to eventually find out he was still alive, he might as well be the one to deliver the message. That was about as far as his rationalization had taken him. After climbing up the stairs, he walked through the first door on the left and into the office of the People United Group. A pear-shaped Hispanic woman in her late forties sat at a modest desk in the reception area. She looked up over her reading glasses.

In a pleasant, but bored tone, she said, "Good afternoon. How can I be of help to you today?"

"Hi," Steve said. "I'm here to see David Reilly. Is he available?"

"Do you have an appointment?"

"Ah, no I don't."

"Whom shall I say is here to see him? And can you please tell me what this is in reference to?"

Steve tried to think on his feet.

"I'm a union representative with the San Francisco Fire Department. Local 7890. I've done a lot of work with the San Francisco PUG. I'm visiting some friends in the area and was looking forward to doing some volunteer work while I'm here. I was told to come here and speak with David Reilly."

She stared at him through narrowed eyes but got up from the desk and walked down the hall. After knocking on the first closed door to the right, she poked her head inside. A short time later the woman motioned for Steve to come and stepped aside to allow him to enter the office. Steve walked in and the receptionist closed the door behind him. The man seated at the desk rose. Steve immediately recognized him as the man in the photos he and Edie had been looking at earlier. David Reilly.

The office was appointed with standard government issued simulated wood furniture. Reilly's desk was at the far end in front of a large window overlooking the parking lot where Steve's Ambassador was parked. A strong smell of stale cigarettes dominated the atmosphere. Groupings of pictures on the wall showed Reilly in a variety of poses with prominent looking men and women. Most of them Steve didn't recognize, but there was one photo encased in an ornate frame of Reilly in a group picture with President John Connor and two other individuals. He didn't recognize the stunning Hispanic woman or the imposing black man who flanked the president but noticed Reilly looked stiff and uncomfortable. He reminded Steve of the class geek who showed up at the prom without a date.

Steve sidestepped the small conference table between the door and the desk as Reilly walked from behind his desk to greet his visitor. Nothing but a short span of the gray carpet separated Steve from the man he suspected had played a role in the events leading to his father's death. A reeking wall of tobacco odor slapped at Steve's senses.

Reilly spoke first. "Miss Dominguez told me you're visiting our area and are willing to volunteer your services."

Steve stared at Reilly.

"You've come at the right time," Reilly said. "The campaigns are gearing up and we're going to be involved in some tough battles between now and election day. Miss Dominguez said you were from San Francisco, but I didn't get your name."

Steve remained motionless for several seconds before answering. "I never gave my name to your receptionist. But I did tell her I was referred to this office by a close friend of yours."

Reilly sensed something was amiss and crept back a few steps until he felt the edge of the desk against the back of his thighs. He grabbed for the pack of cigarettes on his desk and lit one up.

"A close friend?" Reilly asked.

"Well, I may have misled you a bit. This guy didn't personally tell me to come here. I'm sure he would've though. But you see, Reilly, Peter Fenton can no longer speak. He's dead. A tragic—suicide—I believe the authorities are calling it? But also convenient. Wouldn't you say?"

Reilly stiffened and tried his best to look confused. "I'm sorry, but I don't know who you're talking about. I don't know anybody named Peter Fenton."

Reilly tried to restore some degree of control, and said, "Who the hell are you?"

"You don't remember the man who has worked for you for almost ten years?"

"What are you talking about?" Reilly said. "Why would I know somebody who committed suicide in New Jersey?"

"Who the hell said anything about New Jersey? I don't think it was me," Steve said with a tight smile on his face.

"Well… I… ah…wait," Reilly said. "Just a minute. When we first opened this office… ah… yeah. There was this guy named Fenton. But he wasn't here very long. I think somebody told me he went over to Coeur d'Alene to work with a new conservative group there. The Restraint in Government Alliance. Yeah. Now I remember."

"That's your story?" Steve shook his head.

"I guess," Reilly said, "I heard he later went to work for Senator Griffin in New Jersey. You say he killed himself? That's terrible."

Steve crowded up to Reilly. "Nice try. But we both know it's a bullshit story. And guess what? You think this is all behind you? Well, Reilly, it's not. Your associates are ruthless, but they can also be a little sloppy. Or I wouldn't be standing here having this conversation with you."

"What the hell do you want?" Reilly said.

"I needed to see you in person," Steve said, "and tell you to your face—your plan is going to come back and bite you in the ass."

Steve turned to leave the office.

Without much conviction, Reilly said, "Who… who the hell do you think you are coming in here and talking to me like that? You don't know who you're dealing with mister."

Steve stopped at the door and spun around to face Reilly. "Really? My name is Steve Casella. Perhaps you remember my dad. Tom Casella? Well, Reilly, now you know who the hell you're dealing with."

Steve turned and yanked the door open and stepped out with a reverberating slam of the door.

Reilly slumped against his desk and reached for another cigarette. He started grabbing for the phone to call Ben Courtney in D.C. but changed his mind. Marchesi and his partner were still back in New Jersey wrapping up that little incident with Peter Fenton and Tyler Griffin. This was something he could handle himself. Courtney didn't need to be bothered with this little problem while he was busy focusing on the vice president. Besides, Marchesi was the one who let Casella get away. Reilly reflected that D.C. was always trying to control everything. This would be a great opportunity to show them the local boys were better suited for the job. After all, Courtney wouldn't have known Casella was here in the first place if he hadn't been doing his job. He pushed away from the desk and headed toward the lunchroom. He grabbed Cornell and Willie and dragged them back to his office.

"See the guy leaning up against his car?" Reilly said pointing out the window. "I want you guys to follow him and see where he's going. There should be another person staying with him. A girl. They need to disappear. If you can, wait till he leads you to the girl. But if you run into any problems following him, make sure he doesn't get away. You understand? Now get going."

After breathing some fresh air and calming himself down, Steve climbed into the Ambassador. He fiddled with the Bluetooth earpiece while punching the button on his phone to give Edie a call. This could be harder than what he just put himself through in Reilly's office. As he waited for Edie to answer, he pulled out of the parking lot and headed back in the direction of the interstate. He didn't notice the two men getting into the black Honda Civic at the other end of the lot.

"Why the hell do I have to drive?" Cornell said.

"You're left-handed. It'll be easier for me to hold the gun out the window and shoot the bastard."

"We're only supposed to follow him, Willie."

"You heard what Reilly said. If anything goes wrong, we can't let him get away."

"What could go wrong?"

"Look. This is our chance to show them how valuable we are. We take care of this problem, we'll be doing more than the usual hiding in the shadows, planting bugs, and wiping Reilly's ass. You get it, Cornell? This is our ticket. Now let's get going. Don't lose the son of a bitch before we get out of the fucking parking lot."

Cornell jerked the Honda into gear and the car lurched forward. "Jesus, Cornell. Don't fucking rear end him." Willie removed the Walther PK380 ACP semi-automatic pistol from his jacket and placed it on the seat beside him. He kept his right hand resting on the weapon.

Watching from the smoke-clouded office window, Reilly sowed the first seeds of doubt about giving the responsibility of such an important job to those two clowns.

CHAPTER 53

STEVE RUBBED THE EAR IN which the Bluetooth device was hanging from and tried to reduce the volume to a level where it didn't sound like Edie was screaming inside his brain. "I'm leaving the PUG office now, Edie."

"What the hell were you thinking?"

"I had to look this guy in the eye, you know? It's fine. No problem. He was so flustered—he didn't know what hit him."

Steve glanced in the rearview mirror and observed a black Honda turning out of the same parking lot. "Hard to believe this guy is a heavy hitter. But he's gotta be tied up in this somehow."

"Did you ever stop to think he might not have let you get out of the building? And besides. Remember? They thought we were dead. This morning you were saying that was a good thing. And it would be stupid to barge in there and announce they were wrong. I'm beginning to think your dad did the same thing with Fenton. And we both know how things turned out. This is not a good time to be following in his footsteps."

The adrenaline rush subsiding, Steve began to get Edie's point.

"Well, it's over for now. Nothing to worry about. They would've figured it out sooner or later. Anyway, they don't know where to find us."

Steve saw the black Honda moving up closer behind him. He abruptly shifted from the extreme right lane over two lanes to the left. Then back to the middle lane.

"Ah… Hang on a second."

He was traveling south on North Division and had reached the point where the road divided back into the one-way section leading to the interstate on ramp. Steve made his decision. He pulled the wheel hard to the left and turned down the next cross street, narrowly avoiding a collision with a boxy FedEx van traveling in the left lane. At the end of the cross street, he made another hard left. This took him back toward the PUG office building. As he settled into the middle lane, the black Honda careened around the same corner and took up a position several car lengths behind him.

"What the hell's going on there, Steve?"

"I think I got a tail."

Edie looked down at Amber. "Oh. Oh shit. You mean someone's following you?"

"Yep."

"Gee… Who would've thought it possible?"

"Well, they're not doing a very good job. I picked 'em up right away," Steve said.

"So now you're a goddamned critic? When did you become the expert on this?" Edie sounded alarmed. "Jesus. What're you gonna do now?"

Steve passed by the PUG office building. He wasn't aware that Reilly, obscured behind a cloud of smoke, was still woefully looking out his office window, having come to the conclusion this was a bad idea. Reilly tried calling Cornell and Willie on their cell phones but got nothing but a recording. He slammed down the phone.

"At the moment I'm trying to get out of all this city traffic and find a more deserted area where nobody else could get hurt. Sure wish this old car had a GPS unit in it.

I'm heading north, away from the interstate. How long do you think before I get to Canada?"

"Hang on, Steve. Give me the address of the PUG."

Edie dashed over to the computer and opened up Google Maps on the screen. She punched the keys as Steve gave her the information along with the last cross street whizzing by.

"Gottcha. You should be coming up to a major intersection. I want you to make a right. It's called Francis Street."

Just as Edie relayed the directions, he saw the sign for the intersection. Steve swung the Ambassador into the turn. The black Honda negotiated the same turn with a little less fanfare, but Cornell still managed to bounce the rear wheels over the curb.

"Okay," Steve said. "Now what?"

"Stay on this road. In a couple of miles the name is gonna change to Bigelow Gulch Road."

"Good to know. But why the hell is that important?"

"Shut up and listen, Steve. This road will take you out of the city and residential areas. On the map, the area looks rural. It's what you wanted. The map also shows lots of curves and side roads crisscrossing all over the place. Maybe it'll give you a chance to lose 'em."

"Did I ever tell you I loved you, Edie? You're not even here, but we're still a team."

"Just make sure you get your pretty white ass back to me. Oh. And please don't bring any of your buddies home for dinner. I'll be damned if you think I'm cooking tonight."

Edie lowered her head and whispered a prayer.

Chapter 54

"I THINK HE MADE US, WILLIE."

"Christ. What was your first fucking clue? Where the hell did you learn how to follow someone? We're gonna have to take care of him right here. Somehow, I don't think he's heading home to his girlfriend. Thanks to your fucking driving. We should've shot the asshole in the parking lot."

Steve could see green pastures and groves of trees coming into focus as the Ambassador bounced across a busy intersection as the light turned red. The black Honda barely slowed, veering its way through the crossing traffic amidst a serenade of blasting horns and screeching tires. Steve picked up speed on the first open straightaway, thankful the traffic had thinned. He heard what sounded like gunshots and used as much of the road as he dared, swinging the wheel back and forth to minimize himself as an easy target. A few metallic pings rang in his ears.

"What's happening?"

"Hang on, Edie. Don't you know it's not safe to talk on the phone while you're driving? With someone chasing you. And bullets bouncing off your car."

"I didn't get that. What'd you say?"

The straightaway gave way to a sharp right curve, forcing Steve to reduce his speed. As quickly as the road curved right, he bore down on a left curve, almost losing control as the Ambassador's suspension was forced to react to an inertia never engineered into its design. For the moment he was no longer a direct target, but at every curve the black Honda closed the gap.

Although the Honda was better equipped to handle the terrain due to its size and suspension, Cornell was not as capable as Willie thought he should be and offered a few words of encouragement. "You drive like a fuckin' high school kid getting his first blow job behind the wheel. How the hell can I get off a clean shot with you boogying this car all over the road? Listen. I know this road like the back of my hand."

"Yeah?" Cornell shot back. "Then why don't you fucking drive this piece of shit?"

"Just shut the fuck up and listen," Willie said. "In about a half mile we're gonna come up to a long stretch of open road going downhill for a ways. When I give the word, I want you to stomp on the gas pedal. Imagine it's Reilly's fat white face. Then you gotta pull this shit wagon alongside that oversized piece of crap. I'll blast the asshole right in the head. You got it?"

"What if there's a car coming the other way?"

"Well… gee… you can use your turn signal and indicate your desire to pass the vehicle in front of you. Jesus fucking Christ. What the hell do ya think, Cornell? Let 'em get outta your way. This is gonna be our best shot to get him."

Steve glanced in the mirror. He hesitated an instant as the Ambassador swung out of the last curve. At first the open road in front of him didn't register in his brain. That was all the time needed for the black Honda to gain the advantage. Disappearing from Steve's rearview mirror, it was suddenly alongside. He caught a glimpse of steel and an arm extending through the front passenger side window. This time Steve didn't hesitate. Somewhere from deep in his brain, a few synapses did the math. You're behind the wheel of one big motherfucking car—

challenged by a little rice burning tin can. Those words took infinitely longer to think than implementing his primary reaction.

When Steve jerked the wheel to the left—the Honda never stood a chance. Steve heard a crunch as the driver's side fender on the Ambassador crumpled from the impact. Cornell tried to regain control, but overcorrected, sending the Honda reeling into some nasty strands of barbed wire fencing. The taut ribbon of wire snagged itself around the front axle. The car flipped over several times, ending up with its wheels back on the ground.

Steve slowed and pulled the Ambassador to the side of the road about a hundred yards from the wreckage. He jumped out of the car and looked back at the Honda. All his training screamed at him to go back to give assistance, regardless they'd just tried to kill him. His survival instincts were telling him to get back in the car and get as far from here as possible.

He heard the driver's side door squealing in protest as it was forced open. Next the passenger's side door made a similar objection as it was kicked out. Both occupants staggered around the destroyed car waving their arms and screaming at each other. The guy who got out of the passenger side looked up. He saw Steve still within range and reached inside the car. He grabbed his weapon and fired. Steve's training never taught him to be an idiot, so he got back in the car and drove off.

As the wreckage with its two defeated occupants disappeared from his rearview mirror, Steve resumed his chat with Edie. "Hi, Edie. Yeah, I'm on my way home. Need anything at the store? Don't forget Nana will be visiting us tomorrow. Okay, see ya soon."

CHAPTER 55

Washington, D.C.

"GOOD MORNING, MARIA," MATTHEWS SAID. "Everything set on your end?"

"Yes. The president and I were extremely convincing in promoting our bipartisan strategy to the vice president. She was a little concerned about there not being enough time for her security detail to prepare for the trip. Especially when we've got her landing at a civilian airport."

"Did you tell her I—"

"Yes, Matthews. I assured her you would be coordinating the details and the need for enhanced security measures. I also reminded her there was a local security team already in place due to our previous plans to participate in the local celebrations."

"Perfect," Matthews said, handing some papers to Maria. "Here's the planned itinerary for you to give to the vice president's secret service detail. Of particular importance is their cooperation with our ground agents who will be directing the activities scheduled at the airport. David Reilly has been asked to identify a secure location in the terminal for the vice president to be greeted by a spokesperson from the RGA and a few select representatives of one of the more extreme right-wing organizations. David, of course, will represent the PUG faction. After this private session the vice president is scheduled to be taken to a banquet meeting at the Coeur d'Alene Resort where she will address the larger bipartisan audience. After that she is scheduled to speak at the opening ceremony for the Vietnam Traveling Wall Memorial exhibit at the Coeur d'Alene City Park."

"I'm assuming," Maria said, "you don't expect the vice president to attend any of the events in Coeur d'Alene?"

Matthews nodded. "But we are arranging for national live media coverage of the ceremony at the memorial, which if all proceeds according to plan, will be replaced by the first reports of the vice president's assassination. All complementing the president's own address on the South Lawn. Is the president clear on exactly what is going to happen on Friday?"

"I've explained to Connor that if the vice president was not sent to Coeur d'Alene, he would probably not be finishing out his second term. And with the right outcome from his supposed bipartisan outreach, the final aspects of his dream would be that much closer. He asked no further questions but reminded me we'll be meeting tomorrow to prepare the final talking points for his speech, as well as giving him an update on the status for the next important phase of the transformation."

Maria paused, and then asked, "How much trust do you place in this Reilly character?"

"There's only one way I know to make sure our western tracks are completely covered."

CHAPTER 56

Kellogg, Idaho

EDIE WAS UP EARLY, FILLED with a rush of nervous energy. Amber had been fed and pampered and was now scooting about in the confines of her urban jungle. Breakfast preparations were underway, the tempting aroma wafting throughout the large house, reaching the master bedroom and waking Steve from a contented slumber. He had tried to downplay yesterday's events, but Edie was not buying any of his lame excuses. Shuffling into the kitchen, he yawned and stretched his arms in a wide sweeping circle before nesting them around Edie's waist. He eased himself into a cozy embrace while she stirred something on the range top burner.

Still nuzzling her neck and shoulders, he whispered, "I could get used to all these fringe benefits. Why didn't I think of sleeping with you sooner?"

"I could be wrong, but I got the idea you were thinking along those lines when Amber had me pinned to the ground in your front yard."

"No respectable liberal-minded citizen would ever contemplate cozying up to a conspiracy driven right wing black woman. Unless she happened to have one of the tastiest—"

"Unless she happened to have the intelligence, skills, and patience to get this misguided individual to understand his actions were at odds with his core principles. That's what you were going to say, wasn't it?"

Steve spun Edie around and kissed her hard on the lips. He got his first sample of breakfast as a dollop of hot grits dripped off the spoon down his bare back.

******

About an hour later they were locked and loaded into the bruised, but resilient Ambassador. They were cruising east along Interstate 90 through the remaining segment of the Idaho panhandle on their way to the Missoula International Airport to pick up Rosa Margaret Pauling, more affectionately known as Nana.

"Now, let me get this straight," Steve said. "Are you sure Nana told you she was looking forward to meeting me?"

Edie nodded her head.

"She used my name?"

Edie nodded her head.

"So, you told her you were going to San Francisco to meet up with me?"

Edie shook her head.

"What did you tell her yesterday when you talked on the phone?"

Edie shrugged, trying to think.

"Did you ever mention my name?"

Edie shook her head.

"So, she doesn't know we are…"

Edie shook her head and rubbed her mouth.

"I never thought I would say this, but don't you talk anymore?"

"Until you brought it up, I didn't give it much thought," Edie said.

The rest came out in a rush.

"When the convention in San Francisco was over, I told her I met a few new friends and was going to take a little extra time and do some sightseeing. Oh. And I did say we were going to be staying in the Coeur d'Alene area. But I swear I never mentioned your name."

"So, you have no clue as to what's going on?" Steve asked. "Doesn't her coming here sound a little strange to you?"

Edie shrugged. "Yesterday when I talked to Nana, I was so unnerved about her announcing she was on her way out here, I guess it didn't click. One minute I'm thinking Nana is going senile, next she starts issuing me instructions like I'm five years old again. I never even had a chance to ask her why, or more importantly, try to talk her out of coming here. She doesn't know anything about the trouble we're in. I don't want her getting hurt because of me. I wish I could convince her to turn around and go home before something bad happens."

"You think that's possible?" Steve asked.

"Not a chance in hell. If you think I've got an attitude, well, wait until you meet Nana."

"By the way, did you happen to ask her why we're picking her up in Missoula? Wouldn't Spokane be the logical choice?"

"I figured she's a little confused about the geography and all. Maybe her mind really is slipping a bit."

Steve didn't reply but was beginning to wonder about Nana's mental acuity himself—but he was coming to a far different conclusion than Edie.

They arrived at the airport long before the expected arrival of the US Airways connecting flight from Denver.

Steve pulled into the short-term parking lot across from the passenger terminal. The weather was overcast and cool, with a slight drizzle coming down. They cracked the car windows and left Amber in the back seat chewing a rawhide dog treat while they walked over to the arrivals area to wait for Nana.

Walking through the terminal's fine art gallery, Steve guessed Amber would have been impressed by the selection of assorted woodland creatures represented. She might have even been munching on some parts of one of their relatives out in the car. They were sipping their coffees at the sidewalk café, gazing at the bustling activity inside the glassed-in casino area when Edie's phone chirped.

"It's me, Edie. I'm getting off the plane and heading for the arrivals area. Are you here yet?"

"Nana? This isn't your cell phone number."

"No. I picked up one of those prepaid phones before I left. So are you here or should I be looking for a taxi?"

"No, no. We're in the terminal. We're heading over to meet you right now. We'll see you there in a few seconds."

Edie hurried toward the arrival area with Steve several steps in her wake. From behind the security barrier Edie started waving her arms at one of the approaching figures maneuvering a wheeled carry-on bag expertly around some of the slower passengers. Steve stared as the elderly woman approached. He didn't need Edie to identify this person. Except for her hair which was gray, short, and curled, she was the same height, weight, and skin tone as her granddaughter. He got a glimpse into the future, seeing an image of Edie fifty years from now. As she exited the secure area Edie ran up and hugged her. Watching the two of them face-to-face made Steve's head spin. After regaining his composure, he stepped closer but was still unsure of what to do next.

Nana released Edie, handed her the handle of her bag and embraced Steve. "I am pleased to make your acquaintance, Mr. Casella. But if you don't mind, I'll be calling you Steve. As long as you call me Nana."

"Yes, Ma'am. I… ah… mean, Nana. It's good to meet you. Here Edie, let me take Nana's bag." He led the way back to the car.

CHAPTER 57

Missoula, Montana

THEY ARRIVED AT THE CAR and Steve unlocked the trunk. He was placing Nana's bag inside when Amber began one of her barking episodes. Nana stared into the rear window. Amber's barking stopped and she reclined on the seat; ears slanted back with her snout tucked between her outstretched front paws.

Nana turned back to Edie, shaking her head. "What's become of you, child? First, you're sleeping with a white boy, and now you got yourself a white dog?"

About to slam the trunk lid down, Steve changed his mind and began rearranging the sole piece of luggage in the empty trunk space.

"Oh, Steve," Nana said as her head peeked around the trunk lid. "Having trouble squeezing in my bag? Shouldn't we be on our way?"

She looked at the crumpled front fender and turned back to Steve.

"Practicing to be a New York City cab driver?"

Edie replied for him. "Even better, Nana. Steve has figured out the best way to deal with inconsiderate drivers. And he's only been in Idaho a week."

Thankful for any diversion, Steve jumped into the driver's seat. He was coming to the conclusion that he'd be no match for two generations of the Pauling family. He'd have to watch them both carefully. He saw no signs of any mental incapacities in Nana.

Nana insisted on sitting in the rear seat so she could keep an eye on both of them. At first Amber repositioned herself to the far side of the car, but gradually slipped over so her head rested on Nana's lap. She was rewarded with a generous ear massage.

Edie was anxious to prod Nana for an explanation of her cryptic tone and sudden appearance on the scene, but Nana was stalwart in her resolve not to discuss her motives until they had time to relax. And eat dinner. But she was more than willing to listen to what the two of them had been up to over the last week. Willing to listen was not exactly correct. She insisted on a full and detailed accounting of their escapades. At first Edie tried giving a vague and watered-down version, leaving out the menacing facets, but it wasn't long before Nana had them both talking like a couple of drunken sailors whose ship just got into port after six months at sea.

Compared to Nana, Steve was starting to believe living with Edie was a breeze. What he found most interesting was throughout all the harrowing storytelling about their recent adventures, Nana never looked nervous or even surprised.

At least not until they were getting close to their destination in Kellogg. Nana looked out the side window and propped herself up so fast Amber got flipped onto the floorboard.

"Steve. Could you please get off the interstate at this next exit?" she asked.

Steve and Edie focused on the approaching freeway sign for Historic Downtown Wallace.

"If you're hungry, Nana," Edie said, "we'll be home in about fifteen minutes. We don't have to stop here. Steve and I have a great dinner planned."

"I'm sure you do," Nana replied. "But that's not it. You know how I love silver jewelry. I hint at it for every birthday and Christmas. Remember? Well, this little town happens to be famous for having the most unique collection of silver trinkets in the area."

Nana caught Steve's eye in the rearview mirror. "And this might interest you, Steve. At one time they were also famous for their whorehouses. When that occupation was fashionable here, I was about the right age to earn tons of silver rewards. I'm sure I would have been quite popular with all the boys. Don't you think? Especially since the only black people seen around here at the time were the dirty miners coming back out of the tunnels."

"Nana. What are you talking about?" Edie asked. "You must still be a little light-headed from the long flight. How do you even know about this place? Did you buy some kind of tourist book at the airport?"

"You're right about the flight being tiresome. So, I brought my tablet with me. It has this great shopping app I've personalized for my favorites."

This convinced Steve. Nana was a lot more informed about things than she led on. He couldn't figure out why Edie didn't see this. He held that thought and took Nana's advice and steered the Ambassador down the exit ramp and guided them onto Bank Street, emerging in a familiar setting of historic architecture.

"You can park anywhere along here, Steve," Nana said, pointing out the window. "There are silver stores everywhere."

Everywhere turned out to be confined to a three-block section of town, but when Steve tried to park, he found no free spaces. The downtown section was crowded with pedestrians and finding a parking spot on one of the side streets also turned out to be impossible. After much circling, which coming from San Francisco was standard operating procedure for Steve, he maneuvered into a spot underneath the freeway ramp on the outskirts of town. Both Pauling women refused Steve's offer to drop them off closer to the shops. As they walked back toward the center of town, they saw a sign welcoming them to the Gyro Days Carnival.

Nana and Edie paraded through a bunch of stores while Steve walked with Amber up and down the busy street. Amber became fixated on a shop with stuffed and mounted animal species posed in the storefront window. Amber challenged each and every one of them, but had no takers. She settled on a generous piece of antler rack out of a bin in front of the store. Steve paid the shopkeeper. Amber proudly carried her prize as they headed back to the car, taking a shortcut through the carnival attractions. A voice bellowed out from behind Steve. He turned abruptly, about to apologize, thinking Amber probably poked someone with the antlers… again.

Instead, a flamboyantly dressed ride jockey called out, "Hey bud. Where'd ya get dat thing?" He was pointing at the antlers in Amber's mouth.

This was about the fourth person to ask Steve this same question. He had exhausted his supply of smartass answers and decided to go with the truth. "There's a little pawn shop around the corner."

"Whadidya pay for im? Lemme see im. Dey'd go good in my fishin tank heere. Don't ya tink?"

"Ah, sure," Steve answered. "They cost twenty bucks."

"Jeez. Be a lot cheapa ta shoot da elk or deer or whaddeva it was."

Nana chimed in. "Young man. You're making me homesick. You're from the East Coast, aren't you?"

"Born an raised in Coney Island. But now I travel da world. At least where da carny goes."

Nana smiled, and said, "Well it was nice talking to you. You have a lovely carnival here."

"Tanks Ma'am. Hava good day now."

******

Steve and Edie prepared an early dinner as neither of them wanted to face Nana alone. Nana sat in the family room with Amber at her side and channel surfed through all the major news programs. As they worked in the kitchen, Steve whispered to Edie, asking her if she thought it would be acceptable to move his pajamas back down to the master bedroom, seeing their secret was out.

Edie grinned and whispered back, "I don't recall you ever wearing pajamas to bed."

"I've always traveled light."

"I may be old, but I'm not deaf. Are you two sure you don't want my help in there? You keep up with that kind of talk, we'll never get to eat," Nana called in from the family room.

Before they could respond, Nana's phone rang. She answered, ambling out the back door and down the porch steps to the yard. This was her second incoming call since they got home. Intermingled with several outgoing ones.

Amber took this as another opportunity to show off her ball retrieving skills.

Looking back from the window, Edie said to Steve, "How is it she's getting calls on a phone she picked up a few hours ago?"

"Why don't you help me get the rest of the food out to the table? I'm sure we're gonna find out those things and a whole lot more. If she's satisfied with our cooking."

As it turned out, Nana was satisfied, but she then insisted on helping them clean up in the kitchen before they all returned to the family room. Nana sat herself down in one of the leather lounge chairs and invited Steve and Edie to sit facing her on the sofa.

"I'm guessing you two might be interested in why I'm here," Nana said. "Plus, I think I can clear up a few other things for you."

CHAPTER 58

Washington, D.C.

THE FURNITURE IN THE OVAL Office had been returned to its original location, and the symbolic flames were still flickering in the nation's most influential fireplace. This morning the president sat across from his two most trusted allies in their plan to transform the government of the world's most successful implementation of a constitutional republic. The founding fathers were not naïve, nor did they think to rely on the intrinsic morality of any particular government official. They recognized the necessity of limiting the powers of a central government and had devised a formidable scheme of checks and balances to prevent any undo increase in the scope and power of any given branch of the government. They also knew the strength of this system was dependent on the knowledge base of its citizens. An informed populace was more important to the republic than any single leader. If the majority of the citizens lacked the insight and ability to make informed decisions, the course of the nation would soon become aimless and flounder. The best way to transform the populace from one of individual strengths and accomplishments to one of collective meekness and lack of moral character was to increase their dependency on the government for basic human needs through increased regulation and the redistribution of the nation's wealth.

What would it take to bring the nation to the point where the scales were tilted in the direction of absolute government strength and a subservient populace?

The three individuals sitting in this sanctuary of government power had envisioned such a plan and had secretly fostered the energies and the power behind their political party to test the limits of the founding fathers' faith in the American citizens' ability and willingness to recognize this fatal course before the shoals were hit and the nation was grounded in a sea of defeat.

After skimming through the latest drafts of key talking points for tomorrow's address to the nation, President John Connor looked up at his senior advisor and his chief of staff.

"Are you sure we're not cutting this too close?" he asked.

They both knew he was referring to opening his speech with a somber message to the nation regarding the brutal slaying of Vice President Alice Andersen by a group of radical right-wing extremists. Ralph Matthews allowed Maria Santiago to field this one, knowing it was her job to put the president at ease in such a monumental decision. He imagined the president was reluctant to wipe his own ass without Maria's approval, or maybe even her help. It might even be in her job description.

The president nodded his acceptance of Maria's assertion. This speech presented an important opportunity to exhibit his presidential qualities.

"So," the president said, "am I mistaken, or didn't we use a lot of this rhetoric about racism, bigotry, and fascism in a previous Independence Day address?"

"Can't get enough of a good thing," Matthews replied. "Besides, it fits in even better this year with the tragic news you'll be delivering. Plus, it reinforces the seriousness of how a region with a long history of being associated with right-wing extremists can be a threat to the progress we have made in being a nation not bound by reactionary views."

"You know, Ralph," the president said, shaking his head, "sometimes I almost believe your bullshit. But let's look ahead for a moment. Barring any significant negative events, we're poised for a super majority control of congress after the mid-term elections. What's our polling consultants have to say about our less publicized efforts to achieve control over the state legislatures?"

Matthews sat up a little straighter, his voice resounded in the room. "The projections are promising, but we need to increase our local campaign coffers to guarantee victory. There's no doubt we'll get control in more than two-thirds of the states. As of today, we predict a minimum of thirty-eight states will be ours."

"Good news," the president said, bobbing his head.

"But," Matthews cautioned, "as you know, this is our one chance. Getting those pesky constitutional amendments abolished must be done as quickly and as quietly as possible. Nobody's ever tested this backdoor route before, that's why there have been no red flag warnings. We need to keep up the distractions and accusations against our opponents. By the time we cycle through the top dozen or more of the standard ideological talking points, they'll be so dizzy from chasing their tails they won't know what hit them."

"You figure the RGA movement is well controlled?" Maria asked.

Matthews gave her a huge smile and continued, "The best thing for our plan turned out to be the emergence of the RGA and their constant squabbling with the mainstream republicans. While they're busy trying to figure out who's to blame for them losing elections, we'll have succeeded in eliminating the whole fucking bunch of them, as well as any other rivals in the foreseeable future. Who needs two parties when the one in power gives the people everything they need? Or at least what we tell them they should have."

Maria had become mesmerized by Matthews' oration, a heat rising inside. This guy was even more drunk with power than she thought possible. Against all her past emanations about Matthews, listening to the way he was talking was getting her sweaty and bothered. If she got any more aroused, she might give Matthews a chance to rub his gruff hands all over her body. This would be a helluva place for it. Right here in the Oval Office. In front of the fireplace. With the president sitting behind his desk. Signing—

"Maria?" the president said. "Are you okay? You look a little flushed."

"Ah, sorry, John," Maria said in a husky voice. "I was thinking about some last-minute details I still have to work on for your speech. So. We'll have everything in place, and as soon as Matthews gets the signal tomorrow, I'll give you the appropriate set of opening remarks."

Maria rose, trying to appear calm.

"If there's nothing else," she said, "I better get moving on some things."

As the door closed behind Maria, the president shook his head and sighed, "Mother of God. If I weren't happily married, I'd want to get a piece of her."

Matthews nodded, but thought if Maria ever gave Connor half an opening, he'd forget the first lady ever existed and would have her spread over the presidential desk faster than any of his notable predecessors. He'd conjured up a similar scenario in his own office.

CHAPTER 59

Kellogg, Idaho

"EDIE," NANA SAID WITH AN engaging smile. "You might be thinking I'm a little senile, but I didn't forget the question you called me about yesterday. It's as good a place to start as any. In fact, I've been a little concerned that it took you this long to start asking questions. After all, you've been looking at that email for several months now."

"I never mentioned any email to you," Edie responded with a stunned expression. "How do you even know about it?"

"Honey. Just because you don't tell me things, doesn't mean I don't know. Take today for example." She looked at Steve and then at Edie. Seeing the embarrassed expressions on their faces, Nana laughed and waved her arms.

"Now, where was I?" she muttered. "Oh yes. I know you're familiar with where your father was raised. I remember him telling me he brought you to the old neighborhood once and showed you the submarine museum he was always so excited about. But let me tell you a little bit about what you don't know."

Amber settled her head onto Nana's lap. Nana smiled and scratched the dog's ears while she began her story.

"In the early days, your dad wasn't the easiest of my three children to discipline. He had such a wild streak in him I swore he would wind up in prison. Then a young lady moved into the other half of our duplex. She was in her mid-to-late twenties. From the first time your dad set eyes on her, he had the biggest crush you could ever believe. Maybe that was part of what changed him. We never talked about it. But this lady was a prosecutor for the Bergen County District Attorney's Office."

Something triggered in the back of Steve's mind. He sat there trying to concentrate on what Nana was saying. His first impressions may have underestimated the resourcefulness of this woman. The light reflected off Nana's new silver medallion strung on her neck.

"She'd talk to your dad every time the chance came up," Nana was saying, "which happened to be often, being he always seemed to be around whenever she was coming or going. He was like a little puppy dog whenever Alice was around. That was her name. Alice." Nana paused and glanced at Steve and Edie.

They remained silent, so Nana continued, "Anyway, Alice was filled with stories about how it was her job to punish people who thought they didn't have to follow the rules. And she told quite a few harrowing tales. Maybe some of them were even true. The important thing to remember was those stories scared the devil out of your father. She told him it was important to keep busy. So that Satan would leave you alone and not lead you down the wrong path. She was the one who first introduced him to the submarine museum. He became so intrigued by the sacrifices those men made for their country—this I think you already know—it changed his life forever."

Steve placed a hand over Edie's.

Seeing this, Nana smiled. "By the way," she said. "This Alice, I mentioned? Well, she went on to hold a few different jobs before ending up where she is right now. I'm talking about Alice Andersen, our first female vice president of the United States. And she also happens to be the first African American vice president. Not to mention the fact that she is a very dear friend of mine."

Searching for words, Edie replied, "Why… why is it, Dad, or you, never talked about her?"

"It was a long time ago," Nana said, "and I guess we all moved our separate ways. Your dad joined the Navy. Alice moved on to the state legislature and then to the United States senate. It was a different time in his life. I guess he could have said something when he took you back to the old neighborhood. But you know he was a private person. And it wasn't my place to intervene in his personal feelings."

"So… you're good friends with the vice president," Edie said almost to herself.

"It's not like Alice and I hung out every night," Nana said, "as you young folks call it. And after your dad left, as you know, I moved out of our house. But Alice kept in touch. Always a card on the holidays. Always a personal note inside. And she followed your dad's career in the Navy. She was so proud of him."

Nana paused to wipe away a lone tear with a crumpled old tissue. "And when he was killed in the embassy bombing, it hit her as hard as if it were her own brother who died. We've been a lot closer since then. She vowed to find out what went wrong and who was to blame. She had lots of suspicions, but being in a sensitive position, she's tried to tread lightly. But I know she won't quit until the truth comes out. I happened to mention all the frustrations you were going through trying to get answers."

Steve squeezed Edie's hand a little tighter.

"She was aware of this, as well," Nana said, while biting her lip. "I suppose I put the idea in her head to send the email. I knew how upset you were. Feeling so helpless. Looking every which way to find some closure. I also knew someday we would be sitting here, or at least somewhere, and discussing this very thing. Maybe I was wrong, but I thought you needed to find some of this out for yourself. You were never satisfied with doing things the easy way."

Nana stood up, easing Amber's head off her lap. "And now look what's happened," she said taking a deep breath. "We're all in a great big mess. Aren't we?"

All Edie could say was, "But why did you have to come all the way out here to tell me this?"

"Well. There is someone else I need to see as well," Nana said with a renewed energy in her voice. "And you two are going to take me there. Along with all those good things you've dug up."

CHAPTER 60

"THE VICE PRESIDENT IS GOING to be in Spokane tomorrow?" Edie asked.

"Yes," Nana said. "Several days ago, the president decided it was important for Alice to be the White House spokesperson at the Fourth of July celebration in Coeur d'Alene. She became a little suspicious of the president's motivation for sending her on this trip. She didn't go into any more details but knew you were out here following up on her email."

"How did she—" Edie said.

"I informed Alice of what you were up to after you told me your little story about meeting some friends at the convention in San Francisco and deciding to take a road trip up north," Nana said, tilting her head.

Edie stole a quick glance at Steve who was staring down at the floor.

"When you called me yesterday morning, I had just gotten off the phone with her," Nana said. "So I guess I panicked and was afraid to say anything to you on my landline. That's my home phone. You never know when the government is listening. Even Alice wasn't using her regular phone. We all can be a little paranoid from time to time. Which in case you were wondering was why I flew into Missoula instead of the more logical airport in Spokane."

Steve looked up and smiled at Edie. Images of Jimmy Martin rummaging around the community club looking for hidden surveillance equipment were dancing through his head.

"Anyway," Nana said. "Alice realized that what she put in motion with the email was not just a way to help you to get some closure into what happened to your father, but she had sent you right into the middle of a conspiracy which hadn't ended with the video. It's still active and you're in danger."

"All the phone calls today?" Steve questioned.

Nana nodded. "Yes. Earlier I filled Alice in on what you two had found in the way of evidence linking this video to the political activist group in Spokane. She wants us to meet her at the airport when she arrives in Spokane tomorrow and get us all in the protection of her security detail. Then we can figure out what all this means."

PART FOUR

CHAPTER 61

Spokane Airport

AIR FORCE TWO WAS SCHEDULED to land at
Spokane International Airport at 10 A.M. Not wanting to
keep the vice president waiting, they all piled into the
Ambassador, allotting plenty of time to spare following a
special breakfast prepared by Nana. Before leaving, Steve
and Edie scurried about the house trying to tidy it up as
best as they could. They didn't think they would be
returning to Joe Wilton's vacation rental anytime soon.
Amber was relegated to the backyard to minimize the
redistribution of white fur.

The first snag occurred when they got to the airport.
Due to the Fourth of July holiday all spaces in the indoor
parking structures were filled. With the outside
temperatures already in the low eighties, Amber couldn't
be left in the car.

"If I remember," Nana said, "Alice used to be a cat
person, but maybe she's changed since moving to
Washington, D.C. Or is it only the president who
traditionally adds a dog to the family when occupying the
White House?" Ignoring her own question, she
continued, "Well, if she expects to be the next president,
she should get used to the idea."

So with a dog, a briefcase stuffed with evidence, and a
great deal of apprehension, they strode into Terminal

Two and waited outside the security entrance as instructed by the vice president. There would be no gate arrival message for Air Force Two, as once the jumbo jet landed it would taxi to a secured sector at the far end of the airport grounds.

They had been standing around long enough to arouse the suspicions of three Transportation Security Administration agents. The TSA agents appeared to be interested in the dangerous looking old black woman. She was feeding treats to a large white dog performing tricks for the passengers on line at the security checkpoint. As they closed in to incarcerate their first potential terrorist and unauthorized dog of the day, they were pre-empted by two non-descript men wearing loose fitting light gray conservative business suits, sporting reflective sunglasses, and a coil of wire extending from the lobes of their left ears. Except for their demeanor and dress, they weren't actually twins.

The agents first identified their sanctioned package, and then singled out the extra parcel in the mix. Secret service agents never tolerate surprises of any kind. They were already on edge, coming in cold with no prior assessments available. Agent number one spoke into his lapel mike and waited for instructions. After listening to a response, he withdrew a cell phone from his coat pocket, punched a key, and handed it to the elderly black woman.

"Yes. This is Rosa, Madam Vice President. Okay. Of course, Alice. If you don't mind. Yes. We would appreciate it. Thank you. Okay. Yes, I'll see you in a little while. Yes. I'll give the phone back to the nice man with the sunglasses. Yes. Of course they're all wearing sunglasses."

Agents Bixby and Carson led the group, including the dog, into a small interrogation room. They explained the need to perform a thorough screening before proceeding to the secure conference room. The ladies were escorted into an adjoining room by two female security agents while Carson gave Steve a thorough examination. No one got too close to Amber after Bixby tried approaching her with the wand and discovered any metal detected on the dog was not the primary threat potential. None of these people were listed on the approved roster, but the vice president herself had vouched for them. Including the dog.

They were next brought up a flight of stairs to a secure conference area and allowed to enter the Board Room for the Airport Administrative Offices. They were the last of the guests to be ushered into the conference room. Steve winked at a stricken-looking David Reilly who was standing in the front left corner of the room. Steve was tempted to ask Reilly why the two goons who had been shooting at him weren't around today.

Once everything was secured, the vice president would be brought over from Air Force Two. Bixby and Carson handed over their charges to the two agents in the room and left. The taller, deeply tanned man with thick black hair was Anthony Marchesi. The shorter, light complexioned man with clipped sandy blond hair was Gordon Stanford. They were the secret service agents assigned through the local Department of Homeland Security responsible for coordinating the security for the vice president at the airport. In reality, they were working under the direct orders of Ralph Matthews back in Washington, D.C.

As Steve and Edie glanced around the room, they recognized several other familiar faces. There was Sarah Nelson, the director of the RGA in Coeur d'Alene, and Jimmy Martin and Joe Wilton from the Wolf Bay Community Club. The latter two represented the more extreme faction of the local conservative organizations. If they appeared shocked by the presence of Steve and Edie, it was nothing compared to the blanched and stunned expression still plastered on David Reilly's face. Neither Marchesi nor Stanford exhibited any outward signs of distress. However, there was a slight increase in each of their heart rates as the first visible indication of a chink in their armor. Reilly neglected to mention the fact that Steve and Edie had not perished in the fire to anyone else, including Marchesi and Stanford.

Sarah Nelson performed the unnecessary task of introducing Steve and Edie to the director of the local PUG who recovered enough to regain a reasonable degree of composure. Edie introduced Nana to everyone else in the room.

A lot of things had transpired since Steve and Edie first met with Sarah Nelson at the RGA offices. At the moment Steve didn't think this was the appropriate time to confess his new-found revelations to her.

Jimmy Martin had dressed up for the occasion. He wore a light brown sports jacket over a pale blue buttoned-down dress shirt and a pair of dark brown slacks. His tie was a deep maroon with thin white diagonal stripes. Jimmy Martin's jacket hung loosely, and his slacks were too long and starting to fray at the cuffs. The tie looked more like a noose strung around his neck than any customary fashion statement. He appeared nervous and out of place. His hands had a slight tremor and his eyes darted around like he was looking for a cold brew. Edie felt sorry for him being thrown into this uncomfortable situation. She shuddered at the thought of how he would react when the vice president arrived. Steve nodded to Joe Wilton, who looked natural and comfortable in a crisp dark brown business suit.

A sharp knock on the door garnered the attention of Marchesi and Stanford. Marchesi exited the room and Stanford took up a position in front of the closed door.

CHAPTER 62

MARCHESI, DESIGNATED AS THE AGENT-IN-CHARGE for this private meeting at the airport, snapped orders for Bixby and Carson to take up positions outside the secure door located down the hallway at the bottom of the staircase. He also motioned for the third secret service agent at the side of the vice president to do the same.

Instead, the third agent squared off with Marchesi, and countered, "Wherever the vice president goes—I go. I do not leave her side until she is back on board Air Force Two. With all due respect, I don't give a rat's ass what you're in charge of here, Marchesi. Do we understand how this is going to happen?"

Using a measured tone of authority, the vice president said, "Agent Marchesi. I appreciate everyone's effort at assuring my safety. You all have important jobs to do here today, but I have to agree with Agent Finley. He gets his way unless I have a good reason to override his orders. Can we please get started? I don't have a lot of time before we are obligated to leave for the banquet in Coeur d'Alene, and those people inside deserve the respect and the courtesy of their government, of which I now have the honor to represent."

"Of course, Madam Vice President." Although he'd rarely been in the presence of the vice president, he watched her exhibit a more presidential demeanor than the commander-in-chief. He returned a commanding stare to Finley, nodding his head.

"Let's do it, Finley."

By the time they all entered the conference room, Marchesi had reassessed the usefulness of having the vice president's key security agent in the mix. He chastised himself for not thinking of it earlier. It might work out better. After all, Finley wouldn't be around to be reprimanded for his careless behavior.

Stanford closed and locked the heavy oak door after his boss returned with the vice president and the unexpected agent glued to her side. The vice president and Agent Finley stood several steps in front of the door of the twenty- by thirty-foot conference room. A large oak table made up the centerpiece of the room. The remaining guests were lined up along the wall to the left of the long table. David Reilly stood closest to the vice president, while the conservative contingency was next in line, a defining gap separating them from Reilly. The three last-minute additions to the meeting, Nana, Edie, and Steve, brought up the rear. Amber, slightly in front of and to Steve's left, leaned back on her haunches. Her profile obscured by the leather conference chairs around the massive table.

When Steve first entered the room, Amber had reacted to Marchesi by yanking at her lead, ears rigid and forward, with raised hackles and accompanying low, deep growls. Steve thought Marchesi was going to draw his weapon, so he apologized, and with considerable difficulty, led Amber to her present location. He could still feel the tension building in Amber even this far away from the agent. He was starting to recall images of behavioral issues and other things Uncle Bob had warned him about regarding protection training and instincts.

The vice president worked her way down the line, greeting and briefly chatting with each individual. Reilly, who had been working hard at hiding his shock and displeasure at the appearance of his missed quarry, did a credible job of welcoming the vice president to the People United Group district in Spokane. The arrival of the vice president brought back his confidence, and he visibly relaxed.

Sarah Nelson and Joe Wilton were both gracious and comfortable at the opportunity to meet the vice president, while Jimmy Martin had the look of a specimen pinned and stretched on a petri dish placed under a microscope. His jacket and slacks appeared to grow larger as he shrunk inside them. Beads of sweat formed on his forehead. Smiling, the vice president greeted Steve and Edie, and thanked them for coming.

Eyeing the briefcase at Edie's side, the vice president said in a low voice, "I'm anxious to begin our little chat as soon as we finish up with this meeting. Your Nana has already clued me in on some of the details."

She saved Nana for last. The vice president turned back toward her, extended her arms, and scooped her up in a tender embrace. "Rosa Pauling. I can still see you sitting in your rocker on the front porch ready to lace into Chuck as he tried to sneak back into the house after missing your curfew."

After a short pause, she said, "I also have a recollection of you screening each and every one of the men who came calling to my door. Perhaps, it's why I never married. I could never find a man who could stand up to your criteria."

"And I've never stopped looking for the man who'd deserve you, Alice."

This brought a hearty laugh from the vice president.

As she moved past Steve and prepared to take a seat at the end of table, Marchesi nodded to Stanford and both agents drew identical SIG Sauer P229 Scorpion 9mm weapons from their shoulder holsters. Marchesi moved to the right; his weapon pointed directly at Agent Finley. Stanford stepped left and moved back toward the locked door, keeping his weapon rotating across the assembled group. Regardless of Finley's position, one of them would have a clear shot at the vice president.

Reilly began to separate himself from the line-up. He attempted to take a position next to Stanford but was stopped in his tracks by Marchesi.

"David," Marchesi said. "You need to get back to where you were. If you were smarter, you'd have seen this coming. This all plays out much more convincingly if you join the vice president in this tragic saga of right-wing lunacy. According to our associates in D.C., it would complete the portrait of motivation for these fine examples of reactionary extremists within our midst."

Marchesi smiled at the vice president. "If only you were targeted, Ma'am, the country might get the wrong impression and think this was a simple racial attack. As you know, once the race card is drawn, people ignore the remaining cards in their hand. We want to make sure the message we deliver today is clear. These extremists don't approve of any of the president's progressive ideologies. Besides, they keep telling me, nobody in the executive offices tolerates any loose ends."

Waving his pistol at Agent Finley, Marchesi said, "Now, Finley. First, if you so much as glance at your lapel or try to alert the rest of your detail in any way, the vice president takes a bullet to the head. And I hope you believe I mean it. Next, remove your weapon from its holster—"

On instinct, Finley had stepped in front of the vice president at the first sign of trouble. "There is no fucking way I'm going to—"

The vice president interrupted, "Agent Finley. Please do as you're told."

"But Madam—"

"I'm giving you an order," she said. "Please. Do it now."

The vice president was hoping to buy some time as she felt a quick flick of something skim across her right ankle. Amber was poised between her and Steve, still out of Marchesi's direct line of sight. She heard a low rumbling growl emanating from deep within the large white dog.

Finley reached inside his coat. With his thumb and index finger he gripped the handle of his SIG Sauer P229 standard issue firearm and dangled it out to show Marchesi.

"I want you to slide it across the table," Marchesi said. "And make sure you do it nice and easy."

Marchesi was distracted by the impact of Finley's service weapon coming in contact with the table. The sound resounded louder than expected.

A streaking white shadow sprang up from the back of the room.

Powerful rear claws gripped for purchase on the edge of the table. Amber propelled herself over the top, leaping at Marchesi. In doing so she knocked Finley's gun off the side of the table. It disappeared onto one of the chairs.

A formidable set of jaws clamped Marchesi's forearm and his weapon toppled to the floor. Marchesi's screams faded as the sharp canine teeth tearing through his flesh released their grip. Amber's jaw and body slackened in response to the projectile from the weapon fired in Stanford's hand.

In a reflex action Finley pushed the vice president to the floor. He came up shooting at Stanford with the back-up Smith & Wesson revolver hidden against his right ankle. Although not as quick as Amber, Steve came across the table, grabbing for Marchesi's weapon on the floor. At the same time Marchesi lunged for it himself. Steve stepped on the outreached hand before Marchesi could grasp the weapon. He picked the gun up by the muzzle and smashed it across Marchesi's right temple, knocking him unconscious.

In a fluid movement Jimmy Martin sprung forward and grabbed Agent Finley's primary weapon where it had fallen onto the chair. He placed it against Reilly's back, stopping him from making a quick exit.

Steve and Edie crouched anxiously over Amber's body.

CHAPTER 63

THE SOUNDS OF SHOTS FIRED and Finley's radioed commands had Bixby and Carson bounding up the staircase and into the room.

Stanford, dead. Marchesi, unconscious and in handcuffs. David Reilly, collapsed in the corner, babbling non-stop about secret plots in the White House. The names Ralph Matthews and Ben Courtney surfaced numerous times.

After retrieving his primary weapon from Jimmy Martin, and Marchesi's weapon from Steve, Finley shouted, "Get the vice president back to Air Force Two. Now."

"Agent Finley," the vice president said, "the first to get into the limo is the dog and the young man who is applying pressure to the wound."

She turned to Steve and said, "We've got a well-equipped emergency facility on board the plane, as well as two air force medics standing by in the cockpit. Your call, Steve. Veterinary hospital or the plane?"

"Let's get her to the plane."

"You got it." The vice president turned back to Finley and gave orders. "While we take care of this problem, I need the airport locked down. I want no communications to D.C. or leaked to the press until we figure out what we're up against. After we get the dog to the plane, come back and bring the rest of them. This is important. None of what we're doing from this moment on can be observed."

"Understood," Finley said.

"Do we have a cleared area back to the plane, Agent Finley?" the vice president asked.

"It'll be done before you reach the bottom of the stairs." Finley issued commands to his two agents in the room and radioed the appropriate commands to Air Force Two personnel.

In the confusion, none of the agents remembered to secure the Scorpion 9mm hidden under Stanford's body. Before they finished ushering the remaining guests out of the room, the weapon had disappeared.

CHAPTER 64

ABOUT THIRTY MINUTES LATER AGENT Finley escorted Steve and Edie up the spiral staircase and into the vice president's office on Air Force Two. They joined the vice president and Nana who were sitting next to each other on the tiny sofa in the front corner of the small, but elegantly appointed space.

"Amber's doing great, Madam Vice President," Steve said in response to her question. "How's the bruise on your arm?"

"The bruise is nothing. Agent Finley just tried to get a little frisky."

Earlier in the conference room, Finley had pushed the vice president to the floor, trying to shield her. When he yanked the weapon from his ankle holster it scraped up her right arm.

The vice president turned to Finley who stood rigidly in the open doorway. "Thank you, Agent Finley. I appreciate what you did back there. Nice work. The training regimen for the secret service is remarkable, but I find it difficult to believe this scenario could be found in any training manual. Amazing. Shielding the vice president from a rogue secret service agent who shot a white dog biting another rogue agent."

Finley's face twitched, but otherwise his gaze remained steady.

"I guess that's as close to a smile as we'll get from you. Now. You said you've got a preliminary written statement from this Reilly character?"

"Yes, Ma'am." He handed her a single page of a hastily written document. "We have Reilly confined in the secretarial quarters. He's still babbling on about long-standing plots he was a part of with several important people back in D.C. This document is a short version of what he's been saying. Readable, but his hand is still shaking. Marchesi is back in the press room. He's conscious but not talking. The captain tended to his wounds."

Finley allowed himself a thin smile and looked over at Steve. "You and that dog make a damn good team."

He turned back to the vice president. "The others are waiting in the dining room. How do you want to handle the communications? So far we've kept the world in the dark, but when the vice president of the United States becomes invisible for any length of time, a lot of people are going to get nervous."

"Thank you, Agent Finley," she said. "Just give us a little more time here. I'll call you with further instructions. In the meantime, I suggest you be more persuasive with Mr. Marchesi. I might need him to help us out with something. If he continues to resist, I'm sure if you suggest a little visit from Amber, it might change his mind."

As Finley turned to leave, the vice president added, "And on your way back would you please stop in the dining room and ask our remaining three guests to come up to see me?"

She turned to Steve and Edie, pointing to the small meeting table across from the sofa. "Why don't you two have a seat over here? You could have brought Amber up with you, or was she unable to climb those damn stairs because of her injury?"

Edie and Steve looked at each other, and Edie said, "First of all, Madam Vice President, we want to thank you for letting us clean ourselves up in your private suite downstairs. Wow. It's really lovely. Spectacular. Not the typical... what you would expect to find on an—"

Nana interrupted, "Edie? What in God's name are you talking about?"

"Well, Madam Vice President," Edie said. "When we opened the door to your suite, Amber, who can get around remarkably well, jumped up on your bed and won't get off. The captain said it looked like an unusual reaction to some of the medications he gave her after dressing the wound."

"Unusual reaction?" Nana chided. "That dog does whatever she wants."

The vice president smiled. "And I'd say we all should be grateful she does. You know, Rosa, I'm beginning to think I could be convinced to become a dog person. I can't imagine, Curly, my aging calico, being any help back there."

Just as Nana decided to get up to go downstairs and take a peek at Amber, there was a knock on the door. Nana opened the door and let in Sarah Nelson, Joe Wilton, and Jimmy Martin as she excused herself and closed the door behind her. The vice president began by inviting her guests from the local conservative groups to settle in and find some seats and bring them up to date on the little information she could share with them. She had to be careful with what she said, but felt they deserved an explanation. There had been more than enough deceit oozing from the current administration's staff over the last two years.

Jimmy Martin declined to sit down. He stood with his back to the door.

The vice president said, "I apologize for your inconvenience, but we are still trying to sort out exactly what's going on. I can tell you we now believe Peter Fenton had been working with David Reilly at the time the so-called anti-Muslim video was made."

The vice president noticed the sweat pouring down Jimmy Martin's face. She was about to offer him a glass of cold water when he reached under his jacket and pulled out Stanford's semi-automatic weapon.

"I think I've heard enough," Jimmy said with a shaky voice. "I've been telling everyone since this started two years ago. It's the government. It's always the government. They sent Fenton here to use us. He tricked me. And he made Tom do things and say things. He gave us drugs without us knowing it. The government blamed us for the fool who bombed the embassy. They called us racist pigs. Then the government came and took Tom away. They killed him. He didn't die of natural causes in his holding cell. But nobody believed me. I should've stopped it back then. I shouldn't have let them take Tom. It's my fault too. You think you can still trick us? Making us get on this government plane. I know what you're gonna do. You're gonna make us all disappear. So there'll be nobody left to tell everybody what the government's up to. You already tried to kill Steve and Edie. I know the government's responsible for that fire. I'm guessing you pushed the lady who worked at the hotel over the railing too. That was Tom Casella's girlfriend. Why'd you have to kill her?"

Jimmy looked over at his companions. "You see what they're doing here, right? Well. This is gonna stop right here and now. I'm gonna take the lead and stop this government conspiracy. Right here in this room. Who better to start with than the vice president? I'll show 'em they can't push us around anymore."

Under his jacket, sweat plastered Jimmy's shirt against his chest. His entire body shook. He struggled to keep the gun fixed in any one position. Everyone's eyes focused on the trembling finger pressed against the trigger.

On either side of Edie, Steve and Wilton started to rise and move toward Jimmy, but Edie stretched out her arms to stop them. She got to her feet, making sure they'd stay put.

She took a step toward Jimmy and said, "Jimmy. Look at me. You're right. The government is responsible for killing Tom. You know, right around that same time my father died too. Killed by that suicide bomber trying to blow up the embassy."

Edie took another step toward Jimmy.

"You got one thing wrong though," Edie said. "The vice president. She's trying to fix all this. She's the one who led me and Steve here. Without her help we'd never have gotten to talk to all you guys at the community club. Jimmy. It's not the whole government to blame. There are a few bad people. Both sides have extreme elements. A couple of people in power have managed to subvert what some good people are trying to achieve."

Another step toward Jimmy.

"And the vice president?" Edie said, giving the vice president a quick glance. "She was a good friend of my father. She helped him out when he was a boy. And she can help you out too."

She was close enough to feel the cold metal of the gun.

"Look at me, Jimmy." Her voice almost a whisper. "Please. Listen. If the vice president dies here today. They win. You'd be feeding into their madness. The ones in the government who planned this conspiracy. They need her to die so they can tell the whole world you and your friends were responsible. Jimmy. Give the vice president a chance to fix this. You can help her. Please."

Jimmy, still holding the gun in his shaking hand and outstretched arm, turned toward the vice president. Then back to Edie. His eyes settled on the vice president.

"Are you really the good guy?" he asked.

The vice president rose, moving toward Jimmy.

"I agree with Edie, Jimmy. You're right about a conspiracy. But I promise you I am going to fix this."

"But you're one of them. A member of their political party," Jimmy stammered.

"It's not about politics," the vice president said. "Being a republican or democrat doesn't make you good or bad. The people who founded this country disagreed on a lot of issues. It's about a couple of bad people who are obsessed with power and have abused the offices they were entrusted with by the people. They mocked the basic tenets of the people who believed in their party. If you trust me, Jimmy, I want you to hand over the gun. Look at me, Jimmy. I know you want to do what's right."

She stepped the rest of the way to Jimmy and held out her hand.

Again, Jimmy's eyes darted back and forth between the vice president and Edie. He looked at Joe Wilton and Steve sitting on the edge of their seats.

His whole body shivered. Closing his eyes, Jimmy released the weapon into the vice president's hand. He collapsed onto the sofa; face covered by his trembling hands. Placing the gun inside one of the desk drawers, the vice president sat down next to Jimmy and wrapped an arm around his shoulder.

"I must have picked the damn gun up in the conference room as a precautionary measure," she said, appearing to talk to herself. "Finley and I will have a little talk about why I shouldn't have done it. I'll even cut him a break on why he or the other agents neglected to secure it in the first place. Not to mention how they let it get on this plane."

The vice president cleared her throat and looked around to make sure she had everyone's undivided attention.

"None of this happened," she said. "You understand? You guys came in here and we had a nice chat about the incident over in the conference room and how we were going to figure out what this was all about. And then the three of you returned to the dining room, perhaps to have a well-deserved drink or two. Am I clear?"

She made sure everyone in the office, including Jimmy, was paying complete attention to what she said.

As they all nodded in unison, there was a knock on the door and Nana peeked her head in, looking around the room.

"Why the hell is everybody sitting around here doing nothing?" Nana said. "I thought you had work to do?"

After Sarah Nelson, Joe Wilton, and Jimmy Martin left the office, the vice president smiled a sigh of relief, and said, "As usual, Rosa is absolutely right. Shall we get to work now people? It seems we have very little time to figure out how to handle more than two years of incompetency, misdirection, and a good deal of criminal activity."

******

Based on the intelligence information she'd uncovered, and with the evidence gathered today, the vice president was now confident as to who comprised the inner circle of this conspiracy. There were several ways to play these cards, but she decided to raise it to the limit and show her hand. One look at the array of video screens on the wall representing every major news outlet in the world helped to weld her conviction.

Pressing the intercom, she said, "Agent Finley. Come on in here, please. It's time to turn the lights back on. Let's show the world what Independence Day means to America."

Chapter 65

Washington, D.C.

"Goddamn it, Matthews." Maria's voice took on a decided Hispanic accent. "How much longer do we have to wait? You'd think with all the fucking state-of-the-art communication systems we have on board her aircraft we'd be able to make contact with somebody. I thought our people were ordered to report back immediately when their mission was completed."

"Maria, I—"

"And since when," she plowed on, "does the press not have anything to speculate about? There's nothing at all being reported. Don't you have people on the ground leaking information to the media?"

"I'm working on it," Matthews said while Maria took a breath. "We have confirmed Air Force Two is still on the ground in a secure location at the airport. This is good news. We both know if Alice had escaped the trap they would've had her in the air before her butt hit the seat. Courtney is standing by waiting for the signal from Marchesi. He'll buzz me the instant he gets the word."

"The president is ready to shit in his pants. It's all I can do to keep him away from the booze before he gives his speech. He's doing this without a teleprompter, and he won't know until he steps out onto the South Lawn which version to deliver. I knew we were cutting it too close."

"We both agreed—"

"We should've let him give his usual boring Independence Day address to the nation. Let the press do their job and report on this horrific national tragedy," Maria said shaking her head. "We could be working on a spontaneous message delivered by a somber and grieving president. He could've done it later this evening from the Oval Office, where he feels more comfortable pretending to give the nation bad news. You know I'm good at my job, but on more than one occasion the damn teleprompter has done a better job in saving his ass."

"We both agreed if we can pull it off this way," Matthews said, taking advantage of Maria pausing for another breath, "the benefits of crushing our opponents before the campaign even gets started will have us so far ahead those morons will be pondering what the hell happened to the two-party system for the next quarter century. They're way too close to the real conservative movement to get out of the way of this fucking train that's heading right for them. What better way to boost up his ratings than to have the president himself deliver the news as it unfolds?"

The phone in his pocket vibrated.

"Gotcha, Ben," Matthews said. "Did Marchesi say what the hell took so long? Yeah, I guess this might've been more complicated than his last several jobs. Anyway, it's time to sit back and enjoy the show. God. I'm ready to enjoy Independence Day."

Phone plastered to her ear, Maria rushed off in the direction of the South Lawn. She fired off commands for the staff to inform the media the presidential address was about to get under way. Matthews was too consumed with a sense of victory to allow his lustful instincts a chance to surface in the wake of her bobbing departure.

CHAPTER 66

Washington, D.C. and Coeur d'Alene, Idaho

THE PRESIDENT WALKED ONTO THE South Lawn of the White House and stood poised behind the podium. His hooded eyes scanned across the gathered dignitaries spread out before him. He exhaled and lowered his head, gazing into the cameras.

"My fellow Americans," President Connor said. "Today, as this nation celebrates our Independence Day, I come before you with a most shocking and horrific story. It both pains me, as well as stirs up an intense anger at this inevitable outcome of the vile traits of the extremist elements in our great society. Several days ago, the vice president agreed to be an emissary of bipartisanship and reconciliation. She was to speak at a ceremony for an Independence Day celebration featuring our Vietnam Traveling Memorial Wall Exhibit. In an effort to help bridge the gap between our divergent parties, she was also scheduled to host a small private meeting with representatives from a local People United Group and several conservative groups, including the Restraint in Government Alliance. This meeting was to take place in a secure conference room at the Spokane Airport. Later the vice president was to be the keynote speaker at a banquet to reinforce this administration's desire to put aside our partisan divisiveness and attempt to reach across the aisle."

The president paused but continued staring into the cameras.

"We have learned from reliable sources at the Spokane Airport," he said, "the vice president was fatally wounded at this morning's private meeting. There was a communications black-out and the airport was locked down until a few minutes ago. While the details are still somewhat sketchy, one of our secret service agents on the ground in Spokane has verified that the vice president, along with two other secret service agents and the director of the local People United Group in Spokane, were gunned down by a member or members of a local right wing activist group who were invited guests at this meeting. In the course of the ensuing firefight, the suspected assassins, including a high-ranking member of the local Restraint in Government Alliance office, were also killed. The perpetrator commandeered the weapon from one of the vice president's personal secret service agents."

Pausing again, the president collected his thoughts.

"Alice Andersen," he said, adding a slight tremor to his voice, "was a remarkable woman and had dedicated her time in office to reach across the aisle to work with all factions in congress to do what was right for our nation, not for the gain of any political party. Let me say it is time for us as a nation of law to put a stop to the senseless political hostilities erupting from a small, but violent contingency intent on promoting the seeds of hatred and intolerance. We must no longer stand by and permit this venom to infect our nation."

The president reached his arms out to the cameras.

"As your president, I vow to seek out and destroy the root elements in our society who have incited this aggressive disregard for solving our differences in a civil and orderly manner. I will order the Department of Justice to launch a full-scale investigation into not only identifying any and all individuals involved in the assassination of Alice Andersen, but to launch an in-depth investigation of any groups, including the Restraint in Government Alliance, involved in the promotion of violence and hatred in the guise of political ideology. I promise to apply the full force of the executive branch of the federal government to declare a war on the bigoted elements embedded in these so-called political entities."

******

Before a speechless crowd, the vice president stepped up to the podium at City Park in Coeur d'Alene, Idaho, with the Vietnam Traveling Memorial Wall Exhibit as a backdrop. Numerous rumors had been circulating since the arrival of Air Force Two in Spokane this morning, and the subsequent airport lock-down. The onsite media contingency there to cover the opening remarks of the vice president were gaping at the satellite feeds from D.C. that were streaming in to the monitors in their mobile units. A local official stepped down from the podium after making the shocking announcement about the reported assassination of the vice president.

As the vice president prepared to talk, the media crews shifted into gear and secured their uplink feeds for a live telecast of what was about to transpire. The editing rooms in all major news networks across the nation were receiving live feeds of the president's vows to punish all involved with the assassination of the vice president.

In juxtaposition, there was the vice president making an appearance before a crowd of onlookers attending a dedication ceremony in Idaho.

"My fellow Americans," the vice president said, "I apologize for keeping you waiting, but I am not in the habit of pre-empting my boss, the president of the United States. I think on this occasion, however, I will make an exception. So there is no mistake, I am Alice Andersen, and I am alive and still the vice president of the United States."

The murmuring voices in the crowd were hushed.

"What the president is saying is partially correct," she said. "This morning at the Spokane Airport, I had planned to attend a bipartisan meeting. And a clear attempt was made on my life. As you can see, the attempt was unsuccessful. There was one casualty this morning. One of the perpetrators was killed during the incident. There were two other perpetrators involved at the scene, and they are now in custody."

The nation sensed she was directing these next words all the way to Washington, D.C., and the president himself.

"And to clarify another point of misdirection, none of the would-be assassins were members of, or associated with, any right-wing extremist groups. Although the details are not clear at this point, there is strong evidence to link the suspects to a long-standing plot to eradicate the Restraint in Government Alliance and to disembowel the integrity of the remaining elements of the republican party. I have sent a directive to the attorney general of the United States to obtain warrants for the arrests of Ralph Matthews, the president's chief of staff, Maria Santiago, a senior advisor to the president, and Ben Courtney, the Executive Director of the Office of Commitment to Community Progress. I will also be calling on congress to initiate hearings to investigate President John Connor in regard to what knowledge he possessed with respect to today's events, and if he played an active role in any of these devious plots of murder, deceit, and orchestration of steps to bypass our constitutional rights."

******

After calling for a moment of prayer for the slain vice president, President Connor had begun talking again when he noticed his audience becoming distracted. Aside from the occasional heckler in an audience, which was usually a plant to make him look good, Connor never experienced such an overt disregard for the office of the president. Rattled, he glanced to his left where Maria Santiago and Ralph Matthews sat during these events. He saw them both being escorted away from the scene by four men in dark gray conservative business suits. At least two other men, dressed in the same attire, stood in the background, staring in his direction.

******

The vice president continued with her remarks. "I want to take this opportunity to make a statement to the fine people who make up this community. Two years ago you were subjected to a public nightmare caused by alleged allegations of radicalism stirred up by a video released on the internet. This video was circulated by a careless media campaign in an attempt to demonize an entire segment of our population and to indict the regional culture and values of this particular part of our nation. We now suspect this was orchestrated by the same individuals who were responsible for today's actions at the airport. You can be sure I will do everything in my power to vindicate those who were maligned by this conspiracy. As a lasting tribute to the fallen soldiers whose names are engraved on the wall behind me, as well as the countless heroes who have also died and continue to die in a never-ending progression of wars and conflicts, it is my honor and duty to insure that the leaders of our nation do not defile or disregard the legacy of those brave warriors."

The vice president stood in silence at the podium. She was thinking back to a young boy she had known a long time ago and how he represented generations of patriots who selflessly served this nation. They deserved a lot more in return from the country they had died for.

******

As the dusk and ensuing darkness swept its way westward, from our nation's capital, across open plains, over majestic mountains, lakes, and valleys, this inevitable path drew the customary displays of fireworks symbolizing the explosive and fiery birth of our nation. A nation created by men whose ideas were formed by the understanding of tyranny, and with the resolve and foresight to know that while the world progressively evolves, the nature of man remains a constant.

CHAPTER 67

THE ULTIMATE LEGACY OF THIS unique experiment designated as the United States of America is the understanding and confirmation that the basic tenets envisioned by our founding fathers are constant. They were wise enough to understand that future generations would try to impeach the meaning of this doctrine to fit contemporary societal expediencies.

It is the responsibility of any current generation to add to the legacy, and complement its guiding principles, not to chip away at the foundation supporting them.

It is the role of the people to govern, not the government to rule over the people. If the people are blinded either by design or apathy, they will succumb to a government whose power was bled from the masses. The collective strength of a nation emanates from the individual, not the dependency and domination of the government. To clarify and understand the principles of our founding fathers is not the same as corrupting them to justify the behavior of a few, to devour the many.

Those were the exact thoughts Steve contemplated as he turned to Edie and said, "Jesus Christ. Can you imagine what the hell would've happened if Amber didn't bite that son of a bitch?"

They, along with an improbable manifest of passengers, were now traveling eastward on Air Force Two, heading toward our nation's capital after a long and trying day. Besides the participants of the fateful meeting at the airport, the vice president's security detail had also rounded up two additional members of the western operations contingency of co-conspirators. After the dust had settled at the scene in the conference room, Cornell and Willie were apprehended without incident in the airport garage while waiting for David Reilly to return. Stoned out on cocaine. They were offered a free ride on Air Force Two along with their boss.

EPILOGUE

CHAPTER 1

THE JURISDICTIONAL NIGHTMARE THAT WOULD have overwhelmed the local, state, and federal law enforcement agencies was ironically averted, in part, by the alleged conspirators in the current administration who transpired to break a myriad of laws and were now on the verge of being prosecuted themselves.

One of the last pieces of legislation fought for by President Connor and his cabinet was to enact the Domestic Terrorism Subjugation Rights Act. By a narrow margin the bill passed the house and senate in April of this year. The DTSR Act empowered the Department of Homeland Security to coordinate certain activities with the Department of Justice. This included the investigation and subsequent prosecution in the federal court system of crimes deemed to have been committed against any federal employee in the commission of acts purportedly against national security interests.

In addition, the states' rights to prosecution could also be waived for crimes committed by a federal employee, if designated relevant to the Department of Homeland Security's jurisdiction. The authority to make such decisions was placed in the hands of the attorney general of the United States. It was within his power to employ any means necessary to expedite these procedures and drastically reduce the timelines necessary for prosecution.

The justification of this act stemmed from the need for the federal government to have absolute jurisdiction over all matters pertaining to national security. It also ordered that the federal court system, exclusively, should be entrusted with the decision to determine if any classified documents and any other sensitive evidence the attorney general determined to be related to such crimes would be harmful to the nation if brought out in a public trial or hearing. The proposed intent of the law was to give the executive branch of the federal government the power to override the state's jurisdiction in cases of national security concerns for the protection of our national interests.

The actual intent was to further reduce the ability of any individual state to govern its people, thus relinquishing the power of the state to its lowest level in the history of this nation. The fight to appeal this draconian legislation up to the level of the Supreme Court of the United States was in its infancy.

As of now, Air Force Two was streaming back to Washington with a number of alleged co-conspirators and witnesses in federal custody. Back in Washington, three additional alleged co-conspirators had already been taken into custody by federal agents.

Following the abrupt termination of his Independence Day address to the nation, President Connor was ushered back to the privacy of the Oval Office. There was no warming glow of the usual fire, but the stern figure of George Washington scowled down at the current president and sole major co-conspirator elected to a public office. The first lady had been trying to reach him, but he was not ready to talk to anyone about today's events. President Connor informed his secretary to change his scheduled plans and asked her to inform his wife that he would not be joining her at their coastal villa in Malibu.

CHAPTER 2

IN THE FIRST DAYS FOLLOWING the disclosure of criminal behavior against the White House's highest officials, implicating the president himself, political pundits across the nation's vast variety of media outlets debated both the immediate and the long-term consequences of these monumental events. The DTSR Act streamlined the process of handling the arrests, indictments, and prosecution of most of the co-conspirators. The Articles of Impeachment dictated the constitutional steps necessary to remove a sitting president from office. While the Department of Justice stipulated a sitting president was constitutionally immune from indictment and criminal prosecution, the subsequent penalties to be dispensed to one who has been removed from office had never been tested in the history of our nation.

As the enormity of the crimes began to be comprehended, one of the first positive outcomes from this debacle was that all accusations of any criminal activity against Tyler Griffin were dismissed. The New Jersey senator was exonerated of any wrongdoing in the death of his senior advisor, Peter Fenton. By the time the senatorial race officially began in the Fall, there was little chance the incumbent would not be re-elected to his first full term as the senator from New Jersey. He had also garnered the support of a young female journalist from his home state. Her stories on the White House scandal had unraveled the truths from the vast sea of lies the conspirators flooded the nation with for over two years.

In addition to aiding the New Jersey senator, Edie Pauling had gotten the answers to questions frustrating her since the death of her father. She shared her experiences in a number of hard-hitting articles and live reports with a nation thirsty for the truth.

Congress was reconvened on July 7th, following the tumultuous holiday recess. Subsequent to the decision of the House Judiciary Committee to initiate impeachment proceedings, the chairman of the committee proposed a resolution to support the formal inquiry to discuss the impeachment of President Connor. This resulted in an official request of the full house of representatives to debate and vote on the issue to impeach the sitting president. The vote for impeachment was unanimous. In the history of the United States, only two prior presidents, Andrew Johnson and Bill Clinton, had been successfully impeached. President John Connor was now the third.

Next, President Connor was brought before the body of the senate to determine if he should be removed from office. This senate trial was presided over by the chief justice of the Supreme Court of the United States. This time history was made by the senate. They reached the required two-thirds majority vote and John Connor became the first United States president to be removed from office. This vote occurred on November 18th, two years after he had been re-elected to a second term.

A complicated series of arrests, charges, indictments, pleas, immunities, and trials for the remaining co-conspirators were paraded out before the American public over the course of the summer and fall following the July 4th events and disclosures. During the third week of November, ex-president John Connor was formally indicted on a similar number and nature of charges. Thus starting the constitutional struggle of the legality to prosecute a former president for crimes purportedly committed in office, once he had been stripped of his position.

On the same day President Connor was removed from office, Vice President Alice Andersen was sworn in as the forty-fifth president of the United States. She vowed to follow through on her Independence Day promise to start the nation on a path of unification. The new president stated she would refuse to grant pardons to any of the convicted participants of this conspiracy, including the former president himself. In a stunning announcement during her first address to the nation from the Oval Office, she appointed the republican senator from New Jersey, Tyler Griffin, as her new vice president. Thus, her declared war on divisive partisanship was officially inaugurated.

CHAPTER 3

STEVE CLOSED THE LAST STORAGE compartment door on the rear left side. He called Amber and they both climbed into the Itasca Class C recreational vehicle parked next to his home outside Sonoma. He maneuvered the RV onto the narrow winding road leading to the valley floor. It was election day, and Steve was making this his first stop on the long journey he had planned. He could have left two days earlier when his last shift ended, and his final vacation time for the year started, but he'd never been comfortable using the absentee ballots.

This was something instilled into him by his dad. Steve smiled as he remembered his dad always telling him that voting was an important responsibility. It wasn't about politics—it was about expressing your views in a free society. You should take the time and effort to show up at your local polling place and make your mark in person.

The good memories about his dad were returning to him more frequently now than ever. He smiled again.

Steve turned the RV onto Arnold Drive and headed toward Glen Ellen. He passed the old volunteer fire station where he got his first glimpse of the excitement and satisfaction of his chosen vocation. As he entered the tiny village, he looked for a place to pull over the big rig. He would have to walk the final two blocks to the polling place at the Glen Ellen Community Church on O Donnell Lane. This road was narrower than the one he'd ridden down from his mountainside home. After waiting in line, he obtained the ballot and found an open voting booth.

Steve made quick work of marking his personal choices even though the ballot was several pages long and contained numerous propositions in addition to the elective offices. Another bit of advice given to him by his dad: If you're going to take the time to vote your choice, you ought to spend sufficient time to understand what's on the ballot before getting there. Steve did his homework but concluded sometimes the propositions were a wasteful way to make new laws. If the leaders in the state government didn't agree with the outcome from the voters, they could find a way to negate the decision.

After performing his civic duty, Steve found himself back in the RV headed through Sonoma and Napa to pick up the 80 Freeway in Vallejo. This road changed into Interstate 80 once he crossed into Nevada and through the remainder of its path across the country. Although the RV was equipped with the latest GPS device, he wouldn't need it anytime soon. He'd be traveling east on this particular interstate for almost twenty-eight hundred miles before making his next turn.

Steve settled in for the long journey, and Amber relaxed in the spacious cabin. He contemplated the significance of the last two decisions leading him to this excursion. Tapping his fingers on the steering wheel, he pondered on how he came to buy this rig. He never recalled any prior desire to even own an RV, but last month when one of the guys in the squad talked about trading up to a bigger rig, Steve got sucked into the moment and took the plunge.

This brought him to his next decision. What the hell was he doing now? Barreling eastward along the interstate on his way to meet up with Edie back in New Jersey. More to the point, why hadn't he mentioned this little road trip to her? Well, he had at least another forty hours of driving time to figure it out.

The last four months had gone by both quickly and slowly. Since the confrontation at Spokane International Airport on July 4th, Steve and Edie had been involved in a number of interrogations, depositions, hearings, and other legal proceedings. These were related to the tidal wave of federal indictments resulting from the Department of Justice's investigation into the unraveling conspiracy.

Edie got caught up in a whirlwind of journalistic activities. Her career spiraled upwards from a series of written and live accounts of the unfolding events. In addition, she became a leading member of the campaign staff for Senator Tyler Griffin in his successful bid for re-election.

Steve chose a different path from the one he championed two years ago when the video featuring his father was released. This time around Steve refused any interviews and shunned publicity of any kind. He sat back, relaxed, and enjoyed watching Edie take on the world.

Two weeks ago she accepted a new position as a FOX News Contributor. The last time Steve saw Edie's face was four days ago when she appeared on the O'Reilly Factor. He smiled when he recalled her response to being referred to as Pauling by the bold and fresh host. Who's pithy now, Bill?

They tried to spend as much time together as their busy schedules allowed. In addition to Steve's required trips to fulfill his legal obligations for the federal prosecutors, he had flown out to visit Edie on two separate weekend trips. Most of the time spent secluded in Edie's one bedroom apartment. He smiled thinking of the inside of her updated four-unit Victorian-styled building located near the southeast corner of the Morristown Historical District. Steve would be at a loss to describe any details of the apartment's amenities or Edie's decorating skills, other than he felt satisfied with her hospitality. Except for those occasions, busy schedules limited their relationship to a series of almost daily phone calls.

Steve talked to Edie right after her last appearance on FOX News. She convinced him to fly out to New Jersey for the Pauling Thanksgiving Day gathering at Nana's house several weeks from now. He never mentioned anything about his new RV and neglected to inform her of this current revision to their last discussion. With all the trading and shift switching with the rest of the squad to get this time off, he doubted he'd see another free day until the next presidential elections were history.

******

Not hampered by any early season wintry weather, Steve made good time on his first cross-country road trip. He enjoyed the companionship of having Amber along for the ride. He often thought of the bittersweet memory of how their paths first crossed and the experiences they shared.

Steve crossed the Delaware Water Gap and entered into the western boundary of New Jersey. From this perspective one could almost believe it was the Garden State. A lot different from his previous arrivals at Newark Liberty International Airport flanked by groves of oil refinery storage tanks. After a short jaunt paralleling the Delaware River, he swung the RV onto State Highway 94 and headed in a northeasterly direction toward the town

of Newton. The county seat of Sussex County, New
Jersey, and his final destination. Turning control over to
the dash-mounted GPS system, he followed the
instructions and was soon trying to find a space to park
his RV on Townsend Street, in a quiet residential
neighborhood of Newton. He found an open spot about
a half block from Nana's house.

His next biggest decision was to leave Amber in the
RV, thinking it might be too cowardly to use her as a
shield or a crutch. He did remember to bring Nana a
wrapped gift box with a beautiful piece of silver jewelry
picked up on one of his stops along the route. He also
had a small package for Edie—but delivering it would
take more courage than repelling from a helicopter into a
raging wildfire. He decided to leave it in the RV and wait
for the proper moment.

Steve walked down the quiet street admiring the well-
kept homes and tidy grounds maintained by the owners.
Nana's house was no exception. Her house was a single-
story Craftsman styled bungalow with a rare hipped roof
design. It had weathered brown shaker shingle siding and
a full-length front porch with triangular shaped
supporting columns. He cringed seeing the roof was
composed of cedar split shake shingles, but supposed the
increased fire hazard was not a major concern in a
neighborhood so far removed from any wildfire risks.

With great effort Steve knocked on the glazed batten
walnut front door. He tried not to think what would
happen when it opened. He didn't have long to wait. The
door swung open in an authoritative manner, and he was
confronted by an immense black man in his early thirties,
weighing close to 270 pounds and over six foot six. He
had a shaved head, smooth chocolate skin, and a pair of

hawk-like eyes which were focused in a burning glare right at Steve.

Steve smiled and opened his mouth but was cut off before any words reached his lips.

"Hey, Nana. You expecting any honkies here this morning?"

Another male voice boomed back. "Need any help there, Sampson?"

"Nah, Thomas. We're cool. But tell Nana there's a white dude here with his mouth open, but nothing coming out."

Nana and Edie appeared in the entry hall.

"Sampson, where's your manners? Let the gentleman in. Besides, you're letting all the heated air out the open door," Nana said.

As the door closed behind Steve, Edie walked up to him. Her face as immobilized as the granite sculptures on Mount Rushmore.

"What's going on here?" she asked. "When I spoke to you yesterday you told me you were hanging around the house playing with Amber."

"I was… kinda. Except I brought it with me. Parked it down the block."

Edie peered through the curtains. "The RV's yours?"

"Sure is. Remember when you came to Sonoma? I never got the chance to invite you inside my house, and seeing you weren't coming out anytime soon, I thought this might work."

Sampson and Nana retreated to the living room but were still visible beyond the wood framed archway. Steve could hear several other voices in the room.

"I was thinking," Steve said, "maybe you'd want to get away from this cold weather and head south for a few days. We could head for the coast or shore or beach or whatever you call it out here."

"Just like that? You show up and say let's go for a ride? You don't give me any warning? And how did you even know I was—Nana!"

Nana walked back into the entry hall. "You don't need to shout. I'm not deaf. By the way, it won't be necessary to drive me to the hospital. Go get your suitcase out of the trunk so you don't keep this young man waiting."

Nana turned to Steve. "This girl almost messed things up on us. Right after we talked, and I gave you the directions, Edie called me, crying and carrying on. Said she'd packed her suitcase and booked a flight to San Francisco. She was going to leave this morning, for God's sake. Even had the nerve to try and cancel our family dinner plans. Babbled on about how she'd had enough of this coast-to-coast relationship, was missing you, and was going right out there to be with you."

Nana paused and touched Edie's arm. "Now, as you know, I don't like to lie... but. Sorry, Edie, I'm not having any procedure done at Newton Memorial Hospital tomorrow. I had to keep you here for one more day."

Steve placed a hand on Edie's shoulder. "Does it mean you'd like to see the inside of my house?"

Edie leapt into Steve's arms and said, "I really, really missed you, Mr. Casella... and you bet your white ass I'm gonna see the inside of that thing."

She lowered her voice and whispered something in Steve's ear.

Steve glanced over at Nana who had both hands held tightly over her ears.

"Before you go, Edie," Nana said, "it would be nice if you could introduce this fellow to the rest of the clan. And Steve. Make sure you get yourselves back here in time for the best Thanksgiving Day meal ever. And young lady. Before you guys make your first stop, I would appreciate it if you at least drove around the corner. The neighbors can be nosy."

There was a tentative scratch and whimper coming from outside. Edie opened the front door. Amber pounced on her and pinned her down on the entry hall carpet, licking her face and ears. Edie was not wearing her white T-shirt today.

Amber glanced up smiling at a speechless Steve, as if to say: *I knew we were coming here all along. Oh… and didn't I tell you the latch on the RV door was no problem at all?*

THE END

AUTHOR'S NOTES

OPPOSITION REFLEX is the first book in a new thriller saga, The Amber Restrained Series.

The series chronicles the escapades of two disparate individuals, Steve Casella and Edie Pauling, who surmount their differences and form an interminable bond that takes them on a journey to fight the injustices assailing the American dream. Together they challenge the seemingly unending barrage of incompetence and corruption that is ignored, facilitated, or orchestrated by the almost invincible power structure of an encroaching government. Along for the ride is Amber, a dog Steve has rescued from a fatal house fire. The sometimes disobedient canine companion is a constant source of frustration and amusement, but as part of their team, no one is more capable to assist when times get rough. As the nation and the world gather at the brink of extinction, Steve and Edie desperately try to gain traction against the slippery slope toward ultimate destruction.

<<ronvergona.net>>

www.ingramcontent.com/pod-product-compliance
Lightning Source LLC
Chambersburg PA
CBHW030019180626
46810CB00001B/112